DEAD
CENTER

DEAD
CENTER

JOANNA HIGGINS

THE PERMANENT PRESS
Sag Harbor, NY 11963

This is a work of fiction inspired by an actual event. Court testimony where drawn upon has been used imaginatively, and all characters, settings, and actions herein are fictional or used fictitiously. The novel is not intended to depict any person, place, or event associated with the actual case.

For information, address:
   The Permanent Press
   4170 Noyac Road
   Sag Harbor, NY 11963
   www.thepermanentpress.com

Library of Congress Cataloging-in-Publication Data

   Higgins, Joanna–
      Dead center / Joanna Higgins.
         p.   cm.
      ISBN 978-1-57962-212-1 (alk. paper)
         1. Loss (Psychology)—Fiction. 2. Fatherhood—Fiction.
      3. Adopted children—Fiction. 4. Domestic fiction. I. Title.

   PS3558.I3574D43 2011
   813'.54—dc22   2010044092

Printed in the United States of America.

For Jerry

There is no sure foundation set on blood;
No certain life achieved by others' death.

—*King John*, SHAKESPEARE

NORTHERN MICHIGAN
APRIL, 1970

The body lay on its side, blood darkening hair, sideburns, face, and neck. Flies circled in a steady drone, a few cautiously alighting, and then others, to wade through sweet pools and lakes, drinking their fill. On the other side of the clearing, deer emerged from cedar growth and began grazing on new field grasses, while a wood thrush sang its plaintive three notes, always inflecting the third as if in question. High above the woods, a jet drew a chalk line across the late afternoon sky.

At the first sound of vehicles, the wood thrush abandoned its perch and flew deeper into the woods. The deer bounded away. Soon EMS workers were kneeling around the body while game commissioners snapped Polaroids, and people who'd heard of the accident on their police scanners were running up a path toward the clearing. But finally the stir of human activity moved elsewhere as darkness came on and the air cooled.

The night filled with the whir of tree frogs in a marsh to the north of the clearing, their electronic-like pulsations near-deafening to one man who'd returned. He was smoking a cigarette down to the calluses on his fingers, ash falling on new blades of timothy and florets of trefoil and wild strawberry. Then he left, and deer returned to graze in moonlight. Tree frogs kept up their mating racket, stopping only at first light when the man came back, another cigarette between his fingers, to study tree line and clearing and the earth where the body had lain. The tang in his mouth from the night before was still there. Soured milk. Nails. Blood.

And the feeling in his gut.

HILO, HAWAII
1990

BEN AND KAREN

Ben glanced away from the child's nostril, where he had been delicately angling to secure a small object. Charlotte Hoon, his office manager, was hanging onto the doorframe with one hand and leaning into the examining room. "The police, Doctor, they want to see you. They say come get you."

The wobble in her voice caused his heart to lurch into some erratic gallop. "Tell them I'm not finished here."

"But they—"

"Five minutes."

"Okay." She shut the door behind her.

The hand holding the tweezers began quivering. Two decades earlier, when he'd first opened his pediatrics clinic on the Big Island of Hawaii, he'd been haunted, daily, by dread. The envisioned details varying, as well as the intensity of coincident chest and gut pain, but never the overall picture. But after several years, when imagination and reality failed to conjoin, the fear that it *would*, one day, dulled, then finally slipped back into the depths where it riled his dreams at times, but not his overloaded waking hours. A state of mind nearly as troubling as the other, when it occurred to him to think about it. *For it's then that it will happen, probably.*

Something weirdly akin to that old folk saying about a watched pot not boiling.

Tears were seeping from the boy's closed eyelids, making the long lashes spiky and beautiful against perfect skin. Ben didn't look at the mother, crowding him, but sensed her tension, the heat of need and fear rising off her. He tugged gently with the tweezers. It was coming. Emanating its stench.

14

His heartbeat swung into some new rhythm that was hardly rhythm at all. He took deeper breaths yet couldn't get enough. The back of his neck felt frigid. Pain hit exactly where he expected it to, radiating outward from the lower left ventricle. Slowly he raised his head but avoided the mother's puzzled look. Instead, he stared at a poster on the wall above the examining table. Type I Diabetes. The colors red and blue and yellow. Lines. Circles. Print. The vulnerable interior, its small tasks, each crucial to survival.

Red detached itself from the poster and flowed outward. Bright anthurium red. Oxygenated red. Then darker. Old blood, depleted. Lifeless. His heart bounded and spun, tripped, stumbled, raced to catch up, the tachycardia accelerating toward fibrillation. *Look. Colors. Breathe. Breathe.* But he was seeing his own heart, dark red and swollen, fat with scarring and ruin. He willed ease. Willed calm. Willed the coronary arteries to open however much they could, and that crown of thorns, the Kranzarterie wreathing the heart, clawing it. But the image too fanciful, too poetic for the event, which was prosaic, and deadly.

Just breathe.

And then he could envision it: those damaged arteries expanding and pain furling itself again as the organ got enough oxygen to allow the spasm to ease. In the next moment his heart found its rhythm again, and again he leaned over the child. It was coming, this whatever. Giving up its dark niche.

And with it the stink of drainpipes and sewers.

He studied the object between his tweezers—so many things removed from children's nostrils and ears over the years. And like most of those other microbe-laden things, this too was green-black and furred. It dropped soundlessly into the enamel tray his nurse held, somewhat unsteadily, in her hands. He took the tray and scraped at the thing. A bead. A simple craft bead. Turquoise.

The young mother's face brightened with relief and the luxury now, of anger. "I tell him alla time. Stay away from your sister's stuff! But no! What he musta done was hide it up there. Maybe think he take it out later when she don' see. Is that what you think, Roberto? You see what happens?"

A familiar theme—a mother's anger when her child knowingly or unknowingly does something dangerous. He removed his gloves and touched the young mother's shoulder.

"It's all right now. Roberto will be fine. And the smell's gone as well."

"You're all set!" he told the boy. "Just stay away from your sister's stuff." He smiled.

The thought came that it wasn't what it seemed. Despite that reopened investigation in Michigan, officers here for a totally different reason. An accident. Some injury, emergency. That's how it worked, crazy reality. All over the place, and a person's life, with its mammoth concerns, a mere fragment of a speck in it all. Not even that. A microscopic nothing. The day would go on, and he within it. His patients would be seen. Tomorrow there'd be others. And starting right now, the imagination would begin churning out its doomsday scenarios again.

For a moment it was like breathing freely again—what the little boy must then be experiencing. Air flowing cleanly into the lungs and out again. He opened the door and went to meet them, out of habit extending his hand. They drew guns. In the next minute he was escorted out through his reception area, wrists manacled, an agent on either side of him gripping his upper arms. *A warrant for your arrest, Doctor, and an extradition order. You're being charged with first- and third-degree murder . . .*

He saw Karen, his wife, standing alongside Charlotte Hoon. Saw the young mother and Roberto, as well as a number of other children and mothers in the waiting room. Everyone, everything stilled. His heart was working too hard again. He imagined himself dropping to the sidewalk, the rainbow shower tree blossoms there.

"Wait!" he heard his wife calling. The officers paused, and that gave him time to will the necessary relaxing. "You can't . . . you shouldn't . . . he's a *doctor* . . . A *pediatrician*! There's no need for *handcuffs*."

Then Roberto's mother ran up to them. "What you people doing? You crazy? That's Dr. *Weber*. He our doctor! What we gonna do, man, if you take him?"

And then he and his wife were in a car and the car moving.

KAREN HAD always thought it would happen at the clinic and invariably saw herself there, helping Charlotte—as she was on that March day. When Charlotte rolled her chair away from the reception counter, then hurried to the hallway beyond, it was as if it had all happened before, in time. Or else within the images that so often slid readily to mind in those vulnerable predawn moments, the conscious mind newly awake, still snared in dream time and open to whatever darkness the deeper self might want to thrust its way at three or four in the morning. Yet in those dark imaginings, part dream, part hallucination, she hadn't gotten any of the other details right—the vase of green and red anthurium at Charlotte's work area and how, moments after the police and agents arrived, the woman's hand brushed against the stippled milk glass, toppling the birthday array, and then water spilling over various forms, the holy bits of paper that made up so much of their lives. A miniature flood then, a mock natural disaster to mimic the larger devastation rising all around.

We have a warrant for his arrest.

The State of Hawaii officer polite, apology softening the staccato Island cadence. Three other officers and two agents in business suits stood near the counter. The police officers held their revolvers in open view.

Absurd! In a medical office. Children just feet away, in the waiting room. The usually ebullient Hawaiian children frozen statuettes. Then the six officers and her husband leaving the clinic, two of them holding her husband's arms as if he were some feeble patient attempting to negotiate the way back home.

Petals on the wet walkway. Rain cloud draping Hilo Bay. Beyond the Kalanianaole Highway, the water pewter-toned. Upland cane fields gray-green, under the roil of cloud. Out on the bay, a three-masted schooner at anchor, causing in her a moment of profound disorientation. In her predawn imaginings there hadn't been any three-masted schooner. Nor rain. Nor the indifferent river of traffic.

She heard herself shouting at the officers. They regarded her with sympathy but kept walking. Her husband looked at her—*Don't say anything more*—and she went silent.

They allowed her to sit alongside him in the police cruiser, but he seemed wrapped in that same opalescent shroud over the town and bay. Or else she herself was muffled in some distancing cocoon of fear. Anger there, too, secreting its noxious hatred for her former in-laws who obviously couldn't go to their graves without exacting revenge for the loss of their only son. Hatred one of the Deadly Sins, for it deadened, but who could help it. They'd never much liked her. As a young daughter-in-law, she'd done her best, having them over for Sunday meals and holidays, keeping the house clean and cheerful. Giving them two grandchildren they *had* loved. But they'd set their hearts on a different girl, apparently, their son's first sweetheart, and maybe that break-up something of a divorce, to their way of thinking. So then, a withholding. And in the barrens between them, burdock and thistle.

And now this.

Hands clenched. Limbs. Body. A tension that felt like being shaken.

At the terminal, arriving tourists appeared apprehensive as they entered the boarding lounge, walking in a clump toward greeters holding signs and calling out names. *Kamainas* arriving from Oahu or the other islands strode through it all smiling, string-tied pastry boxes in hand. Twenty years ago it had been like that—the confusion and joy of arrival. She could feel Linda's weight in her arms; could see Laura's white-blond hair framing her eyes, those skeptical blue eyes, and pink down-turned mouth as Ben carried her toward the luggage carousels.

Karen had looked back at the massive 747 that had brought them so far. White against jungle green. The sky dove-gray. Air like some moisturizer. And vibrant ferns swaying in it.

This should do, he'd said, smiling.

Now they boarded first, with the agents. She seated on one side of the cabin, with her guard; he on the other. Tourist class. The State of Michigan, she thought, sparing every expense.

Sometime in the night came the thought that it had all been blown away the instant the trigger of the shotgun ignited the small explosion within the shell that had killed her first husband. That shot taking even what would *be*, in time, so that everything that had happened to her afterward, to them both, she and Ben, and to the girls, and to their daughter Katherine, was as if it had never been.

In the plane's twilight, she found tissues in her purse and the rosary tossed there before leaving. Cupping the mother-of-pearl beads in one hand, she began saying the old words to herself. When flight attendants made the rounds of the cabin with hot face cloths, she took one and held it against her skin. Images tumbled, assembled: that day in April. So many people in the house, and she locking herself in the bathroom and holding a cloth to blotched face and closed eyes. And in that dark the truth clear as the window panes she'd washed that day: *Her fault. The death her fault. And so now this, too.*

As the plane sliced downward through thin cloud, descending into Chicago's O'Hare, a vast monochromatic landscape appeared, all segmented grays and browns dusted white—not so much landscape, it seemed, as the gears and bits and innards of some enormous machine. Then the curve of Lake Michigan, its wrinkled surface a hammered silver tray. Soon she had to endure the glances of people crowding the aisle, impatient to deplane.

Finally the aisle was clear and she could see her husband, still in his seat, bracing his chin, elbow propped on folded arm. As if sensing her look, he turned toward her. *It'll be okay. We just have to get through this thing.* Then he, too, stood, and soon the two agents had hustled them to another terminal, where commuters glanced up from paperbacks and newspapers and a little boy called out, "Mom! Look! That guy over there's got *handcuffs* on. Whad'he do?"

Linking her arm through her husband's, she walked with her shoulders well back. *Nothing. He did nothing.*

ANN ARBOR, MICHIGAN

LAURA

Her answering machine flashed with several new messages, all from Charlotte Hoon. *Laura, call me, please. This is my number . . . Laura, please call me . . . Laura, it is urgent you call me. I wait here for your call.*

Outside her study window, a raw March day. Black maple limbs lifting and falling in wind. Low rain cloud like smoke from burning tires, moving fast. But she had just seen masses of emerging crocus along the driveway. Tiny green spikes piercing last year's faded brown leaves. *God, don't let this be terrible!*

The impromptu prayer doing little to stop the shaking, nor the vision forming of her dad in the hospital. His "iffy" heart, as he called it, finally giving way.

Then she was listening, incredulous, to Charlotte Hoon's narrative. "They come with guns! Like in some movie! An' everybody scared, kids, parents! I say, what you doing? He's a doctor, he don' hurt nobody. But they put handcuffs on him, right in front of everybody. I tell them they're crazy. Parents holler at them, too. They take him to the airport with your mother. She tells me to call you. I have her dogs here. I take care of the orchids, yeah? An' I call Lin and Katherine. Your mother, she wants Katherine to stay at school in Kamuela for now."

Charlotte gave careful directions, then lapsed into emotion again. Laura let her talk. It *was* terrible, but a different terrible than a heart attack, imminent death. Relief muted outrage, but the shaking didn't abate as she told Charlotte she'd start out right away and be there for the arraignment in Tunley that night. She agreed that it had to be a mistake. Her father wasn't a murderer. It was just that some people had it in for him.

Two years earlier, news of the reopened investigation had made her physically ill for several days. But after a while, rationality reasserted itself and she'd been able to regard the new investigation into her birth father's death as something engineered by people who needed, still, to assuage loss, find satisfaction in revenge, as in those old blood-soaked Jacobean revenge dramas she'd read in college and thought too over-the-top to be taken as realistic. Eventually she'd convinced herself that it would all pass over like some fierce but brief storm. Her dad was no more a murderer than she was. Or her mother. Her sisters. The law would come to that conclusion, too. But meanwhile it had to go through its torturous—and torturing!—process to satisfy a few vengeful people.

And now, again, the inner moil of terror. So much money already spent on the team of Chicago lawyers apparently unable to halt the legal juggernaut launched by her grandparents. Four hundred and some thousand, which included her own and Lin's trust-fund money. How much more would they need? But more to the point, what did it mean that her grandparents had been able to get this far, with it all? Her mouth could hardly form clear words as she told Charlotte Hoon she'd call Lin.

From Ann Arbor, Laura could make it to the small town in the northern part of Michigan's Lower Peninsula in about five hours, if she started out right away. For Lin, in Ithaca, New York, it would be trickier. She tried Lin's number and, not reaching her, called the co-op where Lin worked, part-time. But she wasn't there, either. There were other calls to make, and it kept terror at some manageable level. Her private piano students had to be notified as well as the voice students at the university she was supposed to accompany in the coming days. Also, she needed to inform the artistic director at the small regional theater where she worked as a musician. *A family matter*, she told everyone. *No, not an illness. Just . . . something I have to help my parents with.* Which sounded lame as well as enigmatic, but she hadn't been able to come up with anything better. After packing her car with a few necessities, she tried the co-op again.

Lin answered. "God, Laura. I got your message and tried to call, but your line was always busy. The thing is, I can't make it up there tonight. Possibly not even this week. I've got three tests. I've got a paper due— How long do they have to be there?"

"You can't? I was thinking you could get a flight out of Syracuse. That would take an hour or so to Detroit. Then you could either drive up from Metro or fly to Petosky. I don't know about those commuter flights, though. Maybe you could get there tomorrow and—"

"Laur, I can't. Really. I've got all this stuff for school plus work. I can't just drop out, take Incompletes."

"We're not talking about the semester, Lin. It's an arraignment and then a hearing. Well, maybe a couple of hearings. There's the matter of bail, so I'm not—"

"What exactly *is* a hearing? You have any idea?"

"I think it's to see if Dad *should* be tried. That's why we need to be there, too. Show our support for him."

"Is Katherine with them?"

"Mom wants her to stay in Hawaii. At school. I think Mom's trying to shield her from this."

"But he's her dad, too!"

"Yes, but maybe Mom thinks that what happened has more to do with us. Or maybe she just wants Katherine spared. She is young, Lin. Only seventeen."

"But *I'm* supposed to put my life on hold here and come."

Laura recalled only too well how her sister had bounced around between schools, had dropped out to get married, then after the divorce, tried a culinary institute, then hotel management, and now physical therapy. After all that fussing around she was suddenly Ms. Conscientious? Anger gave voice to thought, precipitating one of their verbal firestorms for which, minutes later, Laura apologized. "You're right, Lin. You *are* trying. You're on track and want to stay there. I understand, really. I'm just . . . a little freaked right now. And I need to get going. But this isn't about us, is it? It's Dad we need to be thinking about. And Mom, too. Especially Mom, given her health."

"But not our *birth father*?"

At that, Laura clicked off and slammed out of her apartment on the second floor of her house. Crawling through late-afternoon traffic, she berated herself—what they didn't need right now was some stupid fight. They needed to stick together. A thought reminding her of her friend Bogdan and his family. How they were always helping one another with tuition money, apartment money, flight tickets from the Ukraine— His was the one number she hadn't called that afternoon, and now she understood why. He, being Bogdan, would have offered to help, begged to, but how do you explain to someone with a close religious family that your stepfather has just been charged with murdering your birth father twenty years ago. And that he married your mother shortly after. And became your dad. Whom you loved.

Driving too fast, she turned onto 23 and became part of the flow northward. A scrim of fog rose from patchy snow on harvested beet and corn fields and drifted across the highway. The setting sun gave a moment of color to clouds in the west, and then it was dark.

A person thinks too much, driving. She wished Lin were with her, even though Lin was freaking out too. That *but not our birth father?* Where was that coming from? It had never been an issue with her before. The reopened investigation had obviously done a job on her. Well, she wasn't going to let it get to *her*. Their dad was a good man. His actions bore this out. Always.

Still. How much did she really know of the past? Only what she'd been told. At first, just those few terrible words. *Your daddy's in the hospital. Doctors are trying to fix him.*

A lie—a white lie to spare them, get them to sleep—for by then he was dead. Later, the words amended. *Your daddy fell while out shooting. A fatal wound.*

Then there were her stepfather's words when she was ten and had felt grown up and serious, asking him about the shooting.

When my father died, did you see it happen?

No, honey, I didn't. I heard the shot and ran to where I could see him. All I saw at first was how he was lying face down on the ground. I turned him over and tried to get him to breathe. He'd been chasing something—woodchuck or porcupine, I'm not sure what. He must have tripped and the gun went off.

How do you know he was chasing anything, I mean if you didn't see it happen?

Well, I heard him holler something like Hey! There it is! His dad, meaning your grandfather, didn't like woodchucks making holes in the field because you could accidentally step in one and break an ankle. Maybe that's why I thought he must be after a woodchuck. We'd seen one earlier that day. But it could have been a porcupine, too.

Why would he want to shoot a porcupine? Do they make holes?

I don't think so. But they can be dangerous to dogs.

Did father have a dog? I don't remember any dog when we were little.

He didn't, but people who came out there often brought their dogs.

So you think he tripped in a woodchuck hole when he was running.

He might have. But sometimes you can trip when you're just running. You know—you catch your toe on some uneven ground and just go flying.

Did anyone find a woodchuck hole nearby?

That's a good question. Maybe they did. I didn't look, though. At the time, I was just trying to help your father, but he must have died right away. I don't think he suffered at all.

She recalled reading somewhere about certain rare individuals who could pick a day, any day, in their own lives—April 23rd, 1970, for instance—and start the movie going and there it would be, in all its minutiae, as that person lived it. Who, in their right minds, would want that? It would be like the Last Judgment *ad infinitum*: this you did; that you failed to do. Waiting at the dentist's office, you could bring it up. The doctor's. A grocery line. See yourself in all your wondrously glaring flaws. See all the missed chances. The flubs. The tapping of a judge's pencil, the one probably responsible for your not getting into Juilliard. That, she could remember even though she definitely wasn't a savant of any kind. But April 23rd, 1970. You'd see yourself that morning, a toddler, making a mess at the breakfast table. You'd see—

She could only imagine, not know. She did remember marshmallows. A cloud of white froth melting atop hot chocolate in a huge mug. Francine, their neighbor, making them hot chocolate that night—Francine's name supplied years later.

But an ability to fully remember that day from her own perspective wouldn't tell her what had happened in all that space beyond her own small orb of consciousness. For that you'd have to be psychic, or God.

So you need to go on faith. And maybe intuition. Both telling her he was innocent. *Lin, we have to believe him. Don't get crazy now, the way you sometimes do. Don't dramatize this, okay?* Her hands hurt, when she released her hold on the steering wheel. She'd been clutching it hard and driving well over the speed limit, hardly aware of the road. Raising her foot from the accelerator, she focused on the highway. Near Flint, traffic thickened. An angered edge to everyone's driving. And minds, she imagined, correspondingly racing with complaints about the day. How could they know that where they were, in their ordinary, complaint-ridden lives, was in fact a kind of heaven. That, you can't see, though, until something devastating happens. Then you look back with startled regret, realizing how you cheated yourself out of happiness.

North of Bay City, she stopped for gas at a place with a Palladian window and chandelier in its entry. Country music rained down from a canopy above the pumps. Inside, it twanged from the ceiling above shelves of junk food in flashy packaging. A store for kids on a spree. Lin pointing this out once—the American palate wanting only fast hits of sugar, fat, and salt, thanks to a food industry as bad as, or nearly so anyway, as the cigarette industry.

She bought a package of chocolate chip cookies, some packets of cheese and crackers, and a cup of coffee. Before starting up again, she tore into the cookies. *Really, it's just a vendetta, Lin. Our grandparents hate him. Always have. Our father tripped and fell and the gun went off. That's all.*

Then she was driving again, leaving the more populated areas. Occasionally the lit-up eyes of deer hung in the narrow space between interstate and woods like small white Christmas tree lights. She slowed to forty-five though the loss of time was making her panicky.

Three hours later, on a secondary highway, she ran into fog and had to turn down the high beams. She envisioned the small aircraft somewhere above, its landing lights valiantly on, illuminating the fog. Her parents probably holding each other's hand. She glanced at the clock again, then accelerated in a clear patch.

The head of a buck suddenly appeared at the passenger side window. A serene face, the black eye large, the white muzzle right at the window's glass. The thud must have come simultaneously, but it would later seem that several moments lapsed while the head remained framed by the window, floating there, then gone, an image imprinting itself on the retina as she braked, emergency flashers on. The car hadn't lurched. There'd been no sound of crushed metal, just the image of that great head at the window, filling its space, and then the gut-wrenching *thud.*

She was shaking so hard she almost didn't sense the car moving, when she went to get out. Falling back behind the wheel, she braked, and rammed the transmission into Park, then got out again, tremors racking through her and making the ground underfoot seem distant.

She could see nothing on the road except the haze of fog. The animal must have kept going somehow, maybe to fall later and lie in the woods, enduring broken legs and terrible pain. Ultimately some awful death by starvation. Or maybe bobcats and wolverines would feast even before it had died.

Headlights appeared, and she raised both arms, but the truck rattled past in the other lane, its hole-ridden muffler blasting. Then brake lights came on, and after a while, back-up lights. Wretchedness gave way to hope as the driver rolled down his window. The bearded man's face fleshy, his breath foul. Another man sat on the passenger side.

"I hit a deer," she said. "He ran into my car, on the side. He might be up ahead a ways, or just in the woods." She pointed in the direction the truck had been traveling. "If you've got a gun, you might . . . finish it off. Could you take a look?"

The man's stare unnerved her. She turned away, finally, and despite the trembling, jogged to her car. "Too many of them fuckers anyhow," he yelled from the truck. She slammed and locked her car doors, then panicked about the keys. It took a few seconds to realize they were in the ignition, and the car idling. She drove off slowly, keeping an eye on the rearview mirror. The truck didn't move, then finally did, in the opposite direction. After a few miles, she turned back and scanned both sides of the highway.

There it was, a dark hump, the antlers on one side keeping its head partially off the road. As she approached, it tried to rise. Blood pooled under its muzzle. It occurred to her that she could stop somewhere and call the police. She walked back toward her car, but stopped. Then walked on and got the plastic shopping bag kept under the front seat to use as a signal in case her car ever broke down somewhere.

Violent shivering came in spasms as she again approached the animal. And again it tried to stand, the hooves of its hind legs scraping the wet pavement, its front legs working uselessly.

God, let me do this.

Slowly she raised its quivering head, placed the open bag on the pavement, then lowered the muzzle and closed the bag around it. She had to turn away, eyes closed, while the hind legs scrabbled a while longer. Finally the deer lay still.

Quiet gave way to a thrumming, as of electricity galloping through high tension wires. Later, she'd realize the sound was

somehow internal, that wild humming. Taking hold of the antlers, she pulled the carcass farther to the side, then grabbed
hold of the hind legs and pulled. The animal's fur was wet.
Still warm. She scooped up some snow and wiped blood
from her hands. Sensations passing through the skin's barrier,
sinking down through tissue, bone, marrow, and—indelibly—
into memory.

ITHACA, NEW YORK

LIN

"I would if it were my dad. But none of my business, right?"

Yet she'd made it his business by stupidly spilling her guts the previous October—he'd walked into the stockroom and found her kneeling over a crate of organic apples and dabbing away tears. After that, whenever he'd asked how things were going, she—again stupid!—had told him. Creating this bond between them, which she regretted.

She looked at the co-op's wall clock. "It's too late."

"But if it's a hearing, it might last a few days or so, won't it?"

"I have no idea." Geeky Clarence. How like him to know about court hearings.

"Even if it lasts only a *day*, your folks probably need you to be there. For them. And it'd be better than avoidance."

"What're you, Clarence, a Psych major?"

"Haven't declared yet. The thing is, when my grandfather got sick and was in the hospital? I couldn't even stay home an extra day and see him through it. I was on the bus to *college* when he died. Talk about screwing up. The thing is, you do the small things okay. Like birthday gifts and stuff. But then it comes to that one *big* thing and you just . . . blow it." His eyes went shiny, the area around the acne lesions on his face and neck more flushed.

"Clarence, he probably didn't know you weren't there."

"Probably he did! Plus, I knew. Ever read *Lord Jim*? It's in there, too. Jim and this captain dude think their old tub of a boat is going down and nothing to do about it, so they go and jump. Then are rescued. But guess what? The boat *doesn't* sink. It's found with all these pilgrims on it, minus the captain and first mate. Then those two guys are fucked *forever*. Even if other people do forget about it in, like, fifty years or so, *they* won't. That's how I feel. My grandpa used to take care of me all the time, practically, because my parents were always at work. I loved him more than I loved my parents, so why the fuck did I *leave*? I wouldn't just think about it, Lin. I'd go, man."

"My car's a piece of crap."

"Big deal. Take mine."

"I can't take your car, Clarence!"

"You're wasting time."

"My sister wants me to fly up to Michigan, but I don't want to take her money. We don't . . . get along. She's like—"

Clarence pretended to be playing a violin, then said, "Just take the frigging money. Your dad has a bad heart, right? Well, guess what. Anything could happen now. *Anything*."

She looked at the clock again. "Flying is only half of it. From Detroit it's another, I don't know, six hours—of driving. Plus, it's just a hearing, it's not like a real trial, and I have a ton of stuff to do here."

Up went the pretend violin again. "You might be really sorry, I'm telling you."

She capped her marker.

She was eleven when she and her stepfather had talked about the shooting, and she'd never questioned his explanation. Until six months ago. The thing is, why, if it were so straightforward—*a simple hunting accident*—would there be this investigation? But say, just say, that he *had* done it. Couldn't it have been because of love? A crime of passion? Maybe even an accident but passion tangled in there, too? Among the few things she remembered from a religious ed class years earlier was that bit about God not liking lukewarm people. Saints and sinners okay, but cast away the lukewarm, the nothing-people. The soulless automatons. CIA assassins, for example.

She pressed cold fingers against her brow as the jet rode the air over the vast darkness that was Lake Erie.

Who else on her flight could possibly be wondering if one of their parents was a murderer?

Or both, for that matter.

TUNLEY, MICHIGAN

LAURA

When the arraignment hearing was over, officers escorted her dad into the hall outside the magistrate's office and there Laura could finally hug him. Handcuffed, he couldn't return the gesture, but she held onto him despite the awkwardness of his manacled hands.

He lowered his head and kissed her cheek. "I worried about you in that fog, honey."

"Dr. Weber," a man in a blue windbreaker said. "We need to leave now. You can see your family in the morning, at the jail."

She stepped back, seeing once more the handcuffs locked to a steel ring which in turn connected to a leather belt hanging low on the waist, supremely incongruous with the sport coat. The apparatus looked like something designed for a draft animal. The steel cuffs themselves were greater in thickness than she could have imagined. Worse, *leg shackles,* the length of chain between them clinking as he walked. Sudden anger burned away at the mass of soggy emotion she'd become. *Did they really think he was going to try to run?*

Laura walked to the right of her mother and their lawyer's investigator, a short, thick-set man everyone called Midge. But the camcorders were all aimed at the three men in front of them, particularly at her father—the tallest—in the center. The questions addressed to him as they walked toward the sheriff's car.

Head lowered, he said nothing.

At a bed and breakfast place called the Hutchins House, the bedrooms had angled ceilings, dormer windows with window seats, and wallpaper in a flowery Colonial Williams-burg design. Also, gold-framed botanical prints, antique bird's eye-maple dressers, bureaus, and nightstands as well as mul-ticolored, hand-braided rugs. In her mother's room, across the hall from her own, the four-poster bed was high, its posters topped with wooden pineapples, its spread a heavy woven cotton, cream-colored. A charming, fully domesticated room, Laura thought. A theme-park room, and the theme?—innocence, artful simplicity. The larded-on charm was so in contrast to her state of mind that it offended.

Her mother was sitting in a wingback chair, defying house rules and smoking. It scared Laura, her mother smoking again so soon after her hysterectomy. But she couldn't bring herself to start nagging. Instead, with another fingernail, she dug into the skin under a thumbnail as she sat in the room's desk chair, facing her mother.

"Mom, from what you're saying, there might not be a trial?"

"It depends on what they have. They've gotten this far, so they must be fairly confident."

"What do our lawyers think?"

"Well, Russ seems optimistic enough."

Laura stood to open the dormer window. "What evidence can they possibly have?"

"For one thing, the autopsy results."

"In other words, their experts' opinions?"

"And we'll have ours, I suppose."

"Then won't they just cancel each other out?"

"Maybe. I don't know." She balanced the cigarette on the porcelain soap dish she'd been holding.

"Mom, are you hungry? I could try and find something."

"We ate on the flight. I'm okay, honey."

A lie. Her mother never touched airline food. "I just remembered—there's some crackers and cheese in the car. Also cookies."

"Thanks, but I'm fine, really."

She wasn't. Thinner than ever. And under each eye, a cres-cent of bruised skin, the storm-cloud feathering upward as well. The cheekbones prominent. The knuckles of her hands.

"Mom, do we have enough money for dad's bail bond?" A question she immediately regretted.

"If it's entirely cash, we may not. But if the judge allows property collateral, then yes, I think so."

"Property— You mean the house in Hawaii."

"And the clinic as well. Also, you remember the people in Virginia who raised your dad, the professor at the University of Virginia?"

"But they died, didn't they?"

"The man did. The woman is in a personal care home. She's been keeping in touch and now wants to do whatever she can. Through her lawyer, she contacted Russ. I guess her mind is still pretty sharp. She owns some income property and is prepared to offer that as collateral. Even poor Charlotte— Mrs. Hoon—offered her savings."

"Well, but we can't—"

"I know." She drew on the cigarette, let her eyes close for a moment.

"Mom?" *Please put out that cigarette.* "Maybe you shouldn't be smoking so much."

"I probably shouldn't, but it . . . helps."

"Sleep might be better."

"I don't think I can."

"At least you'll rest better than in that chair. How about if I find you something to read? I saw some books out in the hall."

A few minutes later she returned with one of the library discards shelved in a pine bookcase at one end of the hall. Her mother had taken off her suit jacket and was searching her suitcase. Her frailty alarmed Laura, the bones so clearly visible under the thin fabric of her shirt.

"I thought I packed a nightgown, but now I can't find it." Tears came. "We were in . . . such a rush. It was . . ."

"You did, Mom. Look. Here it is, but you might be cold in just this. Wait a second. I might have something." Laura hurried across the hall to her own room and found a cotton turtleneck for her mother to wear over the nightgown.

Finally settled in bed, her mother reached for the porcelain soap dish she'd placed on the nightstand, then for her cigarettes.

"Mom? I'm sorry." She took the pack of cigarettes from her mother's hand and felt terrible doing it. "We don't want to be kicked out of here tomorrow, right?" At the door, she paused. "'Nite. I love you."

Her mother blew her a kiss.

In her own room, Laura lay in the high bed and tried to relax, but every muscle still seemed on alert; and when she closed her eyes, she kept seeing that deer right at the window. After a while she got up and dressed.

KAREN

Lying in the double bed, Karen smoked a stub of a cigarette and regarded the room, its tiger maple highboy, fringed
curtains at the open window, maple washstand, and a quilt,
even, on a quilt stand. Russ's staff had obviously succeeded
in finding a comfortable and exceptionally clean place for her
and Laura, but wasn't it strange how life had a way of taunting
one with irony. Excoriating one with the past. This room might
have been one of the bedrooms in the farmhouse belonging
to Ben and his first wife Marcia, a house she and Pete had
toured the night of the party to celebrate its restoration. The
gabled farmhouse had struck her as something right out of
Country Life—and no expense spared. She had been envious,
of course, and in awe, while at the same time a bit scornful
of the religious attention to detail, the fussiness. Stoneware
pitchers filled with dried flowers and grasses, crewelwork pil-
lows, plaids and prints and decoupage, stenciling and weather-
vanes and wooden cows, sheep, and geese Marcia might have
painted herself. No children, no full-time work, and so lots of
time. Whereas she herself had had little time for even the necessary cleaning. Her baby—Lin—and two-year-old Laura so
needy, especially of a vigilance that often left her exhausted and
then snappish with her husband when he'd return home
late to a haphazardly set table and a meal she'd thrown
together, something, anything, just get through it and into bed.
She loved her children, each so beautiful, a bountiful beauty,
golden, and their liveliness, curiosity, intelligence. She loved
them but they exhausted her, she'd had no idea it would all
be so draining, had once hoped to be the perfect mother and

40

wife in a perfect home. But—hardly. Each minute had become an uphill step. Fourteen hours held eight hundred and forty of them. She needed help during the day, but Pete felt that the children were too young to trust to a sitter, even while Karen was right there in the house. *Wait until they're a little older, okay?*

In her pediatrician's dining room, surrounded by beautifully refinished antique pieces and so many crafted, toy-like objects, she judged herself a failure. *This woman should be a mother, not me.* A perception heightened by the large glass of Chablis she had downed too fast. Glancing around for her husband, she saw instead Dr. Weber approaching. *These look really good, don't they? Let's fix you a plate. What would you like?*

Ben he'd wanted to be called. She couldn't. Had kept it to Dr. Weber. A basketball player's height and sheen and leanness. Hair buzz-cut at the sides. Bony cheekbones and nose. Childless, despite the reminders of fecundity all about.

Actually, it's time we leave. Pete is still skittish about sitters for the girls and—

But it's only nine or so.

I know but I need to be up by 6:30, the latest. Laura's an early riser and Pete's gone by then. If I sleep beyond that, I have to hit the floor running and it's crazy. That's why I like to get up even earlier. It's quiet then and I get to read yesterday's paper.

She'd tried to laugh, but shame suffused her face at that raw rush of self-revelation. And self-pity.

There must have been some witty parry, for it was a party, one celebrating house, home, and new beginnings—another irony. A house, with its golden oak and tiger maple and bird's-eye maple and burled walnut and country curtains and plank floors and simple crafts that may as well have gone up in flames that night, given what was soon to come.

She took another cigarette stub from the soap dish and relit it, the match's flame singeing her fingers. Nicotine spangled the tunnel of throat, the cave of chest, and threw forth its roadblocks in the brain. After a while, she felt calm enough to open the book Laura had brought her and begin reading how Washington, in 1861, was a city rife with sedition.

Sedition. Wasn't that like treason?

Betrayal, then.

And she was back in that Michigan farmhouse the night of the party, studying the man she would soon accept, in a fully volitional act, as her lover.

No—beloved.

LAURA

When she placed a flannel nightgown and pair of slippers on the counter, the clerk asked if she was Dr. Weber's daughter.

"I am. How did you know?"

"I sort of guessed. You look like your dad. I mean your real dad, the one that was shot. His picture's been in the paper. Plus, you're new in town. Here for the hearing, right?"

"Dr. Weber's my real dad."

"Sor-ry. I just meant—"

"I know."

Laura glanced to the side. One other shopper lingered in the seasonal aisle, an older woman holding a plush rabbit and studying the price.

"Listen, I knew your dad. Dr. Weber, I mean. He's gold. Helped me out a lot one time. I was up a creek without a paddle, you know? Even paid my room and board and tuition at the community college over in 'tosky."

The young woman—her name pin said *Ruthie*—was heavy, her plump arms and face garishly white under the fluorescence. A plastic tortoise shell clamp held back a top layer of blond hair. The rest, darker, drizzled down her shoulders in tight waves. Several small ear rings pierced the curve of each ear.

"How did he help you? I mean, in addition to paying for college?"

Ruthie met Laura's eyes, then looked away. "You know."

"Oh. He—" She couldn't form the words.

"The thing is, I can't really talk about it, you know? I mean, the way things are here. Just want you to know I'm on his side. Yours, too."

43

"Well, thanks."

"It's okay. Tell him hi for me if you want."

"Ruthie—"

"Ruth Ronkavich before. Married now. Two kids. Husband workin'—" She laughed. "Which is something, up here."

The other shopper was approaching, rabbit still in hand.

"I'll tell him."

On the way back, she tried to imagine it: Ruth a farm girl with beautiful hair and lush skin but not one of the high school elites in hip-hugging jeans. The popular boys probably hadn't given her a second look, while the unpopular ones had. One boy, in particular. And then Dr. Weber helped her out of a jam.

Laura turned and drove back to the variety store. The lights were out except for a few in back, and the place locked up.

LIN

Her sister hugged her first, a quick cool embrace. Then her mother's, warmer, needier. Her mother seemed to have the flimsiness of balsa wood, which scared Lin. Two years before she had looked wonderful, as usual. Shiny wheat-colored hair. Thin but muscular arms with real strength. Now? A brittleness. As if she could snap into a zillion pieces at any given second.

"Mom," she said. "Sorry I'm late."

"It's all right, honey. You're here now."

"Where's Dad?"

"The county jail," Laura said, her voice low. "We can see him this afternoon."

Her mother squeezed Lin's hand.

"He's okay," Laura said, to divert attention from her mother's welling eyes. "Better than we are, probably. You know Dad."

In the dining room they sat as far as possible from a middle-aged couple who stared at the three of them, then leaned toward one another, whispering. A stocky woman poured their juice and explained about the cereal, pastries, and rolls arranged on an antique sideboard at the far wall. Lin wished she'd brought something non-hydrogenated from the co-op.

"How was your flight?" Laura asked, putting jam on a croissant.

"Uneventful."

Laura looked down at her loaded plate.

"How was your drive up?" Lin said after a moment.

"Lots of fog. And I hit a deer. Actually, it just ran into the side of the car. What would make it do that? Why would it just run at the car like that? It was awful."

The words *death wish* came to mind, which she knew to be stupid. If anything, animals probably had better brains than people, more suited to survival, anyway. "Probably just confused in the fog, maybe." Lin drew fingers across her lips, signaling Laura.

I'll tell you later, Laura mouthed.

Since greeting Lin, her mother hadn't said a word—or eaten much of anything. A bite of Danish she had cut into tiny segments, a sip of coffee. Outside, a dour overcast. Dry sunflower stalks in a back garden stood gray and bowed, their plate-like disks tipped toward the earth. A sparrow clung to one, pecking away.

Eye, Lin thought, in her fatigue. Pecking away at an eye.

THE COUNTY'S new jail had been built in an older neighborhood, rather than out in a field somewhere, with some long access road, as Lin had envisioned. At first she'd thought it must be some angular, avant-garde library, its maroon blocks rising to a narrow band of windows on the second story, its "yard" paved and surrounded by a high wrought-iron, picket-type fence. She supposed the neighborhood residents hated it, so at odds as it was with the surrounding well-kept Victorian houses, most with large porches, yards, and old shade trees.

Just inside the entrance, a grim officer went through their purses, finally allowing them to pass through a metal-detector archway. They signed a register, and then another officer escorted them to an open area holding three rows of molded chairs. Under the fluorescent lighting, aqua color seemed to bleed upward into the room.

"One person at a time," the guard said. "Rule is, no physical contact whatsoever with the prisoner."

Prisoner. "Mom, you go first," Lin said.

Her mother smoothed the trousers of her pantsuit. Lin remembered this outfit, its fabric an expensive blend of silk and lightweight wool in muted pastel shades, but now it hung loosely on her. Yet despite the discoloring under each eye, despite the alarming loss of weight, she was still beautiful in a way that neither she herself nor her sister would ever be. It was mysterious. The exact right alignment of bones. Plus the reserve, possibly some unconscious sense of superiority. Alongside her, Lin always felt more like a peasant trying to dress up for the day, even though a lot of people had told her she was beautiful. She enjoyed these compliments but, next to her mother, recognized the truth. She was okay. Just. Laura, on the other hand, wasn't even that. Frumpy, in fact, in her turtle-necks and long full skirts. Also, too heavy, but far be it for her to say anything and start World War III. Lin knew how much Laura had wanted to become a concert pianist, a star in that competitive world, and how she'd regretted not being glam-orous in some willowy, seductive way. Lin had once said, "But Laur, you don't *have* to be. You just have to play well, don't you? Isn't that how it goes? Talent and ability. What they call mastery?" But Laura had argued that an aspiring performer needed an edge, something *more*, something people would remember. Star quality.

"Oh come on. Sex sells cars, I realize, and movies and hot tubs, but Beethoven?"

"You'd be surprised."

Something else had to have been going on, Lin decided. Some kind of burn-out. All that instruction—the good teachers, the summers at Interlochen, the innumerable hours of prac-tice, the study at Oberlin and the University of Michigan, and yet the thing not happening. Lin saw the turning point as the moment when her sister didn't get into Juilliard. And that was when, Lin thought, her sister had taken the turn back into the world of ordinary mortals—where she was, in the current jargon, a not-altogether-happy camper. Lin tried to keep this in mind whenever the bitchiness kicked in.

Now she took hold of Laura's hand, much warmer than her own. "Laur, this is kind of . . . scary."

"What did you expect?"

The tone flat, non-judgmental, so she went on. "Not that he would be *here*, a *prisoner*. I thought it would be more, I don't know, like we'd just go into a courtroom or something and hear the lawyers out. But this is like he's already guilty, you know?"

"Well, he's not."

"I know that."

"Do you?"

Keep the peace. "The thing is, I'm glad I came. Glad you yelled at me."

Her sister said nothing but didn't pull her hand away. Lin regarded it as a positive sign.

Then it was her turn. She followed the guard into another harshly lighted room where she was told to sit opposite her dad at a cafeteria-type table. He was unrecognizable at first, in an orange jumpsuit, his eyes reddened, his face gray. He raised fingers to his lips, gesturing a kiss. She did the same. The guard stood a few feet away.

"Wish I could give you a hug, honey." His voice rasped with emotion.

"Me, too, Dad."

"You had a long trip."

"You and Mom as well."

He raised a hand to his right eye and blinked. "Honey, take care of your mom, all right? I'm pretty worried about her."

"Her health?"

"That, and all this, too. It's made her start smoking again. Having you girls with her might help."

"If we don't fight."

"You won't. You're big girls now."

"That we are."

"Just try to, gently, keep her off those cigarettes. Her last treatment was four months ago, and things looked pretty good until this. Do what you can, okay?"

"We will."

"And how are you, sweetheart?"

"I'm okay."

"Honest?"

"Honest." She opened her eyes wider to contain tears.

"We'll beat this."

"I know we will."

"I've never let you down, have I?"

"No."

"Nor your mother."

Tears spilled. He extended his handkerchief.

"Sorry, Doc," the guard said, stepping forward and shoving it back to him.

"For Christ's *sake*."

"I don't make the rules."

Her dad's hands were trembling. His eyes looked black.

"It's all right, Dad. I've got tissues somewhere."

"Just hang on, honey. Okay?"

"I will, Dad."

"I love you, sweetie."

"I love you too, Dad."

It was good to turn away, finally.

BEN

*A*ccident. Beyond his control. That's how accidents were. Everything going along okay and then nothing the same afterward. And the thing sinking into every thread of your being. *Muscle memory.* The shotgun there between the two of them, his own gun *but Pete using it that day.*

That's right.

No, wait. Pete had been running. Chasing something. Then he was down.

His hands shook. Again, as before, he's whipping Pete's Jeep into that old guy's driveway and ramming the derelict flatbed truck parked there. The old guy bursts out of his place, then stands there gaping, wiry old guy, looked after the camp when Pete or his parents weren't out there. *Accident! Back in the clearing. Pete tripped and shot himself! You got a phone here?*

The old guy dopey or shocked still at the sight of blood.

Phone! I need to call, dammit! Blood on his hands, darkening. Blood blackening under his fingernails. Blood on his face, smeared blood, and the old guy's mouth open.

Somewhere a phone was ringing. Somewhere men were talking. Everyday words. A guard in gray swung by and gave him an impassive glance. The guard obese, his gut a barge he pushed ahead of him.

His thoughts skittered to cowboy movies, *cowboy movies,* ranch hands branding cattle, the calf on its side, three legs roped, and the smoking branding iron pressing into its haunch, and the animal bleating and trying to kick, while in the movie house's humid dark he and his friends chewed Junior Mints and waited for the good parts to come around again, the chases,

50

the shoot-outs. Pain hadn't figured in; pain had nothing to do with anything.

Unlike now, he, branded by successive images: his wife's face. His daughters'. Bravery struggling with bleakness. Confusion with faith, or its pretense.

He'd told her it would come to this one day. A change in the town's power structure, and things would turn against them.

But what about the truth? Doesn't the truth count?

Of course it does.

Then we'll be all right.

So they'd married, and the girls had become his—and he, theirs. A family.

And now the *this* it had been coming to all along. A guard eyeing him so that he wouldn't do himself in, somehow. An ill wife. And two young women—*his girls*—nearly scared out of their wits.

The gun there between them.

The gun there between them?

Dinner was a cube of tough Swiss steak, with instant mashed potatoes and gravy. He passed on it, then sometime in the night, regretted it, the hunger so gnawing he feared he might vomit up the sour fluids filling his stomach.

But even that preferable to what was slewing about in his brain.

LAURA

On her tongue, the Host, faintly sweet, but in her heart no sweetness, no love for the man kneeling only three feet away—Anton Svoboda—in the rectory's chapel, where weekday Masses at St. Anne's were said. The Deputy Assistant Prosecutor for the State of Michigan in an ordinary beige suit, a frazzle of graying hair, a face in mourning. He hardly looked like an attorney of some status, more like a small town businessman up against hard times. She'd read in sidebar articles how he'd been raised in a suburb of Detroit and had worked with his father at a Ford assembly plant, putting himself through the University of Michigan with the help of a scholarship. After a distinguished tour of duty as a Marine in Vietnam, he returned to Ann Arbor and was accepted into the University of Michigan Law School. Even while in Vietnam, one article noted, he tried to keep up his practice of attending daily Mass—so she shouldn't have been surprised to find him at the rectory that morning.

Kneeling there after Communion, she thought that Christianity—truly following Christ—was impossible. How can you love an enemy? After Mass, she took her time gathering jacket and purse while an elderly woman left the chapel first, followed by Svoboda.

"Was that kind of hard?" The priest's voice without resonance, thinly juvenile, like everything else about him. He grimaced a little, as if involved in some strenuous manual work. She sensed his lack of confidence as she could sense it in her piano students—that tightness and fear of making mistakes. The diffidence and lack of humor. And he was shorter than her

52

by several inches, which added to the overall impression of his being not quite *there* yet.

But was one ever?

"So you recognize me, too, Father." The appellation made them both blush.

"Yes, but I don't recall—I'm sorry—your name?"

"It's Laura. Laura Weber. I should have known he'd be here. I've read articles about him."

"He is quite faithful."

Faithful. "The thing is, I probably won't be back. It's too . . . awkward."

"Do you have time for a cup of coffee or tea? We could talk a bit."

"Thank you, but the hearing, I have to be there in a few minutes."

Forestalling an unexpected surge of emotion, she turned away and was soon hurrying down the rectory's stone steps, the day's cold wind working like a needed compress against burning face.

"We could have Mass over at the church," he called, "if that might be better?"

She shook her head and kept going.

Window boxes along the shops fronting Tunley's main street were barren of flowers, but the earth there black and moist, ready. Ahead, at the end of the street, the red brick court-house, its Ionian columns and pediment white. A few reporters with camcorders stood near the front steps. Hurrying along the side of the courthouse, she came to the unassuming door used by employees and court regulars and, no doubt, the accused, the convicted.

Her mother and dad were seated alongside one another on a couch, but each seemed oblivious of the other. And each looked wrecked. Well, sure, they'd look that way, any-body would, given all they'd been through in the past days. The bail hearing, for instance, sickening in implication. *Three quarters of a million dollars.* But at least property collateral had been allowed. Still—her parents sounding like beggars on the phone, struggling to pull that amount together, which they had, finally. But now all those people knowing that the Court didn't trust them.

Still, fatigue and sadness didn't necessarily equate with guilt.

Minutes later, Russell Lowry entered and threw off his overcoat, a gesture Laura found both theatrical and off-putting, a power thing. He might have just come from a sauna—the shiny forehead and cheekbones, the rose-glow cheeks. A round face, babyish, and thinning blond hair only enhancing that impression. Rimless eyeglasses, though, helped to counterbalance the effect. That, and his obvious confidence.

"Morning, folks!"

Her dad returned Lowry's smile. Her mother didn't. Lin turned from the window and raised her eyebrows a degree, glancing at Laura.

The attorney gestured for them to join him at the long oak table, and when they were all seated, he explained his strategy. Svoboda, he said, was probably going to be fairly contained. Where he went wild, usually, was before a jury. Still, he'd be typically reckless, and Lowry planned to allow him enough rope.

Apart from that, Lowry was simply going to fight him every inch of the way, question every bit of evidence. Mainly photos and ballistics and slides from the second autopsy. But first, he was going to move for dismissal because of the length of time that had passed and also because several key witnesses were either deceased or unable to testify—for one, the county investigator at the time, now mentally incapacitated and residing in a nursing home.

"At this point, do you folks have any questions?"

They all appeared to be studying the table's scratches, but then her dad asked where he was to sit. He hoped, he said, it could be with his family.

"I'm afraid not, Doctor. You'll have to be at the defense table, with us."

"And my wife and daughters?"

"In the gallery, on the right side of the courtroom, as we enter from judge's chambers. We'll all exit the same way. "Mrs.

Weber, during breaks, you , Laura, and Lin are free to come and go by way of the public entrance at the back of the courtroom, but I advise against it. Same thing for the morning; use the rear entry, as you did today. A couple of other things—there's a coffee machine here and spring water dispenser as well as a small fridge. This room also has its own restroom and lounge. If you need anything, please let our paralegal, Bev, know. She'll be happy to help you out. Finally, let me emphasize: while in the courtroom, don't speak with the press, nor respond to anything a spectator might say, friendly or otherwise. You can acknowledge a person with a smile, a nod, but keep some distance. Your main job is to appear attentive and calm. In other words, not rattled, not angry, not bent out of shape in any way. Save emotion for later. All right? Any further questions?"

"How long is it going to take?" Lin asked. "This hearing."

"Possibly a week. But I suspect less."

"A whole *week*?"

Lowry glanced at his thin wristwatch. "It's time, folks."

ENTERING THE courtroom was like tumbling underwater, all sound muted as Laura followed her mother and sister to the first-row bench on the defense's side of the courtroom. Gradually the aural fog lifted, and she could hear people walking—heavily, importantly—down from the big doors at the back. A large woman in a wool skirt and matching jacket. A young man listing under the weight of his lawyer's case. A thin woman in high heels, auburn hair clamped in a bouncy ponytail. Then Svoboda. No-frills Svoboda, bringing up the rear and swinging a white pointer back and forth like a spear.

Laura wasn't in the habit of reading legal thrillers, nor seeing their film versions; nor was she captive to any courtroom dramas on TV. So it was all new, the gravitas, the near-ritualistic language. The legalese flowed so swiftly that it was a while before she realized Russ Lowry had lost his opening gambit—the motion for dismissal curtly denied—and he simply going on to the next thing as if mechanized.

The prosecution's first witness, a board-certified pathologist, spoke with the precise yet musical enunciation peculiar
to residents of former British colonies. Dr. Havani's demeanor
was equally courtly and self-assured. Pete Hyland's wound
had been sewn, he said, by the funeral director twenty-one
years before. But based on photographs taken at the time by
the examining physician, Dr. Millard Howe, the wound had
been an inch wide by an inch-and-a-half long. The photographs
also showed some scalloping from entering shot pellets but no
darkening, no deposits caused by still-burning gases. Thus, the
range of fire was, in his opinion, between three and five feet
away. And the shot's trajectory, in his determination, was from
high to low and from front to back. The exploded shell had
amputated half the heart. "Blew it away," Dr. Havani stated
calmly. It also perforated the left lung and deposited shot pellets under the armpit.

All this Svoboda elicited without mishap, and Laura began
to wonder if what Russ had said about Svoboda's recklessness
had been somewhat exaggerated.

At the cross, Russ Lowry, holding a book, rose to ask if
Dr. Havani knew the exact diameter of the shotgun's muzzle.

"No. I do not."

"Well, I have it right here. Would you care to have a look
at this information?"

Dr. Havani bowed his head slightly, thanked Russell Lowry,
and replied that he didn't need to know that in order to draw
his conclusion. He had seen no evidence of smoke or unburned
gunpowder—the dark "tattooing" that sometimes gets under
the skin around the wound or along the wound track. Nor had
he seen it on the clothing. Also, there were no burns on the skin.
No muzzle abrasion, which occurs when a gun is fired with its
muzzle directly against the skin. Gases become trapped under
the skin, the skin then balloons and pushes against the muzzle.
But he did not see any evidence of that either in the photos
Dr. Howe took during the initial autopsy nor during the second
autopsy he himself did.

Laura let her eyes shut for a few seconds, knowing that she shouldn't. The press, seated in the well and able to look out over the gallery, might note it and spin the detail into their articles, but my God, skin ballooning against gunmetal. Envisioning it, she missed most of what Havani had gone on to say about shot cups, the plastic containers for the pellets, opening "like flower petals." When he stepped down to draw illustrations on a marker board, she didn't listen. Let Russ fight the battle. The important thing was that *he* believed this case should never go to trial.

She'd made a point of asking him directly, the day after the arraignment. "You wouldn't take on this case, Mr. Lowry, would you, if you thought my dad were in fact guilty? Or am I being naïve?" Even as she said those words, she understood that she probably *was* being naïve. Lawyers needed high-profile cases. The question of actual guilt or innocence was probably irrelevant. All they cared about, maybe, was whether or not they could win.

"Your dad," he said, "made a plausible statement at the time. It's still plausible today."

"But do you believe him?"

"I'm here, aren't I?"

"Yes, but is that any measure of your *belief*?"

"It is, indeed. You'd make a good lawyer, incidentally."

She'd been the one to lower her eyes first. And that night, at least, she'd fallen asleep without too much difficulty. Things had seemed possible again, and it wasn't a forced march to believe they'd soon be on the other side of it all.

Now she took her mother's hand and tried to distract herself from Havani's testimony by imagining how it would be when it was all over. Her parents would fly back to the Big Island. Her dad would return to his clinic, her mother to her volunteer work, her orchids, and her two dogs. Lin would go back to school and maybe stay put this time. And she herself?—she'd resume her own life. It would be like coming back from somewhere far away.

KAREN

That couldn't be right. *High to low; front to back.* Pete *had* to have been running after something. Pete the hunter. The sportsman. Chasing some small creature. Porcupine. Groundhog. Grouse. He'd been proud of his aim. Had hunted since he was twelve at least, if not before, with B-B guns. It hadn't exactly shocked her to learn of this in high school. Most boys up there hunted. It was just that he hadn't seemed the type. He'd been in Chorus—a wonderful tenor. French Club. Honor Society. She remembered how he'd talked about museums, complaining that there were none of any significance for hundreds of miles in any direction. While at Michigan State, he'd made trips to Chicago to see the Monet *Water Lilies* there, and to the Detroit Art Institute. He'd recounted the French Club's trip to Montreal and said how he wanted to take her there after they were married. On their New England honeymoon, they'd spent a day at Boston's Isabella Stewart Gardner museum. He couldn't get over its oriental collection and fantasized about a trip to Japan, when they had a little money. The passion for hunting seemed some aberration.

She supposed he'd been indoctrinated into it by his father, a rough-edged sort who for years had driven a dairy tanker until farming in the area went into decline. Then he began selling insurance to the farmers, or former farmers, he'd known on his route, eventually took over the small insurance business, built it up, then brought in his only child, after Pete graduated from MSU. She'd always thought that Pete went along with the hunting to please his father. But knowing how it displeased her each November to see the bloodied deer carcasses roped to cars—and up there that was as much a trophy as the antlers which eventually were nailed to rec room walls—she thought he might give it up. Yet, if anything, he became more avid, extending his range to Ontario, Montana, and Idaho with his buddies, and collecting even larger sets of antlers. There was less and less talk of visiting museums, particularly after the birth of the two children.

. . . *high to low, front to back* . . . But if you fell, you'd be gut-shot, wouldn't you? Sometimes he'd talked about that, stupid guys running with loaded guns, the safety off. Shaking his head—guys like that definitely didn't belong in the woods. Guys like that got what they deserved.

Karen took a tissue from her purse and crushed it between blue fingertips. She knew she mustn't show any emotion; the reporters, the spectators, her in-laws would seize upon it. *Hey look. She's crying. Well, so what. Women like that get what they deserve.*

The Pete of that April wasn't the considerate, even-tempered man she'd married. He'd gotten moody, the mood swings frightening her and the girls. He'd go on hunting trips and not call to say where he was or when he'd be back. Or, he'd call from work and say he'd be staying late, then arrive home early, saying the meeting had been cancelled. Sometimes he'd want to make love at odd times of the day, the children playing in nearby rooms. Once she found a bottle of gin in a drawer of his roll-top desk, then didn't look again, knowing that it—or a replacement—would probably be there.

Then there was that party in Travers, on a yacht moored in the harbor, he dropping their hotel key in a dish where other keys lay, and Richard Geffe picking it up, then seeking her out. But Ben had been there, too, had driven her back to Tunley, to the children and their sitter.

So, yes. It made sense that he would have been chasing some animal that day out at the camp, for so much of what he did in those days was off-kilter, as if he'd become someone else who just happened to have the same name.

Because of her? *Because of?*

For years dormant, the question clawed its way out of the murk.

Why else would she have wanted to kill herself that night? Actually take her own life—unless she had felt certain.

That night. Death a sea lapping all around. And she wanting to plunge in. More than wanting. *Needing*, for she didn't know how she was going to be able to live in all the hours of that night, in all the hours of the next day, and the next and the next. A form of agony, that mental assault. The word now devalued; common—*it was agonizing*. Still, agony. Every cell in pain, every muscle writhing with knowledge. *Pete is dead. Pete is dead.* But it was their faces, finally, her children's faces in sleep, that had saved her, rather than any fear for her immortal soul. Those tear-reddened faces in their little deaths, at the mercy of dreams.

An image that became for her an amulet.

And then, some months later, Ben had come into her children's lives not as Dr. Weber but simply as Ben, and their broken world began to heal.

LAURA

For their lunch, Midge, Russ's investigator, brought in sandwiches and soft drinks from a restaurant down the street. Also, giant brownies corseted in clear plastic. Lin took one look at the array on the long oak table and said she was going for a walk and might pick up a salad on the way back.

After she had gone, Laura said, "These ham sandwiches look pretty good, Mom. Would you rather a soft drink or coffee with yours?"

"Just some coffee will be fine."

Her dad put half a sandwich on a paper plate. "Have a few bites anyway," he said. "You don't want to get lightheaded."

Laura tried to think of something to spark a little conversation, but each thought seemed more banal and ridiculous than the previous. *What was the weather like in Hilo when you left? Aren't those beds at the guesthouse comfortable?* Finally she said, "Looks like they might be repaving Main Street soon. I saw a lot of heavy equipment this morning when I walked here from Mass."

Her mother regarded the triangle of ham sandwich on the paper plate before her. "They're doing it for the cameras. So everything will look just wonderful."

"I'm sure, honey," Ben said, "they've got better reasons than that."

"People here were always meanspirited, under it all," Karen said. "Calculating. Clannish. Hypocritical. I might add arrogant and proud, too. Of course they'll want the street perfectly paved, putting so much stock, as they do, in appearances. It's too bad they're only now just starting, with the TV crews already here."

Laura finished her sandwich and eyed one of the oily-looking brownies. "Dad," she finally said. "Can I split one of those with you?"

He pushed an entire brownie across the table. She felt guilty unwrapping it while her mother just gazed down at her own sandwich. Then Laura saw the tears. She slid her chair closer to her mother's and put an arm around her. "Mom? C'mon, okay? Everything's going to work out."

"Your sister couldn't even stand to be here."

"That's not true. You know how she is about *food*."

"Then why isn't she bringing something back here to eat? Because she doesn't want to be with us."

"Mom, she does. She came all the way from Ithaca."

The silence deepened again until her mother said, "Can I smoke up here, do you think?"

"I'm sure you can," Ben replied. "But just a few puffs, all right?"

Laura couldn't stop eating bits of the cloying brownie.

THAT AFTERNOON Havani explained, in his precise manner, that if one is running while carrying a gun, the barrel of the gun most likely will be tilted downward and would have to rotate 180 degrees in order for someone to get a wound angle such as the deceased had—up to down. Police cadets attempted to re-create the scenario by running and falling but in each instance could not. Also, if one is running and the gun leaves one's hand, it would tend to fall farther away, the muzzle facing in the wrong direction.

Laura listened despite herself.

". . . Now if the gun drops away from one, during that fall, what will happen if one pulls the gun toward oneself, in the process of trying to stand up? First, this assumes that the barrel would be pointing toward the person, a faulty assumption, I believe. Also, you would have to assume that something gets caught in the trigger guard, forcing the trigger back. Still, should the gun fire because of the object, the twig or whatever, caught within the trigger guard, the wound track would be in the *opposite* direction—low to high. In this scenario, there is the additional assumption that someone who knew about guns since childhood would even make such a mistake as pulling the barrel of a gun toward oneself."

Across the aisle, Laura's grandfather was shaking his head. She supposed it was the first thing young hunters learned— never to aim a gun at yourself or anyone else regardless of whether or not it was loaded and the safety on.

At the cross examination, Havani admitted that the examining physician *had* noted what he termed "some darkening" around the wound. Darkening, Lowry would have the magistrate understand, was indisputable evidence of a close-contact shot.

Lowry then asked a number of questions relating to terrain and weather conditions. Had the doctor gone to the scene himself to determine the contour of the land? No. Could he have done so? Presumably he could have, yes. How many photos had he examined? As many as the police had given him. Did he know if these photos were all the photos available? No, he did not. Might there be other photos in existence that he hadn't seen? Yes, presumably. And the weather conditions—did he know what kind of day it had been? A fine, early summer day. Well, it was actually spring, by the calendar, was it not? Late April? Yes, by the calendar. Had he made any attempt to determine wind velocity that day? No. Had he made any attempt to determine wind *direction*? No. Does the examining physician's report state that the shooting was an accident, a homicide, or a suicide?

"It states only *gunshot wound to chest.*"

"Thank you."

At the Hutchins House, Laura raised the inner window and then the storm window several inches to rid her room of its stuffy heat, then lay in bed, listening to the swish and whistle of a white pine just outside. Lace curtains billowed at each gust, and in the hall something was bumping, which allowed the day to continue spilling through her: Svoboda kneeling so piously at Mass, those window box planters along Main Street—the dark earth there, the paving machines, the insurance place that had once been her father's office, the wound hole, shadowed on one side. She got up and went into the hall. The lower dowel of a quilt hanging was rhythmically striking the wall. She closed the hall window, and in the quiet heard her mother saying something in the room she now shared with her husband, words indistinguishable for the most part except for three . . . *don't think . . . should . . .*

Soundlessly, Laura went back into her own room and lay down again. It was late. They were talking. So it had to be something important. But it needn't be. Couldn't they just be *talking*?

Thought melded into dream—a cloud forming low to the earth. It gave meaning to the cliché *inky* for it appeared suffused with black India ink. A twister spun down from its belly and swaggered toward her, dragging the cloud with it, while she just stood there, fearing the cellar as a potential tomb.

Waking, her heartbeat wild, she tried to calm herself by analyzing the images—typical of powerlessness, she decided. Yet so acutely real, the gut feeling of it. The scare. But the blackness of that cloud—an omen? Or maybe just the brain's way of dealing with all that gruesome courtroom imagery. Creating its own therapeutic art, though she failed to see anything the least therapeutic about it.

Rain made a delicate plinking against the eaves trough. Repetitive, atonal, like Cage's music. The sound, maybe, of all those involuntary systems operating blindly within the body. Faithfully doing their jobs. And then the music winding down, music-box fashion, to the inevitable silence.

Though for her father, the process foreshortened, the box crushed.

She got up and shut her window, stilling the curtains' flight.

KAREN

Rain, now.

Only two seasons up here, her father-in-law used to joke, *winter and bad sledding. Still, it's God's country, make no mistake.* Then God must be an idiot.

But she'd never dared reply to any of his pontifications, thinly masked as jokes. Had only smiled and let others do the ha-ha-ing.

She touched Ben's back, as always a kind of prayer just before sleep: that they both sleep deeply and well and awaken in the morning right there, together. Tonight, though, it brought not peace but the burn of memory. She lying alongside Pete, he asleep; she not. She praying to Mary, asking—it had been more like begging—to know what would be best for the girls, the family, her marriage. And what to do about Pete's drinking. Also, the drugs. Marijuana for certain, but what if other things, too, more potent? Pete had rolled onto his back and, in dream, groaned, extending his right arm. She'd spent the next hours awake, thinking of her marriage vows, her once-flaring love, the children born of it, her small house, each object within it, except the strewn-about toys and books, carefully placed. You might even say *with love.* True, once. If she walked away from it all—just left—he'd get custody. He knew everyone who counted in town. All of them buddies. Magistrate, judge, lawyers—

And there it was: she might be able to leave him, the way he'd become, but never *them.* Her girls.

Then, too, that blind gesture of reaching out. This she'd finally taken as a sign, and so said the Act of Contrition to herself and resolved to go to confession as soon as possible, painful as it would be—*excruciating*, the word. The next morning she drove the girls to the clinic, having invented a pretense, and there spoke the few words wrenched from the previous night's turmoil. *Ben, I'm sorry. I need to stay with my husband.* Whispering. Her back to the girls who were both up on the examination table, drawing rainbows on its white paper.

But do you really want to?

I . . . yes.

The bone under his eye seemed to move, the skin there twitching. And then all attention turned upon "his little ladies" while she waited, sickened by what she had just done. Asking herself why she felt so abandoned when she herself had done the abandoning.

Her throat raw that day. Bloated with emotion. And she incapable of further words. But in her mind, protest. *A good man . . . such a good man.* Then leaving the clinic, her girls in hand, *the last time we'll be here,* and trying to prepare a lie for when they asked the reason, as they inevitably would. Walking was like trying to move through deep snow. But at the same time, relief setting in, as if the snow were in fact quicksand and with each step the three of them were getting closer to firm ground.

BEN

"Are you going to Mass today, Laura?"

"I haven't decided yet. Why?"

"I was thinking I'd go with you. Maybe we all could."

"That might not be such a good idea, Dad. Yesterday Svoboda was there. He'll probably be there today, too."

"I'm okay with it, as long as it doesn't make you uncomfortable."

No one spoke, then, until Laura said, "Dad, it's in the rectory. Everybody has to sit close together in this little chapel. You might have to sit right next to him. Or Mom might."

"And what if," Lin said, "there are reporters, afterward? They'd get us coming out together. Wouldn't that be a scene and a half."

"Maybe you shouldn't, Ben," Karen said. "Actually, I think I'd prefer not to, if it's at the rectory."

"No way do *I* want to go," Lin said.

He caught the warning look Laura gave her sister and hoped they'd know better than to start sniping at one another. The onus on him to keep them together. Buttress his family. He knew how much Laura's Catholicism meant to her, and it hurt to think of her attending Mass alone, with Svoboda there. Set against this, though, was his own reluctance to go, for at the heart of the ritual was the moment the priest raised the Host at the Consecration, making it *God,* and then offering this God to the believers, one of whom he, a convert in name but not in spirit, would necessarily have to pretend to be.

For his family.

Converted wasn't exactly right, though, for he'd been nothing before. Still, he'd gone through the various hoops—studying

67

texts, answering questions, allowing himself to be prayed over before Masses—all culminating with his baptism into Roman Catholicism at an Easter Vigil Mass one Holy Saturday. There had been the power of ritual, of course, causing him to feel somewhat different that night. Better, he supposed. Worthier. Definitely closer to Karen and the children he hoped would eventually become his own in time. That is, his own in love if not biology. But as for *belief* . . . he wanted to believe, if that counted. He said he did—in hopes that it would somehow jell for him—belief, *faith*. Still, he'd felt like an imposter that night, a feeling that persisted every Sunday and Holy Day since.

"I'll go with you, Dad, if you still want to," Laura said.

He looked at his wife, then Lin. "How about you guys? Last chance."

"All right," Karen said. "I'll get ready."

"C'mon, Lin," Laura said. "You, too, okay? Let's show some solidarity."

He saw Lin's displeasure, impatience; saw her mask it with a breezy, "As long as we're not late for the Svoboda Show later."

They went in Laura's Volvo. Getting out of the car, Ben breathed deeply of the cold air off the lake. *This is what it is to be alive. Inhaling this air. Getting out of a car with your family. Taking your wife's arm and guiding her around puddles.* The precariousness of it all. His wife's fragility, his daughters' need for assurance. Protection, really. He had to summon strength. *Will* success. Beat the damn threat so far into the ground it could never rise again.

And Svoboda with it.

The chapel's kneelers and chairs had been set up in two rows facing a rectangular table covered with a starched white cloth. On the wall behind the table was a black crucifix, Christ's limp body the color of a cadaver. Ben deliberately took the chair next to the prosecutor and when, after the Our Father, the young priest asked everyone—his voice breaking—to show one another some sign of peace, Ben first embraced his wife, then his daughters, then turned to his right and extended his hand to Svoboda. The man grasped it, and Ben heard himself saying *Peace be with you,* a lie that didn't prevent him, later, from accepting the Host he could not believe was the Body of Christ. But these actions not blasphemous, he reasoned, nor a sin; merely those of a man doing his best to hold his family together.

And if in fact He did exist, He would understand and forgive the lie. Also that greater failure—of faith.

For was He not a God of Love?

LIN

That morning the magistrate wore a white shirt under his black robe. Small town big time, and so white shirt. Lin had liked him better in the plaid one. For some reason the plaid had given her hope, but now it looked like he was putting on airs. Possibly because of Russ Lowry and his team in their showy suits. She told herself to get a grip. These were dumb thoughts.

Soon photos of the body were being entered as evidence, and she remembered how she'd once been drawn to a file box of photos so that she might study one in particular, that of her birth father—a stranger, as so many of their Michigan relatives had become, after the move to Hawaii. His blond hair and popular kid's smile, the perfect teeth and confidence: *my father?* A word encompassing, it seemed, some huge mystery. How could he just die like that? Disappear from her life? Become a face in a photograph to which little if any emotion accrued. At times she'd come close to posing these questions to a school counselor, but had always offered other nuggets for scrutiny instead. Because if she'd gotten started, she might have gone on and on. . . . *and then my mom married the man who was out there that day. Now he's our dad and it's sort of weird. Sometimes a little scary. When I think about it too much? Which I definitely don't like doing.*

So—no. Better not to stand out in any strange way. Better to keep the lips zipped.

She had, but here it all was, now, anyway.

As Svoboda handed up one of the eight-by-ten glossies to the magistrate, a spike of red appeared to flare across its surface for an instant. *From the Exit sign?* She slid a bit to the right as another photo was handed up.

There it was again. Like a sudden burst of heat lightning, only red.

Svoboda took the photograph from the magistrate and gave it to the defense. Lin tried to read her dad's face, but it showed nothing, all thought closed to the outer world. The witness on the stand, a retired state trooper, though, delivered his description of the clay pigeons under the body's right wrist— one broken, one intact—smugly, with a thread of a smile and narrowed, amused eyes. "There was no blood on the ear," he added, "and on that part of the face covered by the hearing protector."

Photographs of the gun followed those of the body. "No blood," the witness stated, "on the gun's muzzle."

The flash of red settled, for a moment, on each photo. She began shivering.

When Svoboda came to the eight-by-ten photo of the boot, he asked his witness to describe what he'd seen, in relation to that boot, that day in the clearing.

"It looked staged, to me. Right away that's what I thought, *staged.* You got those lower laces, the eyelet ones, still tight, but the upper ones are draped down straight. So that's what I thought, that it was staged." He went on to narrate how he'd taken photos of the body and how the coroner told him not to bother because it was an accident. But he'd gone on photographing anyway because, well, it didn't sit right. And besides, that was his job.

Lin did some mental calculations and concluded that the trooper had been in his forties, back then. Not exactly a rookie, unless he'd joined later in life. But maybe a rookie in spirit, enjoying the little power trip of having everybody standing around, waiting for him to finish.

At the break for lunch, Lin took her mother's arm and guided her past her grandparents' bench, her grandparents waiting, she sensed, for them to pass before exiting themselves. The air felt prickly with awareness. The back of her neck bristled.

They had two hours. Odd how time was fractured now, into theirs and not-theirs. Private and public. Odd how this process said something about freedom. How you weren't free, most of the time. And how time itself was always being divvied up. And not fairly.

Midge drove them to a restaurant far enough away to afford a degree of privacy but no real chance to talk to one another, with him there. She wished she could ask her dad about those laces. You could fall and still have part of your boot stay tight, couldn't you? Also, if you're running, there could be some clay pigeons around, and you could fall near them, couldn't you?

The restaurant's menu was beyond depressing, with its fried entrees, but even more depressing was seeing how little her mother managed to eat. Some cottage cheese, a few pieces of pale fruit that had come with it. Lin ordered the chicken soup and was nearly blasted out of her seat by the salt content, as she phrased it to the waitress.

"Just add some water, hon, if you don't like it that salty," the woman said.

"Order something else, Lin," her dad said.

Midge looked up from his hamburger and fries, his face bunchy. "Don't have time, Doctor. Sorry."

In Midge's Buick, Laura reached for her hand, and it freaked Lin, as if this were some funeral or something, and the floaty Buick in the cortege. And then she remembered her older sister doing just that at their father's funeral, grabbing her hand and squeezing it, in the big car that wasn't theirs. Now Lin gently tugged her hand away and looked out at scrubby farmland, still brown, but yards greening, and shirts and jeans on laundry lines, swaying like prayer flags in the sun.

That afternoon she had to give Russ credit for doing his best. Keeping his voice devoid of any Svoboda-tremolo of emotion, he got the trooper to reiterate that the coroner had said Pete Hyland had been running with the gun. Russ also won a fifteen-minute skirmish concerning the photo of the gun, finally getting it labeled, *Used by Hyland*. And he pointed out a bit of "brush" in a photo of the hearing protectors.

Svoboda objected to the term. It looked more like a twig to him. The former officer was philosophical. "Depends on what you call brush."

"Did you use a measure while photographing the hearing protectors or sunglasses or anything else that evening?" Russ asked.

"No, sir."

"Is it standard operating procedure for the state police to use a scale or measure in its photographs?"

"Not necessarily."

"But if you are trying to show relative sizes, would you?"

"Yes, sir."

"Did you use a measure when you photographed the wound?"

"I was going to do that the following day, when the wound area had been cleaned."

"Did you?"

"Ah, no. Dr. Howe gave us the exact measurements."

"All right. Returning to the scene of the shooting, could you determine whether or not anything had been moved at the site, prior to your arrival?"

"No, sir."

Referring to each of the photographs, Russ was able to get the former officer to say that he couldn't be sure whether or not a particular object had been moved, handled, or manipulated before he arrived at the scene. He could only state that from the time he himself got there, no one had touched or changed anything.

"But are you certain that someone *did* touch the boot prior to your arrival?"

"Yes, sir."

"Did you ever file a written complaint or objection as to the handling of this case?"

The trooper's thin smile returned. "Not a written one, no, I did not."

"Did the state police have a procedure for lodging such complaints?"

"Yes, sir. You could lodge it verbally or in writing."

"Did you ever state your complaint in a letter?"

"Asked and answered!" Svoboda called out.

The magistrate allowed the witness to respond.

"I was constantly advising them orally."

"Did you do anything else in addition to advising them orally? For example, did you go to the media?"

"No, sir."

"Did you go to the F.B.I.?"

"No."

"Did you ever call or send a note to the state attorney general's office?"

"No, sir."

"Did you ever put down anything in writing—"

"Objection!"

"Allow me to finish my question, please."

"Overruled. Proceed."

"Did you ever put down anything in writing, such as in a journal or notebook of your own?"

"No, sir. I just told people."

"Are you retired now, Mr. Kahn?"

"Yes, sir."

"One final question—were you ever made aware, as a state trooper in a training session, for example, of procedures for lodging complaints?"

"I was made aware, yes sir."

"Thank you. No further questions."

"Why wouldn't he put anything in writing or go to the F.B.I. all those years?" Lin asked her sister that evening as they drove to a pharmacy.

"Because he was scared?"

"Of *what*?"

"I don't know. If he didn't do it right away, maybe he was frightened to, later."

"It kind of makes it seem sinister, though, doesn't it? I mean, that he might have been scared? It makes it sound like some conspiracy was happening, or something."

"Oh, please."

"Okay. So let's say he *wasn't* afraid, but just didn't bother to file any written complaint. What does *that* make it seem like?"

"That maybe he's perjuring himself now? I don't know, Lin. He's a former trooper."

"I can see a trooper lying on the stand, can't you? I mean if they can tamper with evidence, what're a few *words*?"

"Lin, c'mon. I think we have to assume he's telling the truth—as he sees it."

At the pharmacy, the dazzle of so many small objects stymied her. She could only stand there.

"Lin? What are you doing?"

"Looking for toothpaste."

"It's over there. Just pick one. We need to get back."

Lin extended her hand, then had to blink to clear away what appeared to be lodged amid the elongated boxes. *Hearing protector.*

"Laur," she whispered. "How could he do that? *Run* with them on?"

"With what on?"

Lin cupped hands over her ears. "Those. Those things he was wearing on his head. Oh, *God*, Laur!"

Laura grabbed a box of toothpaste. "Let's go." In the car, she raged. "You can't just fall apart like that in public, Lin! You need to control yourself!"

"I couldn't help it! Did Dad ever mention those things? I mean, to you?"

"A hearing protector? I don't remember. I don't think so. He just said he was walking toward the cabin when he heard our father yell something. And then there was a shot. Before that, I guess they were shooting at clay pigeons."

"Then why would clay pigeons be under his arm? I mean, if he took off running after something?"

"How do clay pigeons work—don't they fly out of some machine? Maybe there were some in the field."

"That trooper said one was unbroken."

"Well, maybe they don't always break each time. Listen, don't you realize they're making a case any way they can?"

"Okay. So assuming our father was running with a hearing protector on, aren't they like ear muffs?—wouldn't the thing fall off? Does it go on that tightly?"

"Maybe it's designed to stay on."

"So you run and fall and it just stays on your head and your ear doesn't get bloody, but your face does and your hair and everything?"

"If it stays on, I suppose so. Lin—"

"What about that there wasn't any blood on the gun? In that one photo, remember?"

"Dad probably wiped it off."

"Why would he bother to do that? I mean, like, take the time to? It's not making sense, Laur. I'm getting kind of freaked, here."

"Lin, please. You're letting Svoboda get to you. He just needs to wrack up another conviction any way he can. Such a hypocrite, going to Mass every day and then tearing into people! We know how Dad has been—with us, with all those little kids in Hilo. How could he possibly be a *murderer?* We owe him our loyalty, Lin. We're family."

"I know, but—"

"*What.*"

"Our father was family, too. Still is. He's our birth father!"

"Lin, that's beside the point right now."

"It is not! You're the one who was just talking about *loyalty.*"

"I meant that we've seen, for all these years, how Dad is, what kind of person. We have to give him the benefit, don't you think, and not be totally swayed by Svoboda."

"The thing is, Laur, I'm kind of scared. I saw something in the courtroom. And then just now in the pharmacy."

"That's what you get for doing drugs."

"I don't do drugs anymore! That was a long time ago. But I saw something when I was looking for toothpaste. And guess what it was?—*a hearing protector.* I really did, and the thing is, it seems a sign. Maybe from our father."

"Oh, Lin. C'mon. That's crazy."

"Is it? What if he's trying to tell us something? And we just ignore it?"

"Please don't go into your outer space mode, okay? Mom and Dad need both of us, and they need us sane, not freaking out. Katherine does, too. Forget what you saw, or think you saw. Go with your heart."

I am. Words she knew would make her sister go ballistic, so she held them back, with difficulty.

Parked in the graveled lot at the side of the Hutchins House were four other cars. More people, Lin thought, to stare at them at breakfast.

"Remember," she heard her sister saying, "no long face."

Laura crunched through gravel to the guesthouse. Lin wiped her eyes but couldn't expunge the uncoiling certainty that he had been trying to tell her something. Speak in the only way the dead can. Through strange images. Oblique notions. Even coincidence. And the brain's circuits all wild, trying to figure it out.

Blood speaking to blood. How weird is that, Laur?

Weird, she had to admit. Maybe like the truth, most times.

LAURA

Doubt bleeding inward and congealing about those three images: boots, hearing protectors, bloodless gun. Now the prosecution's apparent confidence further unnerving her, their offering only the two witnesses. And so, already, time for closing arguments. Why hadn't Russ countered with any witnesses for the defense? Or was his job simply to cross-examine Svoboda's witnesses? Baffling, the legal process. She told herself not to listen to Svoboda's verbal thrusts, and for a while succeeded. But then he raised his white pointer and angled it like a shotgun. "Weber wanted Pete dead and so he loaded a number-four shot, a more powerful shot than normally used for target practice, and—*blam*—amputated half the heart . . . like this . . ."

Russ jumped to his feet. Reprimanded but unfazed, Svoboda took off his jacket and flung it in the direction of his chair. "A mist of blood all over the place . . . some on Benjamin Weber's boots. He couldn't have been as far away as he said. The man's a liar, a liar and a murderer. . . ."

Thirty minutes later, the prosecutor's arms crashed downward. In the wake of the Svoboda-storm, the air itself felt pummeled. Laura turned her head slightly to the right. Her mother's face shock-still, the large-knuckled fingers interlocked. Laura placed her right hand over her mother's hard grip, pried away one hand and held onto it. She tried taking her sister's hand, but Lin stuck it under her thigh. Laura didn't risk a look at her sister's face; in fact was afraid to know what might be exposed there. Through an open window came the rattling of a leaf rake's metal tines. The courtroom brightened for an instant as cloud gave way to a flick of sunlight.

LAURA 79

Laura thought there might be a recess, a torturous half-hour or more in that upstairs lounge, confined with her silent parents; but the magistrate immediately called on the defense, and Russ was soon speaking in a voice cushioned in rationality and moderation as he reiterated his earlier argument for dismissal of charges. The magistrate leaned far forward, arms and hands making a tripod for his chin. His apparent concentration gave her hope. Maybe he'd had to hear out the prosecution's witnesses before, but now could dismiss.

Yet he didn't. He denied Russ's motion, and denied it swiftly, as if he'd long before decided upon his answer.

Russ placed the first three pages of his legal-pad paper at the bottom of his sheaf and went on as calmly as before, only the coloring at hairline and ears betraying him. The evidence, he argued, incomplete. The box of ammunition used that day missing, so how can we know if the number-four shotgun shell was the exception to the ammunition used that day? Why wasn't a measure used in the photography? Why wasn't the wound itself photographed? Or the terrain? How can we be sure the body wasn't moved before the EMS people arrived? Why didn't trooper Kahn put his reservations concerning the way the case was being handled in writing and send his statement through the prescribed channels? Or contact the F.B.I. or the attorney general's office? Why did the State wait twenty years to prosecute the case? Was it waiting for key witnesses to die?

Svoboda called out, "That is ridiculous! The State didn't deliberately sit around waiting for people to die. It has better things to do than that!"

A clap of gavel against oak finally silenced both attorneys as well as the courtroom. Russ was able to conclude his argument the way he'd begun, with an appeal to reason. "Any trial now, of Dr. Benjamin Weber, would be grossly unjust, a miscarriage of justice. All charges should be dropped and the case dismissed."

Dimpled window glass showed cumulus cloud and blue sky, a tree knobbed with maroon buds, its thinner branches resembling rosary beads. Hopeful images, but a thudding had begun in her chest and pulsed at her temples. Recess, she thought, then decision. It was like waiting for test results, academic or medical. The answer right there, but just out of view. Lip of waterfall or safe harbor, and each second sliding you closer.

There'd be no recess. The magistrate apparently didn't need any time to ponder anything, for in the next instant Laura heard the magistrate saying, ". . . Benjamin Weber to stand trial on charges of first- and third-degree murder."

Across the aisle people were congratulating her grand-parents. Some hugged them. And then Laura was moving toward the defense table, where her dad was smiling as if nothing at all had just happened.

When they reached the Hutchins House, Lin wasn't with them, following in her rental car. They stayed an extra day, enduring stares and whispered comments, but there was no call from her, either.

Laura blamed herself.

AFTER DRIVING her parents to Petosky and watching them board the commuter flight to Chicago, she returned to the variety store. Ruthie was stacking garish cardboard boxes, each depicting some violent action scene.

"Hi, again."

"Oh—hi! Um, sorry . . . I mean about what happened."

"Thank you. I was wondering. Exactly how did he help you, Dr. Weber."

Ruthie kept working. "There was this place? Where you could go? He drove me there. First, he talked to my folks. Then afterward, thanks to him, I was able to go to the community college and live away from home. Which was fine with me. So, yeah, I'm on his side. You bet."

"You were . . . pregnant?"

An index finger with a black and silver ring touched an eyelid. "There was this guy that worked for my dad? On our farm? At first he said he'd marry me, I mean, that's what he told me, but then to my parents he denied that he was the father. My parents decided to believe him, God knows why. I mean, isn't that strange? We could of gone on living there, with them. I would of married him, but he got this thing, I don't know, and denied it all. I guess he was mad at me for the trouble of it, who knows, or maybe he had somebody else, that was probably it, and finally just hauled ass out of there, nobody knew where, and my folks were really pissed. Supposedly he was, like, this super worker."

"But it wasn't, or was it—an abortion?"

"I asked him to, but he wouldn't. I heard he would so that's why I went to see him. But he said no."

"You heard he would?"

"Yeah. You know how you hear stuff. He said I was too far along." She found a tissue in the pocket of her smock and blew her nose. "He saved my life anyhow. Because I was ready to . . . you know."

"What about your baby?"

"Oh, it got adopted. I don't even know if it was a girl or a boy. They didn't let me see it or nothin'. That killed me for a long time. I kept dreaming about it, but I couldn't *see* it. It was always sort of like a ghost or something."

"That must have been pretty awful."

"It was. But things did get better. Except I'm still on the outs with my folks and that's a little hard, like around the holidays. I mean for my kids, not so much for me. But they don't deserve to be grandparents, is what I think. And the kids got Jeff's folks, anyway."

Laura bought a few snacks for her trip, then turned onto the empty highway. *I heard he would.* There seemed something truthful about the vagueness, the very ambiguity. Rumors a kid on the fringes of high school social life would pick up. Whispered words in the air, seed-like.

He said I was too far along.

A few minutes later, she pulled over to the shoulder and turned off the engine. Gusts buffeted the car. Gray-bottomed clouds in the shape of zeppelins cast shadows over woods and rocky pastureland. A log truck dragged past, leaving a trail of mud on the asphalt. She started her car and turned back.

At the cemetery, she drove slowly through the lanes, scanning gravestones, but it seemed hopeless. Finally, she parked and began walking in the newer section, its headstones all low thick slabs of granite in gray or rose or polished black. A few headstones had been cut in the shape of conjoined hearts; others were engraved with woodland scenes—deer, lakes, leaping fish. White pines keened in the wind, but everywhere, green grass and strong spring sunlight. Purple and gold crocus flourished in the sunny shelter of a few gravestones. She paused at one, then continued on.

A plastic statuette caught her eye. It looked like one of the action toys at the variety store, and she thought at first that the grave must be that of a child, and someone had left a favorite toy there. But no. It was St. Michael the Archangel, aiming his spear earthward. St. Michael, who had chased Lucifer and his rebellious horde out of heaven, sending them all tumbling into a hell of their own making.

Then she saw the name on the stone: *Peter Hyland*. But the earth there recently disturbed, its patches of sod new. Her father's body, she remembered, had been interred in some other, unmarked grave after the last autopsy.

Still, it was something. The name. The stone. That earth where his body had lain for two decades.

Father, I'm sorry I don't remember you very well. I do remember you took us sledding once. Lin fell off her green saucer sled, and you carried her but went on pulling me. I remember being jealous. I remember the sunset. It looked like one of our finger paintings. Red and orange and pink all streaky. Snow got in my boots and I cried. And then Lin cried because she didn't want to leave, but I did. There we were, sledding on perfect snow with you but managing to make it miserable for everybody. You got quiet and sad, then left us with Mom, after. And then . . .

Ben stopping by the house—*Dr. Weber*—with brownies for them. Brownies and something for their father, but he wasn't home. So he'd talked with their mother while she and Lin ate the brownies and begged for more and got their wish.

And never questioned why their doctor had come to the house. He just had, and they liked him. He was fun.

Before leaving the gravesite, she touched the headstone.

BEN AND KAREN

From her cabin window Karen watched the Big Island take shape in the distance—gray and abstract, set within a luminous plain of ocean. Soon Mauna Loa and white-tipped Mauna Kea became distinct humps. Then gray gave birth to emerald; silver to sapphire, and there it was, their home, their island, with its pearl necklace of surf. But this time she felt no rising exhilaration at the sight, the miracle of it. Only a profound sense of loss, exclusion, and dread.

Hawaiian music came on in the cabin. Smiling flight attendants in fresh aloha outfits walked up and down aisles, checking tray positions and seat belts. Then the Big Island's high windward cliffs seemed to approach, bearing their gifts of verdant valleys and slender waterfalls, some pluming down to the ring of surf. The aircraft leveled, floating beyond the cliffs and then above a sugar cane field, the plane's shadow a cross rippling over its silvered expanse.

She flinched when her husband placed his hand on hers.

HOLDING HIS wife's hand, willing warmth into it, Ben resolved, for the hundredth time, at least, to project only composure and determination. And hope. For really, what *had* happened? Simply that the State of Michigan had gotten its way, thanks and no thanks to Svoboda, and so now a trial. A speck of doubt, go to trial. Keep people working. Justify the attorney general's office. Russ had been disappointed but not unduly surprised.

So why get bent out of shape?

As for the mini-blackouts—The heart flutters, etc., etc.—
Stress. Nothing routine wouldn't cure. And this air. This
place. As it had before.

But into these musings came bits of music far removed from
anything emerging, just then, from the cabin's P.A. system. Jim
Morrison and the Doors. Somewhere deep within Ben, Morrison was singing, in his dead man's voice, about the end, and
this being it.

The aircraft banked, then sped downward to touch the
earth.

TUNLEY, MICHIGAN
AUGUST, 1990

BEN

"Doctor, the prosecution has just given us some material that raises a number of questions."

Russ's tone, measured as usual but with some new and definitely strident edge to it, immediately put him on guard. He looked up from his blank legal pad into Russ's eyes—that pale, somewhat off-putting Nordic blue behind the rimless lenses—and felt himself tensing.

They were seated around the fully extended dining room table at Russ's rented house just outside Tunley, where the trial was going to be held. The room's chandelier had been replaced with a contemporary fixture holding large-wattage bulbs. Russ sat at the head of the table, with another lawyer, their paralegal, and Midge to his left. Laura and Karen were on his right. At the opposite end of the table, Ben placed his hands in his lap to hide the tremor, but then thought better of it and scrawled the word *questions* at the top of his pad. The handwriting came out erratic but not much worse than his usual physician scribble. He kept his right hand poised over the pad.

"First, I need to tell you something about one of their forensics experts, Dr. Chip Willsey. A *magna cum laude* undergrad degree. Harvard Med on scholarship. Then the navy and a residency at a U.S. naval hospital, plus another degree in plastic surgery. Served in the military, part of the time in Vietnam as a triage officer. A quarter of his cases there involved bullet wounds. Also, he was a professor of forensics for a time at Berkeley. At the Presidio, in California, he directed the wound ballistics lab for several years. He and another doctor there experimented on a gel that mimics pig muscle and tissue. Why is that important? Because according to those in the field,

88

pig muscle and tissue most closely resemble human muscle and tissue. With that gel, they can learn a lot about a bullet's penetration and how it behaves within the tissue. Whether it fragments, for example, or changes form. And—now here's the kicker—with that gel, they can also figure out distances. Much of this has been written up in various journals, the *Wound Ballistics Review,* for example, and *Annals of Emergency Medicine.* So there's no way I can attack this man's credentials. That's one thing. Secondly, he's going to blow *us* out of the water with his testimony. Look." Russ slid several black and white photographs down to Midge who, in turn, handed them to Ben.

"Flash photography," Russ went on, "at one-half of a millionth of a second. It shows what happens to shot cups—the plastic wad holding the brass pellets—at various distances. Now, what Willsey is going to say is that the shot cup's lack of deformation indicates that the distance was farther away than a contact or near-contact shot would show."

Russ took an actual shot cup out of a plastic bag and demonstrated how its "petals" folded back in flight, and then how the shot cup dropped away entirely when the target was, say, twenty feet away. When the target was nearer, the opening petals might "slap" the target, making a mark there as well as getting crumpled in the process. Ben recalled some of this information from Havani's testimony during the hearing. Then, it had caused his gut to clench, as now.

"It's all pretty technical. The jury might be glazed-over by the time Willsey finishes. But the man knows his stuff and will come across well. Also, he'll be corroborating Havani's testimony of three-to-five feet, which isn't consistent, they'll argue, with a fall and near-contact wound. In and of itself this evidence worries me. When placed in conjunction with evidence from another expert, it's giving me a terrific headache."

Ben kept his eyes on Russ. To look at Karen now, or Laura, might be disastrous, yet he was aware of them there, Laura's arm, Karen's thin hand, both too white under the lighting. *The gun right there between them. His. Pete asking to use it that day because . . . because why? Had he asked? Or had he just—*

"Professor McBride," Russ said. "You folks ever hear of him?" *McBride,* he tried to write.

"We've hired him as an expert witness in previous cases. The Blood Man, he's known as in the trade. And he's the best there is. Made a science out of reading blood spatter. That is, the patterns blood makes when it's sprayed onto some surface in a high-speed velocity situation, i.e., from a rifle, handgun, or shotgun blast. Or semi-automatic weapon. It sounds a little farfetched to say that blood can speak, but in fact it makes perfect scientific sense, as he will tell the jurors. The man instructs police officers and detectives. He's written a textbook and has his own lab where crime workers from all over the world come to study and observe demonstrations. So. Professor Sidney McBride, criminologist and forensic scientist, with an academic background in chemistry and physics, will be testifying, Doctor, that you were not some fifty yards away but right up close. Why? Because some of Pete Hyland's vaporized blood still exists on the boots you were wearing that day. Notice I say *vaporized,* not brushed on as you might get by accidentally touching bloody fabric, but vaporized, according to McBride, into miniscule particles by some high-speed blast creating a mist of these droplets. Some of this we learned during the pretrial. But I didn't know how much damage we had to contain until discovery, when they need to turn over material they're going to use so we can prepare our defense. Actually, there's more—I'm sorry Mrs. Weber, Laura, but we need to address it. A bit of human tissue, Doctor, was found in the weave of the jeans you were wearing that day, down near the hem of the right pant leg."

. . . *vaporized blood . . . human tissue . . .* The county detective Delrosier coming to the apartment and asking for the clothing and boots a few nights after the accident. The gray-haired guy in his slate-blue suit, small-town investigator, refusing to enter but instead standing stubbornly in the hall.

Boots there, too?

You want those as well?

Everything.

Well, wait a second. The boots are out on the back porch, I think.
And they were, his Red Wings, on their sides, mud on the soles and laces. But under the porch light nothing else visible except scuffing. Then he'd gotten the jeans, shirt, jacket, underwear and socks from the laundry hamper, a sick feeling in his gut.

How long you going to keep all this?

Long as we have to. I'll get back to you if we need anything else.

He had met the guy's eyes for about half a second before nodding good-night and shutting the beveled, heavily varnished door. What he saw there hadn't been reassuring. The county detective obviously didn't believe his statement though everyone else apparently did, including the coroner and D.A. Clearly, the investigator was out to get him. Probably bought off by Earl Hyland.

Then for years—nothing. Until now. And there they were—the boots, the jeans—in the photographs Russ had sent down the table. Black and white shots. Small arrows pointing to vague specks.

. . . microscopic, not brushed on . . . The figure in the clearing ran through April grasses. Ran, fell, then rose only to evaporate like some highway mirage. . . . *the gun his own gun between them . . . Pete asking to use it because he wanted to try it out.*

"Russ. I have something to tell you." He cleared his throat but said nothing further. His heart was on its rampage. *Breathe . . . breathe . . . breathe.*

"What is it?" Russ finally said, his voice compressed, it seemed, by vocal chords too taut for clear speech. His forehead scalded pink.

Ben saw Laura look up from the sketch of a tree and stare at him.

"Excuse me a minute."

In a small bathroom off the kitchen, he sat on the closed toilet seat and willed calm, willed breath, order, control. The figure in the clearing had been replaced by the figures of two men, a gun between them. As details came clear, the thrashing in his chest slowed. The arcs of pain shortened, the duration between them lengthened. After a few more minutes, he flushed the toilet, ran water and washed his hands and face.

In the dining room, he took his seat. "I apologize, Russ. I, well, twenty years ago what I said seemed the best course. I realize now I should have told you this sooner."

"You mean you lied, Doctor? Back then and now as well? To me?"

"Back then my judgment must have been totally impaired—not by booze but by what happened. I thought it would be best for Karen not to know what really took place out there that day. I was afraid she might blame herself. Maybe even, well, do herself harm. I couldn't risk that. Her kids needed her. So I invented a little. But the truth is, Pete hadn't been chasing any animal. And I wasn't thirty or so yards away. I was right there alongside him when he was shot.

"The thing is, I believe—I've always believed this—that he wanted to kill me. Kill me and maybe take his own life, I don't know. But definitely kill me. There was this . . . struggle."

"You fought with Pete Hyland?"

"It all happened so fast there wasn't any real fight. We struggled, I don't know, a couple of seconds, maybe, over the gun."

"Who was holding the gun?"

"He was, at first. That's when I thought he meant to kill me. It was aimed, cocked, the whole bit. He just . . . turned on me. All that pent-up feeling, I guess. I had to get the gun away from him, and that's how the struggle came about. 'Pete,' I said. 'What're you doing? Stop!' But then, somehow, well, it went off and there he was on the ground. I threw the gun aside and turned him over. First, I tried to resuscitate but that didn't work. I had to get help. But I knew by then that he was dead. Still, I drove to a neighbor's so they could call the rescue squad people. There might be a chance, I thought—I hoped—even though I knew there wasn't. He had no pulse. He wasn't breathing. But still I ran for help.

"I'm sorry not to have told you up front. But I guess I felt, I don't know, it seemed . . ."

The attorney didn't move. Didn't drop his gaze.

"The thing is, I thought it would be best for everyone."

"And for you, too?"

"My own well-being wasn't first and foremost, believe me."

"Did you untie those laces? Stage that detail to suggest he'd tripped?"

"No. If I untied the laces, I probably just wanted to get his boots off."

"*If?* Do you mean to say you don't remember if you did or didn't untie them?"

"I don't, actually. Pete's boots—that's kind of a blur."

"Do you think anyone else untied the laces?"

"I don't know."

"Was anyone else out there that day, Doctor?"

"No. We were alone out there."

"You and Pete."

"Yes. The boots—I don't know. What I do remember are the moments immediately afterward when I tried to resuscitate, then ran for help."

"Doctor, there's no evidence of blood on your shirt or jacket. If you leaned in close to resuscitate, why didn't it get on you?"

"Well it did. On my face and hands, but I washed it off at the neighbor's. As to why not on my jacket or shirt, that I can't tell you. I jut don't know."

"Has your family known this all along?"

"No, not until just now."

"Not even your wife Karen?"

He shook his head.

"Mrs. Weber, did your husband tell you about a struggle with your former husband, Pete?"

"No, he didn't."

"He never told you this before today?"

"No."

"Do you have anything to add to what he just said?"

"No, I don't."

"Given what you know about your former husband, is a struggle consistent with his behavior in the days leading up to the shooting?"

"I think it is."

"Can you explain, please?"

"He was unhappy. Drinking more than usual. He said—"

"Go on, Mrs. Weber, please."

"He said that he didn't want to lose it all. *Can't* was his word."

"Did you understand what he meant by *can't lose it all*?"

"I believe he meant the children and, oh, our marriage, the strong connections to the community. All that."

"And you as well?"

"Yes."

"So he said, 'I can't lose it all,'" meaning, I can't bear to lose it all? Or, I *won't* lose it all."

"I'm not sure how, exactly, he meant those words."

"Did he sound determined?"

Ben waited, along with everyone else, for her answer. When she finally said that he had sounded determined, he let his eyes close for a moment. It struck him that if he should die then and there of some massive infarction, it might be best for everyone.

"Did you regard his words as a threat of any kind?"

"Maybe not an actual threat, but I was frightened."

"Did you want a divorce?"

"I knew I couldn't have one."

"What do you mean?"

"I was, and still am, a Roman Catholic."

"So you didn't want a divorce, then?"

"Yes. That is what I meant to say."

"You didn't want to divorce your husband mainly because of your faith? Is that right?"

She hesitated. "Also because of the children. They loved their father."

"Did Dr. Weber know how you felt?—about your faith as well as about the children?"

"I believe he understood."

"Yet you two were in love."

"We loved one another, yes."

"Your husband Pete was also a Catholic, was he not?"

"He was."

"Yet he might resort to murder, risking the damnation of hell?"

"I can't say what he thought that day. I just don't know."

"Do you remember his last words to you that day?"

"He said he wouldn't be home for dinner and that I shouldn't expect him any time early. I should just feed the children. He said—"

She seemed to be through speaking.

Russ finally said, "Please tell us, Mrs. Weber. At this point we need to know anything of relevance."

"He said he loved me very much."

"Did he sound sincere?"

"Yes."

"Not sarcastic, not angry?"

"No, he wasn't angry or being sarcastic."

"So you believed him."

"I did."

"And you were willing to—"

"Russ, for God's sake," Ben interposed.

". . . patch it up, Mrs. Weber?"

"I don't know if I had any thoughts. I was a little numb."

"Numb. Why?"

"We'd been through so much."

"You'd been arguing."

"Yes."

"About his drinking? Or, your seeing Dr. Weber?"

"Both. Everything."

"Did you ask him for a divorce?"

"No, I didn't."

"And—this is my final question for now—prior to the shooting, did you speak to Dr. Weber about your intention to remain in your marriage?"

It took all Ben's willpower to keep himself still. *No,* he heard her say. *I did not.*

"All right. Thank you." He looked to the left side of the table, where his team sat. "Any thoughts? Should we just pack up and head out? Allow Dr. Weber to retain another team and start from scratch with this new version?"

Ben hoped this was residual anger, bluster.

Russ went into the living room where he stood looking at the low fire in the fireplace. After a while, he tossed in another log and returned to the table.

"All right. Square one."

Russ was still angry, the strain and wobble in his voice said so, but a rush of relief washed through Ben, weakening every muscle. It was out. He'd confessed. And the two decades between that moment and this might be enough padding—for Karen, Laura, and Lin. Katherine, too. Surely it wouldn't hurt them quite as much.

Accident . . . but of another kind.

LAURA

She called her sister's apartment in Ithaca, then tried the co-op, then the apartment again at hourly intervals. Sometime after two in the morning, her sister answered. "Lin," Laura said, before words eluded her.

"Laur? What's going on? Are you okay?"

After a while she was able to speak. "Dad told us about that day. What really happened was, our father—Pete—tried to kill *him*. They had this struggle. Our father was really upset about the way his marriage was going and he aimed the gun at Dad, and Dad grabbed for it and it somehow went off. So it's manslaughter, not murder. If even that. Maybe even self-defense. There was no intent, no malice, nothing like that, Lin. It really was an accident but a different kind than the first . . . are you still there?"

"What do you mean, he aimed the gun at Dad, and Dad grabbed for it and it went off. Wouldn't *Dad* have been the one to get shot, then?"

"Dad said he had to get it away from him. The gun must have gotten turned around as they were struggling over it."

"I can't believe it."

"You mean you can't *believe* it or emphasis on the *can't.*"

"On the *can't.*"

"*Why?* Dad told Russ tonight. We were all there. The evidence led him to finally tell us. He was trying to protect Mom all this time. Why can't you believe it, Lin?"

"Because why would he wait this long to tell? You'd think with all those doctors we had to pay and Russ's forensic guys, he'd want to tell the truth, not let it go on for well over a year or more? I mean, that's sort of crazy, don't you think?"

"He was protecting Mom."

"I don't think I can buy it, Laur."

"And us, too."

"Maybe he's been trying to protect himself."

"Maybe you don't want to believe him."

"The thing is, he should have told us a hell of a long time before now! We're adults, not kids anymore. He should have told Mom, anyway. Had he?"

"She said he didn't."

"You believe her?"

"C'mon, Lin. Everybody's lying? Besides, what good would it have done? It wouldn't have brought our father back. It would have hurt Mom to no end. And maybe too, Dad didn't want us to have an image of our father as this murderous, enraged guy. But despite this picture of our father, Dad's confession tonight was a huge relief to me. I was almost happy, after all the worry. Tonight was good. And now you're doing your best to wreck it. Look, let's talk later. I can't, anymore, right now."

A few minutes later Laura's phone rang.

"I'm sorry," Lin said. "It's just, I've got problems with it all."

"Come to the trial, Lin. Let's hear it all out."

"I'll think about it."

"Please come."

"I can't promise. I have to think. Did you tell Katherine?"

"Mom did."

"Is she going to be there?"

"Mom and Dad think it's better if it's just us, for now. Listen. At least come and talk to Dad. Ask him to explain it to you. This is so important, Lin. And he loves you."

"It's just too strange, you know? Suddenly this new version?"

"It's not a version. He had to tell the truth, finally. What he said before wouldn't work, given the new evidence."

"Exactly."

Moods, the weather of the soul, Laura thought later, exhausted but unable to sleep. The beat of a mosquito's wing somewhere changing the whole mental atmosphere. In this case, her sister's words, again, the doubt embedded within, their dull tone, the leaden pessimism and distrust, her weird need not to believe, all easily overtaking her own defenses, the incipient happiness, moving in upon it like cold drizzle. She kept hearing her dad's voice, kept trying to visualize exactly how it happened, but it would blur, images on water. And there was her mother's voice as well, that *don't think you should,* or something close to it, overheard the previous spring at the bed and breakfast place. Could they have been talking about exactly this?

If so, then tonight maybe her mother had lied to Russ, maybe she had known of this new version, or whatever it was. And if she had lied about that to Russ, then maybe about other things as well.

Crickets, outside. Their nocturnal busyness each late summer and fall. The tiny creatures readying themselves for death, but first—the mating. Her bedroom on the second floor of the house they'd rented in Tunley had lace curtains, but the furnishings could only euphemistically be called antiques. Tubular iron bedstead, rickety nightstand, its varnish beaded black in places, an oak veneer bureau, a dressing table that had been painted bubble-gum pink. A thin mattress atop open springs, which swayed and squeaked. Yet she had moved her things into this room three days earlier with a small degree of pleasure, for the place seemed temporary, as cottages were meant to be, both the nice ones and the slightly crummy, which this definitely was, with its warping veneers and thin braided rug, its colors faded to near-gray. *It won't be forever.* But now after the call, the house seemed iconic in a more troubling, even menacing way.

That faint sweet stink of mice droppings. Old face powder. Dry rot.

LIN

Her mother and Laura were seated in their usual bench up front, her dad with his lawyers. Pain slammed in again. She considered going upstairs and finding some unobtrusive spot, but every bench downstairs, except theirs, was filled, and no reason to think upstairs would be less crowded. She finally walked the length of the courtroom and slid in alongside her mother. It felt the same as being late to church. People watching but pretending not to. Her sister leaned forward to give her a smile. Her mother took her hand.

Just call me the world's greatest hypocrite. Or maybe that title should go to Dad.

A thought taking color from her face and giving it the sheen of nausea while the work of the court went implacably on. Incomprehensible, to her. Lawyers rising, then responding to the white-haired judge, a woman with beautiful shoulder-length hair. Lin gave up trying to understand the proceedings and instead took in what she could of the courtroom. Sage-green walls. A visual pun, maybe? Grecian columns behind the judge's high bench. A full-length portrait of some historical figure in black enshrined there. Two other paintings, smaller, above the doors to either side of the bench. One, a frontier courthouse in a field, with a passing wagon. The other, a north woods scene of firs and a clearing of stumps. Details gone unnoticed the previous spring.

Muscles that had been gradually relaxing tensed again when the judge dismissed the lawyers, and the courtroom seemed to come to attention. On the flight to Michigan, she'd read an article—a terrible one to have in an in-flight magazine, she'd thought—on wind shear. How winds can blow in two different directions at the same time, and if something gets caught in the middle, well, hey. That's all there is, folks.

Which is what she felt now, when Svoboda rose and pushed away the lectern that had been placed facing the jurors. He carried no notes. "I never use these things," he began in a low rumble. Then looking directly at the jurors, he said, "I am Anton Svoboda, Assistant District Attorney for the State of Michigan. That is my title, but, really, I am only a servant of the public who will present the evidence to you."

He went on calmly enough, stating that he wanted to give them an overview so they'd be able to see the big picture. "And what is this big picture? The *truth*. You're not here to search out doubts. You're here to search out the truth." He strode to the defense table and, facing Ben Weber, identified him for the jurors lest they mistake him for one of the lawyers. Soon, words erupted from the prosaic calm. While still looking at the defendant, Svoboda all but shouted, "The Law never forgets! *Never.* There is nothing more precious than a human life. And there is *no* statute of limitations on murder!"

Svoboda was spinning himself into hurricane force as he strode back and forth in front of the lectern, setting forth what the State was going to prove; first, the blatant and often shameless affair between Benjamin Weber and another man's wife. "The doctor didn't care *who* saw them carrying on at the clinic, he didn't care! He thought only of himself and what he wanted, and what Benjamin Weber wanted, he'd get. He'd come up to Karen Hyland, kiss her in front of the nurses, in front of her *children*, he didn't care! He wanted Karen Hyland, and he was going to get her, no matter what."

A painful certainty rushed through Lin. Svoboda would win, regardless of her dad's innocence or guilt, because he was wrathful. Emotion winning out over reason. Just as it probably had in the clearing that late afternoon when her father had died.

". . . Pete Hyland, though, was a simple guy. He loved his wife and daughters. He was the kind of guy who thought

well of people, and so he didn't suspect at first. Didn't suspect that there are people whose hearts might be full of *evil*.
Didn't suspect that a man he thought of as a friend might in
fact want to *kill* him." Svoboda raised the white pointer, aiming
it at himself. Russ objected and called for a mistrial. The judge
sustained the objection but denied the motion.

Sure, Lin thought. *The thing unstoppable, now.* And her
mother crying while trying to remain still and silent. Lin had
nothing to offer, but Laura pulled out a small packet of tissues and put several in her mother's hands. Karen didn't raise
them to her face, maybe was afraid to, Lin thought. Was she
crying because it was true, or false? To Lin, the person Svoboda
was describing sounded more like some sociopathic stranger.
Didn't care who saw them? Thought only of himself? A heart
full of evil? That couldn't be her dad. Something was wrong
with Svoboda's story. No, his melodrama. And though part of
her believed Havani's testimony during the hearing, and that
trooper's, what Svoboda was saying now didn't seem the way
to any big picture except, maybe, the one in Svoboda's head.
Which was nauseating because if these guys couldn't get it
right, then who could?

She watched the jurors for a while, but their expressions
remained blank, cryptic. Ordinary people. Men who might
work in auto supply places or nurseries or farm stores; women
who might be homemakers or schoolteachers. Maybe watched
the soaps. Churchgoers, probably. Conservatives. And each
maybe thinking, *You read about things like this . . . You see it on
TV. It's what happens.*

But you never think it'll happen to you and your family.

Her *dad*—bandaging some childhood scratch, reading to
her, proudly showing her off at the clinic, teaching her to ride
her bike, make an omelet, and, later, drive a car.

". . . she wasn't going to get a divorce. She was a practicing Catholic, and in those days annulments weren't so easy
to come by. So she tells him, No divorce, and that's what drives
him to . . ."

Russ was on his feet again. The judge sustained his objection, then reminded the jurors that opening statements were not to be taken as evidence.

"Judge, may we approach?"

Whatever was said, there at the bench, seemed to have had no effect on Svoboda. He simply unbuttoned his jacket and steamed along.

"So, no divorce. Otherwise, you wouldn't be able to be a member of the church in full standing, wouldn't be able to take communion, and if you did remarry, well, you'd be excommunicated. So Pete gives her an ultimatum—"

"Objection!"

"It's a reasonable inference! One based on the evidence to come."

"Counsel, please approach."

Five minutes later, Svoboda again charged forward. "So because there'd be no divorce, Benjamin Weber decided that, Hell no, it ain't gonna *be* that way, and out comes the number-four shot, he shoves it in and then *blam!* The high-speed force vaporizes the blood, and it's these particles, these high-speed impact particles of vaporized blood that will prove the defendant to be a liar and a murderer. The evidence shows this, and we will ask you to return a verdict of murder in the first degree. Yes, some twenty years have passed, but it could be a hundred years. That doesn't matter. The evidence says that Benjamin Weber is guilty of murder, and we will ask you to tell him that, and tell him that not in this country, not in any civilized country in the world, is he above the *law*."

Svoboda returned to his table. He grasped the spindles of his chair and seemed to want to hurl it across the courtroom. The jurors, in contrast, might have been cast in resin.

At the recess, her mother stumbled across Lin's feet as she went directly to the defense table. Lin observed the way her dad smiled and extended his hand to take hers. She saw how her mother focused on him to the exclusion of everyone else. Here was a truth. They loved one another—still. Of course her mother believed whatever he said. Of course she thought him innocent and probably forever would.

At the rented house in Tunley, Laura apologized for the tuna salad she'd fixed that morning, saying they hadn't been shopping at any health food store.

"It's fine," Lin said. "I'm not into that so much anymore."

They all gave her a look at those words. Her sister sighed. No one seemed to want to mention Svoboda, so she said nothing. Her mother ate a bit of her green salad; her sister, the tuna salad on white bread. Her dad poured everyone coffee. Only Laura had one of the grocery-store cookies. Then it was time to go back, and they readied themselves for that. Once she had been into Zen Buddhism, and this moment brought back how she'd once tried to be conscious of the *moment*, whether good or bad, just accept it. Forgive yourself, if you have to, and let it go. That's how her mother and dad struck her now—accepting, forgiving, maybe, and continuing on. He held her wool jacket for her and saw her safely out the door and down the steps as if she still were the most precious thing in his life.

Outside on the walkway, Laura squeezed her arm. "God, I'm glad you're here."

Russ exuded calm, competence, reason. There was a guileless air about him, despite the tailoring and expensive footwear. To Lin, he looked like the quintessential good guy, blond hair and open expression, still-boyish face. "My name is Russell Lowry," he told the jurors, "and I will use the lectern." No hint of a smile, then, to suggest some joke at the prosecution's expense. He glanced down at his notes on the lectern and stated that what he was about to present would be an outline, not an argument. And he was going to be respectful. Of the law and of the courtroom itself. In the old days, courtrooms often doubled as places of worship; there was something reverential, still, about any courtroom, and he wanted that reverence maintained.

A juror swiveled his chair around slightly and seemed to be considering the color-tinged maples outside.

Bored already, Lin thought. Supporting, pretty much, her earlier theory about emotion versus reason.

"I'm sure," Russ went on, "that you will follow the judge's instructions to disregard certain statements by the prosecution, in its opening statement."

How could they, Lin wondered. It'd be like trying to disregard a thunderstorm.

". . . In contrast to the prosecution, the defense will ask you to consider, always, the details, not the so-called big picture. And we will insist on accuracy of detail, always. For instance, there's no evidence whatsoever that Mrs. Hyland ever considered an annulment. There is no evidence whatsoever that Mrs. Hyland ever discussed this matter with her parish priest. I point it out now as an example of how bombast and speculation obscures, not clarifies."

Putting out fires already.

". . . So then, details. We're going to examine each bit of evidence the prosecution puts forth and will ask you to determine whether or not it is strong enough to prove *willful, intentional, premeditated, and with malice.* And if it is not, then you, as jurors, can acquit Dr. Weber. Our defense will be grounded in honesty. We will admit that he did have sexual relations with Pete Hyland's wife Karen. He does not win a star for good behavior in this regard. We admit that. But this does not prove that he is also guilty, beyond a reasonable doubt, of *murder.*"

Lin tried to view it from that perspective. An innocent man. A man in love. Another man—her father—in despair. Angry at his wife. Enraged by his former friend, Ben Weber. Every word, every glance between his wife and Ben driving him, literally, crazy. *Wind shear.*

". . . You can also acquit on the basis of character. In the course of our defense, we will show you a great deal about Dr. Weber's character as indicated by his actions over decades. And finally, we will present testimony from the one person who can tell us what happened that April afternoon, the one person who was there at the time and saw everything. That person is Dr. Benjamin Weber. Dr. Weber will waive his right to remain silent and he will tell us. He does not need to do this; the burden of proof is on the prosecution, but he is going to take the stand in his own defense in order to tell us exactly what happened that day at the Lake Marion hunting camp."

Mildly, Russ stated that if there are two reasonable arguments, one concluding guilt, the other innocence, the jurors must go with the argument concluding innocence. "That's how the Law works." He gathered his papers and walked soundlessly back to his table.

The first witness for the prosecution took the stand.

LAURA

Woman after woman testifying to the affair. Nurses, neighbors, a former notary public who had taken Dr. Weber's divorce affidavit wherein he had sworn, under oath, that there had been no affair, that his wife Marcia had been spreading rumors.

It might as well be daytime TV, Laura thought, and then, as if this thought had conjured the reality, Svoboda's assistants were positioning a screen so that both the judge and the jurors could see it. Soon the screen bloomed with a larger-than-life image of a woman, a dying woman, whose deposition had been video-taped at a nursing home. She'd dressed nicely for the occasion in a blue sweater with a lacy white shawl collar. Her hands, face, and upper body remained still as she responded to each question with the detachment of someone more than halfway to the land of shades. Nor did her eyes falter in embarrassment as she spoke of numerous "breaches of professionalism"—the young doctor ignoring his other patients in order to stay at length with Mrs. Hyland and her children, the young doctor embracing Mrs. Hyland in the hallway off the waiting room, kissing her, grasping her breasts.

The woman's image gave way to blinding whiteness. Still the jurors stared at it. If what the witness had stated was true—and why wouldn't it be, given her circumstances?—such behavior demonstrated a total lack of judgment, good sense. She herself had never been passionately in love and so couldn't understand. Clichés gave a clue—*swept away, head-over-heels, blinded*—a kind of temporary insanity, maybe? And if so, then possibly— But Laura didn't want to follow that line of thinking.

No, she couldn't understand and so felt repulsed, shamed. Her dad amoral, totally not caring. Her dad in the throes not of love, maybe, but lust. Totally out of control. And if her father knew—and how could he not, eventually?—no wonder he'd become murderous.

And her mother powerless to stop it all?

Or not wanting to.

THAT EVENING Laura found it hard to look at him.

"Girls, I need to say something." They were sitting out on the enclosed porch at the back of the house, a room with windows overlooking a small yard bordered by a cornfield. "It was rough today, and I'm sorry," he told them. "I hate that you have to go through it, you and your mother. You deserve better. You are the best things in my life and I love you, and it's hard as hell to sit there listening when I know you're right behind me, having to hear those words. I'll never be able to make it up to you. For as long as I live I won't be able to. If I knew of some way to make all this easier to bear . . . but I don't. I know you're here not just for me but for us as a family. Only, I wish you didn't have to be. I wish I could spare you all this. At least Katherine has been spared, somewhat."

His shoulders curved forward, and then he was crying. Like a little kid, Laura thought, the way a kid fights it and then caves in. Alongside him on the wicker couch, Karen held him. Laura and Lin looked at one another.

"Wow. I really know how to ruin a party, don't I?" He wiped his eyes with a tissue Karen had given him. "The thing is, I just need you to know how much I love you. If anything should ever happen to me, please don't doubt these words."

"What do you mean, Dad," Laura said after a while, "if anything should happen to you?"

"Well, as you know, my heart is a little off-kilter. Dr. Aigaki, in Hilo, has been treating me. He's good, no worry there. But with a heart condition, the thing is, one never knows, and too . . ."

He was looking at the row of black windows reflecting the room's two floor lamps and something of their faces.

"*And too* what, Dad?" Lin said.

"Are you guys getting chilly? Maybe we should go into the living room. I could make us a fire."

He doesn't like all these windows, Laura thought. *Why?*

THAT NIGHT sporadic rain, fitful and wind-driven, kept striking the side of the house. Lin came into Laura's bedroom and closed the door.

"I'm freaking out. Did it seem to you that he wanted to tell us something? Something more than about his heart condition? It was just kind of weird, like he was spooked or something."

Laura thought so too but decided not to fan the flames. "What I'm really worried about is Mom. She hardly ate anything at dinner."

"I know. Maybe because today was really sickening, all those women testifying against Dad."

"Yes, but keep in mind they were testifying about the affair, right? And Dad's going to admit that, so it's almost irrelevant, isn't it."

"I guess. Only, they made it sound just so awful."

Again, Laura silently agreed. "Lin, you should get to sleep. Tomorrow will probably be brutal again."

"Can I stay here with you?"

"Oh, please."

"Is that a no or a yes?"

"Do you snore?"

"I don't think so."

"Because I need to be through with this day."

LIN

Svoboda hefted a large box onto the prosecution's table, opened its flaps, and lifted out an actual tree stump marked with orange numerals and notations. He had to strain—on his tiptoes, hefting, red of face. It seemed as though the box wanted to swallow him. With the introduction of this exhibit, the proceedings had taken on a tragic-comic aspect. The prosecutor might have been a character out of one of those strange plays her sister's theater sometimes put on. Finally the thing was on the floor, too heavy to be hefted up onto the witness stand. Soon, the former trooper who'd testified at the pre-trial hearing was stating that Pete Hyland's body was found near the stump, and near that had been a clay-pigeon throwing machine.

How had she missed this? Wasn't she there during the hearing when this was brought up? Or was it? Maybe Svoboda had saved it for now. She did remember the words about one broken and one intact clay pigeon found near her father's wrist.

Fingers gripped cold fingers. But she was doing okay, she told herself. She wasn't going to freak. Not in front of everybody.

Svoboda had lifted a shirt from the box and handed it up to the witness, who unfolded it and held it before him. A tan corduroy shirt splotched with dark stains.

"Whose shirt was this, sir?"

"Pete Hyland's."

Lin sensed breath entering but not emerging. Sun had brightened the courtroom. The witness was still holding up the shirt clouded with her father's blood.

That he was right there, her father, only a few yards away, defied reason, yet a shadowy figure was somehow assuming form, molecules finding each other again, assembling about the object the witness was holding for all to see. The former trooper finally lowered it only to have to raise it again when Svoboda asked about the hole in the fabric. By then she was hardly listening to the testimony. The thing had become luminous. It's the only way the dead can speak, after all—through electrical impulses that carry no rational bundles of information but only startle, cause the body to sway, to want to weep. A need she tried to overcome but couldn't.

Laura was gripping her arm. Still she couldn't stop.

At the two-hour break for lunch, everyone was eating egg salad sandwiches, but the smell of them made her want to gag. She dropped hers in a wastebasket and looked at her watch. An hour yet to be in the room with them.

"Lin," her dad said. "There's some issues of *People* here."

She left her spot at the window and took the magazines he was holding out for her. Their covers wrinkled, torn.

"Thanks." She sat on the hard leather couch, paging through the old issues, pausing here and there and pretending to read.

That afternoon the bloodied shirt just there, still. A presence whenever she tried to focus on the testimony. It even superimposed itself over the Winchester shotgun the jurors handed around to each other. She was definitely losing it. She definitely shouldn't be there. Soon, testimony turned to the hearing protector and the blood on it. Lin had to keep mopping her face and swallowing.

LAURA

Outside, wind was blowing a fine drizzle at the courthouse.

"Lin! Wait!" Laura ran across the street and caught up with her. "Where're you going?"

"Back to Ithaca."

"Why!"

"I can't stay. It's awful. He's guilty, Laur. I just know it!"

"C'mon, Lin! You're not even giving Dad a chance. Would he just run away if you were in trouble? Accept what others say about you and take off?"

Lin stood there looking at the sidewalk. "This is awful."

"It's a trial, Lin. Each side tugging back and forth. Only right now it's the other side's turn."

"Yeah, right."

"I'll tell you what. Let's get some coffee and then go back. Mom needs us. Dad does, too. "We really don't have to listen to the testimony, you know. We can block it out."

"Does that mean you're having problems with it, too?"

"Of course I am, but that's because this is a trial. Think of the word. *Trial.* Svoboda pulling one way, and Russ the other. That's how it's supposed to go. But it's hard on everyone."

"Wind shear. Pulled both ways. Or pushed."

"Exactly. C'mon. Let's get that coffee and then do what's hardest, the thing we're most afraid of. If I had done that with the piano, who knows?"

In the next days Laura focused on the Exit sign to one side of the judge's bench and kept telling herself *Soon our turn.*

112

Sometimes she hummed to herself—opera arias, themes from symphonies and concerti, Schubert's Trout Quintet—as witness after witness testified. The Affair. The Ballistics. The Pathologists' Reports. Outward to inward it went, the testimony. The man, the weapon, the bodily effect on her father. Svoboda's architecture clear, sturdy, deadly, but she told herself she didn't care because it was all wrong. When her dad finally testified, Svoboda himself would be blown away. Just wait. At her center, a core of warmth she knew to be hope. On her lap, fingers raced through the Trout, creating bubbles and spirals and glittering fantails of sun-struck water.

Then during the tedium of one afternoon came the thought that maybe she should talk to her dad's former wife. Why not? She might say something that would help Lin—and herself, too. So what if the woman probably would be testifying for the prosecution. That didn't mean, did it, that Laura couldn't go see her, and she did live nearby. That much Laura knew from the articles she'd once made a point of reading the previous spring. The court might have its strict protocol about who could take the stand and who couldn't—they themselves, for example, couldn't, which was hard to understand let alone accept—but that hardly held, out in the real world.

AT A grocery store in a town about ten miles away, a clerk pointed to a cork board near the entrance where, among advertisements for small businesses and services, were pamphlets about Marcia Lund's business, *Dream Weavers. Day and Evening Classes. Wool and Supplies. Gallery.*

That Saturday cars were parked in a graveled lot near a large barn. Across the driveway was a Victorian farmhouse Laura couldn't help admiring. It was painted a soft tan with maroon and brown trim, and chrysanthemums filled the front garden and surrounded a sign that said CENTURY FARM. In a pasture were four mottled gray horses with arched tails, short necks, and finely shaped heads. In another field, grazing sheep. Then woods and a distant view of Lake Michigan, sapphire

that cloudless day. Envy made its inroads. Sadness. Her parents with so little now, in contrast.

The person who answered Laura's knock was too young to
be Marcia Lund—a daughter? Laura wondered. The girl wore
her ponytail pulled through a baseball cap and had the exu-
berance of a pretty adolescent just glad to *be*. Laura asked for
Marcia, and the girl told her she was over in the gallery, with
customers.

"Oh, then she's busy. I should probably just—"

"No, no! Go on over. She's always happy to meet new
people, show them around."

"Could you do me a favor? Could you go over there and
give her this for me?"

On a blank page in the notebook she always kept in her
purse, she wrote her name and asked to talk with Marcia
in private.

"Sure!" the girl said, taking the folded piece of paper. Laura
watched her cross the driveway and go into the barn. Minutes
later a woman emerged alone. A short woman with graying
hair cut short. She wore jeans, sneakers, and an obviously hand
knit, multicolored sweater. "Hi," she said. "I'm Marcia. And
you're Laura. Wow, all grown up. Would you like to come
inside or should we walk? It's a great day for it."

Laura took the hint. "Let's walk. I've been inside too much
lately." Words she immediately regretted.

But the woman only said, "Me, too. We could head down
to the lake. It's a nice trail."

An understatement. A wide path covered with shredded
bark curved through pines and oak, with weathered benches
placed at intervals. Squirrels scrounged in fallen leaves. Chip-
munks gave their high whistles. And in the branches overhead,
chickadees called.

"Do you ride your horses here?"

"Every morning, depending on the weather. They love it.
So do the dogs."

"How many dogs do you have?"

"Oh, I'm incorrigible. I have, would you believe, six."

"Six dogs!"

"Oh, a few are elderly and just sleep a lot. They're all res-cued dogs. You know—taken out of rotten situations. Some-times we have to bring them back, more or less, from the dead. Oh, God. Sorry. Stupid of me to say that."

"It's all right." She kept her eyes on the path. A black dog raced up from behind and sped past.

"Thomas, heel!" Marcia shouted. "Heel!"

The lab swung around and loped back, then leapt up against Marcia, knocking her backward. "Oof! Down, you rascal." And when he obeyed, she lavished praise on him. "This guy's still in training but I love him all the same. *Don't* I, Thomas?" She rubbed the dog's onyx back, his neck, his head. The dog fairly pranced.

"Let's sit a minute. I need to catch my breath."

Laura was astonished by Marcia's eyes, a tropical green verging on turquoise, and wondered if she might be wearing colored contacts. Her features weren't delicate but still hand-some and included a sprinkling of freckles that made her seem quite youthful. Twenty years ago she must have been really nice-looking. The dark hair and green eyes, the energy, maybe even vivacity.

"You probably want to ask me some questions. The thing is, I'm not allowed to talk about the case. I'll be giving testimony."

"I realize that. I shouldn't even be here, probably. It's just that I have so many questions and don't know who to ask."

"Thomas! Stay!" The dog had heard something in the woods and sat there quivering, looking in that direction. His hind-quarters rose a little off the ground, and he began whimpering. Marcia leaned to pat his head. "Good dog! Stay, now."

To Laura, she said, "I'm afraid that'll have to wait until after the trial—if you still want to talk to me then."

"I was wondering if you could tell me, at least, if my father—my birth father—was really depressed around that time."

"Oh, gosh. I'm not a psychologist and have no idea what might have been going through his head, but was he down? Probably. I'm sure it messed him up."

"It?"

"Well, the whole thing."

"Did he know about the affair for quite a while?"

"A lot of people did. It messed me up, too. The thing is, I loved my husband very much, and a spouse's infidelity, well, it's plain awful to go through. Add to that the shooting, the talk, and my own craziness at the time, and you've got hell on earth. But at least it enabled me to deepen my work. The world taketh and giveth, right?"

"So my father must have been really hurting, too. Did you two ever discuss what was going on?"

"That I can't answer. Not today."

"Which probably means you did."

"It means you'll have to wait for the testimony."

"Do you really think your former husband *murdered* my father? I mean, you knew your husband, the way he was as a person, his character."

"Laura, I really can't talk about it now. I've already said tons too much."

"From what you've already told me, my father *could* have been suicidal that day."

"I see I've raised your hopes. I'm sorry. That's words for you. I shouldn't have said anything. Before you go, would you like to see the gallery?"

Not really. But out of politeness she said she would, and they walked back up the trail in a breeze that blew late-season gnats behind them. Laura thought of the mythical Furies, crowding around some hapless mortal and wreaking their punishments.

The gallery displayed works by several women, all of whom took classes there, Marcia explained. "We change our exhibits every three months or so." Marcia's own tapestries took up whole walls. These were intricate fabrications of woven wool, twigs, branches with and without bark, stones, ceramic beads, wire, deer antlers, animal bones, even strips of aluminum cans pounded flat and gleaming like tin foil. Laura supposed that the tapestries of pain and loss might be the ones in Death

Valley beiges and rusts, incorporating the bones and bleached antlers and burnt wire. People buying them for living rooms or atriums, though, might never suspect their genesis, for they weren't, somehow, quite wrenching enough. A ragged tapestry might be better. Something on the order of those ancient flags she'd seen in English cathedrals, ripped and falling apart and testimony to terrible losses. So, then, a tapestry half-ripped apart and not at all artful. Or maybe Marcia wasn't quite up to that because it was no longer inside her, really, the pain.

"They're wonderful," Laura said, when she had gazed a respectful few moments at each. Marcia stood with her hands cupped together, Thomas at her side. The girl who'd answered the door approached with a tray of mugs and a plate of sliced bread and lavender butter.

"I can't stay," Laura said, "but thank you."

On the road back to Tunley, she thought how she'd expected to find a woman soured by life, a vulnerable, weak woman only just maintaining some equilibrium. Someone any man might have been glad to leave. But no. Hardly. Under other circumstances Laura might even have liked her a lot. Outdoorsy, a lover of animals, creative and enterprising. Also clearly independent.

In town she stopped at the library and turned through issues of the Tunley *Courier* from 1970. The librarian recognized her and so did the three older people working on genealogies at the next table. But everyone got busy with their own tasks, allowing her to turn through the newspaper's discoloring pages in relative peace. In 1970 men were wearing prominent sideburns and longish hair. Shirt collars were outsized. Ankle boots popular. Older women were still trying to look like Jackie Kennedy, with their flip hairdos and short suits. Younger women might have had Cher as a role model, that exotic waterfall hair. And yet the sideburned men maintained their car lots and stores and farms. The bouffant-coiffed women put on church dinners and bake sales, kept things going in schools, offices, the library, the hospital. Laura studied the photos as if they might open into her parents' world at that time.

The *Courier* treated the story matter-of-factly. *Pete Hyland, a local businessman, died when a shotgun he was carrying accidentally discharged at a hunting camp near Lake Marion on Thursday of last week. Dr. Benjamin Weber, who accompanied Mr. Hyland on the shooting excursion, attempted to staunch the wound and resuscitate but to no avail. An autopsy, conducted the following day by Dr. Millard Howe, brought to light no evidence that the shooting was anything but accidental. Dr. Weber voluntarily submitted to questioning by County Investigator Jackson "Jack" Delrosier. State police are investigating the matter.*

Stated baldly, it seemed graven. Resolved. Except for that sentence about the state police. Laura felt belief sinking in again, settling around the heart, cushioning it. She turned through pages, looking for other references, but except for the obituary and article on the funeral, one of the largest the town had seen in years, there were none.

An article the following year noted Jackson Delrosier's retirement. *Mr. Delrosier, sixty-three, an avid reader of history, plans to do more of that now, as well as travel to many of Michigan's historical sites with his wife of forty years, Margaret Stepaniak Delrosier.* The article made reference to some of Delrosier's earlier, celebrated feats: single-handedly stopping a gang of kids on motorcycles who'd robbed a party store by intercepting them on a bridge, vintage-model machine gun in hand. Another time he'd stopped a hit-and-run car by shooting out a front tire. *Jack Delrosier is a man of whom it can be said he knows no fear.*

And he, too, had dropped the investigation.

Or had he? And wasn't sixty-three rather young to retire? Ill, maybe? But no. He was going to travel. Enjoy himself.

Disquietude replaced the momentary certainty, and then she came upon a wedding photo of her mother and stepfather identical to the one positioned to one side of an antique table at their home in Hawaii. Her mother in a Mandarin-style suit jacket and short skirt, holding a bouquet of freesias and asparagus fern. Ben Weber in dark suit and tie, a broad smile. . . . *The couple, along with Karen Hyland's two young children Laura and Linda, from her previous marriage to local businessman Peter*

Hyland, are planning to reside in Hawaii, where Dr. Weber will resume his practice in pediatrics. Peter Hyland died two years ago in a shooting accident at a hunting camp belonging to his parents, Mr. and Mrs. Earl Hyland.

Laura leaned back from the page, stunned at finding her name there, and Lin's. All of them intermeshed like that.

And then a door into the past did open. Lunchtime. Ben there. And she and Lin. Her mother turning away from the kitchen table and standing at the sink, her back to them. She'd just served hamburgers, and then for no reason Laura could understand had started crying, and Ben said *I'll talk to him,* and at the sink her mother replied *No, don't.* Laura had felt a pang of terror. *What happened?* But no one explaining anything and she unable to eat the hamburger. Then later in her room, the shade and curtains drawn, she understood that whatever had happened must involve not only their father, but all of them. And she was scared because something was going to happen, only she didn't know what.

Jack Delrosier. Find him. Boldly, even defiantly, she asked the librarian if she knew where he was living.

Janet's Creekside Nursing Home was a converted farmhouse with two added-on brick wings. A willow draped the stream in back. On a patio, aluminum chairs in primary colors. A receptionist said that Mr. Delrosier was indeed a resident there. Was she a reporter? Relieved not to have been recognized, Laura said that she was.

"Well, fifteen minute's the limit. That's about all he can handle at a time."

She escorted Laura through one of the wings where open doors revealed dorm-like rooms and, often, an elderly resident in a recliner chair, gazing out. From most rooms issued the sounds of TVs. An entire life, Laura thought, compressed, now, into a single room.

"This here's the men's wing. Ladies in the other one. They join up for meals and activities in the main house, those that can."

Jack Delrosier was sitting in a rocker, eyes closed, lap covered with an olive green afghan. The TV presented a blank screen, but a small tape player emitted big band music—brass in tight unison, the understated tinkling of a piano tapping in a few chords unmistakably the Duke's.

"He ain't sleepin'. That's just how he likes to sit an' listen to his music. Jack! *Jack!* You got a visitor. Open your eyes!"

Laura glanced at the book on a night table. *Letters and Treatises of Cicero and Pliny.* The woman turned down the tape player's volume and urged him again to open his eyes. Finally he did.

He had the passive demeanor of an infant, eyes wide open but little going on behind them, it seemed, except simple interest. And like an infant's, his eyes were murky, swimming in too much liquid. His hair had mostly fallen out; what little remained lay close to his head. He began squeezing a rubber ball in his right hand, then transferred it to his left and did the same thing.

She took the small desk chair and sat facing him. "Mr. Delrosier? My name is Laura. I used to be Laura Hyland. My father was killed in a shooting accident you investigated twenty years ago. Do you remember that at all?"

He shook his head and kept squeezing the ball. She glanced up at the clock.

"The man who was shot was Pete Hyland. I'm one of his daughters."

"You look like Pete."

"Then you remember?"

"There's no statute of limitations on murder, you know."

"I do know that, yes."

"They ever get the other guy?"

"What other guy?"

"The one that killed him."

"Not yet. That's why I thought—"

"Go ask Doc Weber about it. He's the one you want to talk to."

"Dr. Weber, the pediatrician?"

"That's the one. That case had everything."

"Can you recall any specifics, Mr. Delrosier?"

"He behind bars yet?"

"Who?"

"Doc Weber."

"Ah, no, he isn't."

"Well, he should be. You look like your dad. Same eyes."

"Mr. Delrosier? If Dr. Weber was the murderer, why was there no full investigation at the time? Why did people just let it go? Even you did, right?"

"You want to ask Geffe that. Or go out to Kinkle's." He raised a speckled hand. "Listen to that. Now that's music. She always goes and turns it down on me. Turn it up, would you, young lady?"

She did. He closed his eyes, and she watched him slip back into his private heaven. Soon the woman returned. Walking Laura to the main part of the house, the woman said, "You need to take everything he says with a grain of salt. That's what I tell people who come here to see him. He mostly don't know what he's sayin'. They wouldn't even come here and deposition him. Oh, he raged, then forgot, I guess. But like I said, sometimes he'll just say words for the fun of it, like."

At the reception desk, Laura paused. "Can I ask you a question? Do you know anything about a Mr. Geffe or a place called Kinkle's?"

"Geffe, I have no idea. Kinkle's you don't want to go messing around with. That's all I can tell you." She turned to her desk.

A headache had dug in, double pronged, radiant with pain probing each eye as if what she could not see were the cause.

KAREN

Hair rose on the back of her neck. Her fingers blue with fear. There she was—*Marcia*. Looking like Joan of Arc, that cap of hair, the black outfit. The woman he had loved once, enough to marry. Had *they* met first, God, all this would not be.

Nor Laura. Nor Lin.

No, but other children. Four. Five. Maybe several adopted. Many. Many *keikis* filling their house. Ka Lani—the heavenly place. A different life altogether, with no undercurrents, no shifting bottom.

And now Marcia saying how happy they'd been, as newlyweds, after the residency in St. Louis. ". . . we were in love, working together on common goals . . . very happy in Boston. I set up a literacy program for the mothers . . ."

He had talked little about that time. As if it had been a secondary reality, easily discarded. Nor had she asked much about his previous life as young Dr. Weber in a dangerous section of Boston, risking his life, in fact, caring for those children, those mothers. The Dr. Weber she had known was a different man—so full of need, as if all those years of giving had drained him.

". . . when our social life began to revolve almost exclusively around the Hylands after we moved to Tunley, I became suspicious . . ."

Yes, and tongues wagging like crazy, in that small town. But how insane, the laws of chance, Dr. and Mrs. Weber wanting some small town and landing precisely there. Where *she* had become so unhappy, uncertain, exhausted, and under it all, astonished by what was happening in her life, to her, to whom so much had been promised. The degree of failure a daily shock, as if each morning she found herself jumping into Lake Michigan regardless of the season.

". . . We had two angora show cats—I'd brought them with us from Boston—and I purchased a few angora rabbits in order to use their fur combings in my weaving. It bothered him. He always wanted the house just so. Then one day the cats were missing and—"

No. He wouldn't have done that. No a thousand times. Let those cats out. Or worse, as Marcia was now implying.

You're lying. You liar.

Hatred roared through her. She crushed the tissue in her hands.

". . . I could do nothing right. He criticized me all the time. It got so I was afraid. He was strong-willed and . . ."

Hatred gave way to her usual state of grief, as she had named it—the opposite of state of grace. His love for that woman had died because of her. She herself the killer frost.

". . . One evening I asked him if he was in love with Karen Hyland. He said he wasn't sure. That was the closest we'd come in months to talking about it. It gave me hope . . ."

She could picture it. The two of them at that table she'd refinished. The maple farm table. Butter yellow. Pottery coffee mugs. Her blotched face. She, afraid to reach for his hand. He, leaning back from the table.

Because of her.

A busyness in the well. Objections. Counter objections. Lawyers all but bumping up against one another like battleships.

Trying to keep words out.

And then an unwelcome recess and Marcia walking back up the center aisle, looking straight ahead.

Karen composed herself and stood. Looking at Laura, she attempted a small smile, sensed it pulling through dry skin, and feared it must look grotesque. Soon, the court settling again like crows, ravens, raptors of all kinds, she thought, on dead branches. Silent before the kill.

". . . He said he could treat me himself for depression. I took the various drugs he brought home—Valium, Elavil,

Librium—but felt no different possibly because, well, *he* wasn't changing. I wanted to stop taking the drugs. He told me I was being perverse and stubborn. Then one day, on the counter, a bottle of sleeping pills . . ."

Blame it on him! She could have gotten the pills and invented this embellishment. But it had to have happened on the night of the shooting, her overdose. How lucky for the town. What scintillating stuff!

Blame, regret, hatred, guilt. Hardly room in that vortex for love. Love which absorbed all, transmuting it into light. Where it should have been, the steadiness, the radiance, a hellish absence.

God, please. Not that, too.

LAURA AND LIN

The October afternoon warm and humid, amber leaves tearing away from tree limbs and careening like flocks of playful birds.

"So," Lin said as they walked. "How much of her story do you believe?"

"The part about the cats, no. But the sleeping pills, I don't know. It seems kind of over the top."

"I think the jurors bought it."

"How could you tell?"

"I don't know, but I've never seen them paying closer attention. It's the kind of thing you get on daytime TV, and seven of the jurors are women."

"That's a rather sexist remark, don't you think?"

"Still. It blew me away, and I don't even watch that stuff."

"You really believed her, Lin? I mean, apart from the cats?"

"It all fit."

"Maybe too well. Life's not that neat or definite. She painted an awful picture of Dad. He's not like that, is he."

"No, but she wouldn't lie on the stand, though, would she, Laur? Isn't that a crime or something?"

"It is. Perjury. But maybe she wants to get back at him. But wait a second. She also said that our father, Pete, *did* talk to her about the affair. Do you remember? So that could corroborate Dad's testimony about wondering if our father meant to take his own life."

"But the thing is, what if Dad changed, afterward. Became a totally different person because what happened out at that camp was just too awful. You know? I mean, you have to live with yourself after you do something terrible, right? So he became extra nice to us and Mom and everything."

"Lin, except for Marcia, nobody testified that Dad was an awful person, mean to cats and so on. I'm thinking she made that part up."

"I don't know. She was pretty convincing."

"Why do I get the feeling that you want Dad to be guilty?"

"I don't! It's just that I keep thinking about our father, and how it must have been for him, and now all this evidence and stuff. Also, I've been thinking about evil and how people come around to accepting it as not-evil."

"I can't listen to this anymore. I'm going back."

By then they'd reached the cemetery on the north side of town. Laura turned, but Lin said she was going to stay and try to find their father's new grave.

"It's getting dark, Lin! And it's probably unmarked."

"Why would she do that, Laur? Bury him in some secret place? *God.*"

"Because she didn't want his body autopsied yet again?"

"She didn't tell us she was going to do that, bury him in a different spot."

"She hasn't been well. She's probably depressed and so not thinking properly. C'mon. Let's go back."

"I'm going to see if I can find it. You go if you want."

Laura couldn't leave her there alone. They walked past century-old headstones, the plinths and thin, tablet-like stones darkened and tilted, their inscriptions weathered away to a faint cursive. In the newer section, they soon came to the Hylands' family plot, St. Michael still there, doing battle. Their father's former grave was demarked by a sandy line of soil around patches of sod.

Clouds in the west had turned nearly black, against washed blue sky, hanging there like three-dimensional stage props. The sun dropped below the tree line, and it was suddenly evening, and colder.

"Let's go, Lin."

"Wait. It's got to be around here somewhere."

"Not necessarily. It might be in some other cemetery altogether."

"It's *here*. I know it is." Something prickled through Lin. A chill of *knowing*. He had to be speaking to her again.

"Mom probably didn't want us here for the re-internment," Laura was saying, "because of the press and all."

"She could have at least told us where."

Laura agreed but said nothing. A mound of vibrant gladioli and chrysanthemums covering a new grave caught her eye, and roses and baby's breath. *All these acts of doomed love.* But maybe not. Those flowers would surely die, and quickly, hardly having a chance to scent the autumn air, pathway of that particular soul, but the love they emblemized possibly would continue to exist. Maybe forever, who knew? For it wasn't corporeal. As much as she'd loved her dad as profoundly as if he'd been her birth father, she felt, then, that he had in fact stolen the two of them, kidnapped them, and so denied their birth father the love due him by his children.

Lin was walking toward a narrow road on the east side, where they'd already been. Following, Laura saw her stop and then grip her elbows. Laura came up beside her.

"Lin, we really need to leave. They're going to be worried about us."

"This is it, Laur."

On the family stone, the word *Deller*. The grass in front of it looked sparse, patchy and yellowed, as it had in front of the Hylands' plot.

"Something made me stop right here. I know this is it."

A swell of anger transformed itself, almost at once, into pity. Laura put an arm around her sister.

"It was the weirdest thing, Laura. It was like he was telling me where. Wasn't Deller some relation of Mom's?" She knelt down and covered her face with her hands.

Laura knelt alongside her. *Lord, please help Lin. I don't know how she's going to survive this. How we are. And Father, I'm sorry for everything.* When she looked up, the air seemed disturbed, thickening, molecules shimmering—something. A chill came, then sudden warmth: she a little kid again, in the tub, her father shampooing her hair, and silken warm water skimming down over head, face, body.

LIN

At the courthouse the next morning Lin found three children's books where she usually sat. *Treasure Island, Pete the Engineer. All About Boats.* On a yellow stick-on note, upright handwriting. *These were your father's. I found them in a box up in the attic. You and your sister might like to have them. If not, please give them to some children you may know or to charity. Your Grandmother and Grandfather.*

Laura leaned forward and mouthed the word *what.* Lin handed her the note, then looked over at her grandparents. They were sitting as if at church, intent on their priest, Svoboda. Her grandmother didn't turn to see how the books might have been received.

There had been an old carpet in her grandparents' attic, she remembered, patterned with large pink roses and gray leaves, moth-holed and threadbare. Cardboard boxes of stored things had been stacked to either side of the space, under the slope of roof. Sunlight from the four-paned window falling on the rug sometimes became their campfire, sometimes their fireplace, depending on the pretend game they were playing. They used to take couch cushions and prop them against the boxes—these became chairs or beds. Both of them had liked reading there. These books. The worn paper covers soft as cloth.

And now cardboard boxes again—being opened, down in the well. The needle of time skipping from one place to another, as on the vinyl record albums they sometimes played on an old hi-fi. *Peter, Paul and Mary. Sgt. Pepper's Lonely Hearts Club Band.* So, yes, time was really like those circles on the records, circles flowing into one another in the spin of things. These boxes, now, holding not old drapes or records or Christmas decorations, but her dad's old canvas jacket, denim shirt, jeans, and leather boots.

Soon the next witness was taking the stand. The Blood Man.

In his navy blazer, Oxford-cloth shirt, striped tie, and chinos, the man might have just stepped from some college classroom. Hair and trimmed beard shading to silver. A voice honed in classrooms. The recitation of his credentials took twenty minutes, and when Russ immediately, and warmly, accepted him as an expert in blood and ballistics, Russ's tone seemed far more cozy than necessary, telling her how these guys probably all stick together, finally.

Soon Sidney McBride had engaged the courtroom in a lecture on what he called the geometry of blood. A drop of blood is not tear-shaped. *Tears* aren't tear-shaped. That's simply artistic rendering. A drop of blood is perfectly round. If your finger bleeds and you let the drops fall straight down, each will be circular in shape. Each will be, in fact, a small round ball bound into that shape by strong surface tension. It takes a great deal of energy to shatter surface tension. You can suspend a razor blade or needle on it. Insects skate on it. A droplet three-quarters of an inch in diameter won't decrease in size unless there's velocity, which can reduce it to mere millimeters. Additional energy that overcomes surface tension will cause "mist." Gunshots, for example, with their high-speed velocity, literally vaporize blood into small particulate matter.

Lin looked from the witness to the jurors. Each seemed alert and interested as McBride went on at length. Drops falling straight down produce circles; drops falling at an angle will have narrow shapes. There can be triangulation, where the blood fans out. Also, aspirated blood, gushing blood, and prints of blood. "Transfer" blood, which is blood wiped from one surface onto another. Or "back-spatter" blood, which flies backward toward the source of energy. And there can be blood that goes straight through the body, coming out the other side.

He deals with this everyday. Imagine. A life given over to the language of blood. No way could she leave the courtroom now, but the temptation to do so was becoming acute. Soon the images imposing themselves on the staid courtroom scene became grisly. Her father's blood spraying outward, front and side, geyser-like, misting the day, the field grasses, the stump, his own boots, and those of another man, who was hanging onto the gun and who, somehow, had just shot him through the chest.

"Now this here," Svoboda was saying of a large poster board affixed with enlarged photos, "this first photo is from a micron microscope?"

"Objection to the form of the question."

"Sustained."

"This . . ." Svoboda began, then stopped. "Professor McBride, tell us, please, if you will, what this is."

"That is an enlarged photograph done with a micron microscope."

The gallery tittered.

"And it is of high-speed velocity blood?"

"Objection!"

"Sustained."

"Professor, what is it a photograph—an enlarged photograph—of?"

"It is an enlarged photograph of high-speed velocity blood."

Again came the tittering and rap of gavel.

"Professor—but wait. I need to phrase this right or else Mr. Lowry, over there, will have another of his fits—"

"Objection! I move for a mistrial!"

"Objection sustained; motion denied."

"Professor, can you tell us about blood, whether it is, for example, a durable—"

"Objection."

"Overruled."

"Is blood a durable substance, Professor?"

"Oh yes! Blood is a most durable substance."

"Do you mean to say that it lasts over a long period—"

"Objection to the form of the question."

"Sustained."

Svoboda swiped at his hair. "*Does* blood last over a long period of time and if so, how—"

"Objection!"

"Denied. Mr. Svoboda, one question at a time, please."

"Your Honor," Russ said, "this is a courtroom, not a classroom."

The gallery groaned its displeasure.

"Counsel," the judge said, weariness in her voice, "please approach."

When Svoboda returned to his position before the witness, he said, calmly, "Professor, is blood a durable substance?"

"Asked and answered!"

"Sustained."

"Professor, can you tell us about the . . . longevity of blood?"

McBride perked up from his slump. "It's highly durable, if dry, and various things don't interfere with it, such as moisture, bacteria, silverfish, or various other insects. It can last for hundreds, even thousands, of years. It has been found on tombs and on centuries-old documents. It's safe to say that blood may last forever, given the right conditions."

An index finger braced her dad's cheekbone; the thumb, his chin. He appeared to be regarding the professor with detachment even when photos of the boot were entered as evidence, with their microscopic drops of her father's blood.

But then McBride became too much the academic, to Svoboda's annoyance, swerving into the physics of dispersion and distance, trajectories and wind resistance. Long minutes were given over to objections and approaches, while the professor's earlier words—and the sense they'd made—seemed to disappear, vaporized by legalese.

"Professor!" Svoboda said, his tone menacing, "is it your opinion, excuse me, *in* your opinion, given all the evidence you have reviewed, and to a reasonable degree of medical—"

"Objection!"

"What?"

"I can't tell you if you don't know."

"Your Honor!"

"Counsel, approach."

Minutes later, Svoboda rephrased his question. "Professor, in your opinion, given all the evidence you've reviewed, and to a reasonable degree of *scientific* certainty, can you tell us what is the logical source of these nineteen droplets?"

McBride took no offense at Svoboda's confrontational tone. "A shotgun blast to the heart. The body absorbs energy, the energy causes back-spatter; that is, blood sent back toward the muzzle of the gun. The concentration of blood builds up at five or six feet. At greater distances than five or six feet, you'll see less of it."

"Could it go a hundred feet, a hundred and fifty?"

"Objection!"

"Sustained."

"Professor, in your scientific opinion, could this back-spatter blood reach a distance of one hundred feet?"

"In my opinion, it could possibly reach seventy or seventy-five feet, but it would be very minimal because of air resistance."

"What direction would this minimal blood go, in your scientific opinion?"

"It would go back toward the shooter."

"All right. Now say that the wound of entry is low—"

"Objection. Move for a mistrial."

"Objection sustained; motion denied."

The gallery laughed at the judge's tone, so rote.

"Your Honor," Russ called out. "I move for a mistrial! The gallery is laughing. This is prejudicial."

"Motion denied."

Svoboda's bumbling, Russ's need to get all those moves-for-a-mistrial in the record were turning the trial into a circus. But her grandparents sitting there stoically, her grandmother's back rigid, her grandfather slumped forward, the two of them willing to go through anything, it seemed, however grisly, indecent, or insulting. While wherever she looked—the wood fronting their bench, her sister's tweed jacket, the weave of her own jeans—she was seeing spatter shapes, round, elongated, triangular, or almost too small to see, but there.

KAREN AND BEN

She could hear the girls still moving about from bathroom to bedrooms. Lying in semi-dark, light from a street light framing the room's two green shades, she recalled how, when the girls were children, she had tried to get them in bed by eight and how excruciating it had been, sometimes, to observe Laura's fastidious attention to detail. How she'd admire her long fingers as she swished them through soapy water. How she'd scrutinize the bristles on her toothbrush for any stray bits of toothpaste. For her children, time was a boundless playground. But Karen needed them in bed, craved her few hours alone, if Pete was working late or on one of his hunting trips. It made no sense, though, for those hours were always when the haunting began. The mind no longer busy with *doing* and so open to every ambush. Then she'd hear herself saying—the voice in her head the same as now: *We've had this time and it's been good. Many people never even have that much.* And then he, Ben: *Don't say that. It's not over.* But she needing resolution. Ashes, not the flames. Yet afraid it was too late. Ben wasn't going to give up. Go back to before. A sense of inertia, then. Passive acquiescence. A dangerous fatalism couched in grief.

Sin of omission.

But no. She *had* gone to the clinic and said what needed to be said. Yet how weak she must have been in those days, how irresolute for so long. And now, too—weak. Believing, disbelieving. Trusting, distrusting. Hoping, despairing.

He'd said, *I'll be home late. I love you.*

And she had thought, *All right. It's to be this way, then.* And she'd felt lighter, not joyous, but relieved. Still, she hadn't said

I love you too, Pete. Instead, she'd set the table in the dining room, placed kindling and logs in the fireplace. Made egg salad for the girls. Real pain hadn't yet set in. The Novocain of shock still in effect.

It had all seemed to prove *rightness.* The way things needed to be.

That evening she'd pushed Lin in the stroller while Laura followed on her pink and white tricycle, its plastic ribbons streaming from the handlebar grips in Easter colors. And then the police had come and her house filled up with people bringing casseroles and crock pots and sweet breads, and Earl hollered the words that may as well have been shot pellets. *You're the ones that done it, you and Weber. I never want to see you again unless it's behind bars.*

Now she lay there not wanting to disturb anyone by getting up, particularly not her husband, who seemed deeply asleep, free of it all for a while. Eyes open upon a clarity that had nothing to do with the room's shadows and half-formed shapes, she allowed the words to repeat themselves: *I'll be home late. I love you.*

Words with no ominous undercurrent. Words holding only themselves. Words you'd say after some bad quarrel had passed over, squall-like. He'd been planning to come home that day. He loved her. He was not a man about to take his own life and that of another man.

This she knew.

ALONGSIDE HER, Ben was aware of her wakefulness, the tension of it, the lie. So he was afraid to move, to show in any way that he, too, was lying there in thought, trying to keep his breathing deeper than ordinary breathing.

The day's testimony wouldn't let go. Blood this, blood that. Shapes. Attributes. The bastard so sure of himself. One thing, though, to live in a textbook world and quite another to live in the real, the *now*, the red, wet, pulsing heat of it. The body's magisterial order collapsing, bombarded by those bits of speeded-up brass. *The gun there. The gun there between them.*

Ben's right hand twitched, an involuntary scrabbling against the sheet. His wife changed position a little, but he did not.

He could hear the tick of his wristwatch on the nightstand. Inexorable as water drops.

Or blood.

The tick began to sound like someone plodding along a road, then uphill. Then it became footsteps on a stairs, brisk, businesslike, indefatigable. Climbing to where he lay waiting, defenseless.

He eased one hand to his chest.

LAURA AND LIN

Only the root vegetables looked decent enough to purchase. Laura chose a few red potatoes, a bag of carrots, several parsnips, and three white turnips tinted a deep shade of lilac. Amazing, that such colors should form in the earth. Burgundy, lilac, candle-white, and orange the color of goldfish. The vegetables lost their substantiality, becoming pure color blurring and streaming away somewhere. She had wanted to pull together some nice dinner that would satisfy her mom and dad and finicky Lin, and so the idea of a vegetable soup, the ideal of it: a small family seated at a round table, darkness at the windows but steam rising from broth and vegetables, herb-scented steam. Now she was afraid she wouldn't be able to even finish shopping.

Someone touched her arm. "Laura, are you all right?"

Her grandmother—in tailored suit and shimmering weather coat. Laura hadn't recognized her at first, the context all wrong.

"I'm okay."

"You look very pale. Let me walk you to your car. I'll pay for these. Do you need anything else?"

"Really, I'm fine." She became aware of someone else standing nearby, a pink-faced man with white hair and moustache. The left pocket of his white coat embroidered in red stitching. *Manager.* Then she was in his cubicle, holding a Styrofoam cup of water while, far off, the Temptations were singing "My Girl."

"I'm really okay. I know I can drive."

"Yes," her grandmother said. "But I'm going to." She helped her to the car, and then at the house asked if Laura could make

137

it up the porch steps by herself. Laura nodded and didn't turn to watch the woman walk away. Her hand burned where her grandmother had touched it.

Her dad brought her water and aspirin. Her mother was there, too, with a cold washcloth. One of them took her temperature every hour. Once, she woke in the night and saw her dad still sitting in the ruffled chair in a corner. Hand propping his jaw, his legs stretched out. She said he should go and get some sleep.

"I was just about to." He didn't move.

"Dad?"

"I'm right here, honey."

"Good night."

"Nite. See you in the morning."

Still he didn't move.

The next morning she stayed in bed while everyone else left for the courthouse. That afternoon Lin came back alone, giving Laura a scare. "Where are they?" she asked.

"Midge took them apple picking."

"*Apple* picking?"

"Midge's idea. After court adjourned early today, he asked if we 'wanna' go get some apples. I think he sort of feels sorry for Mom and maybe even has a little crush on her. Mom said they weren't dressed for apple picking. She didn't sound too enthusiastic, so Midge right away said they could just buy them there, too."

"How come you didn't go with them?"

Lin smiled. "Not organic."

Laura thought she'd been told to stay behind, check on her. "How was it today?"

"Oh, they brought in another expert. This one came in by private jet, we heard. Even carried this little flight bag thingy into court. Why else but to show off. A medical examiner from Chicago. Awfully big time, given his credentials. He had a funny way of speaking directly to the jury whenever Svoboda asked him a question. He'd look at Svoboda for about half a second and then right away turn to the jury and respond.

Probably making eye contact like crazy. He had this haughty manner, though, and seemed arrogant as hell, with this aristocratic, down-turned mouth. Only, when he addressed the jurors, he wasn't arrogant at all but friendly and warm. I'm sure he gave them the impression that they're the most important people there."

"Well, they are, pretty much."

"True."

"So what did he say?"

"Just that after reviewing all the evidence, blah blah blah, all the reports, etc., etc., etc., he was able to reach an opinion that it's homicide."

Laura closed her eyes for a moment. "Of course he'd reach that conclusion. How did Russ do with him?"

"Oh, you know. Russ and his books. He pulled out this big book and read a section, then asked if the guy recognized the words. The guy said yes. And then Russ goes, You wrote that, didn't you. Going for, like, high drama. As far as I could tell, it had to do with examining wounds on the body, at the time. The guy didn't even blink when Russ went on, saying that father's body had been washed before the photos he examined—the guy, that is—were taken. Am I making sense?"

"The man's name is Huddle, I think. I remember Russ mentioned him."

"So anyway, he didn't blink. Washed and embalmed, he said, sort of cheerfully, implying to his buddies, the jurors, that it didn't make the least bit of difference—to him. That's pretty much how he handled each of Russ's little jabs. Svoboda came on and asked if knowing that the body had been washed and embalmed before the photos were taken affected his opinion in any way. The guy said no. It wasn't going to cause any change in that scalloping from the pellets. It wasn't going to wash away any soot on the inside. And remember that thing about tattooing? Well, that goes right into the skin, so washing the spot wasn't going to change any of that."

"There wasn't any tattooing in the first place, was there?"

"Right. So Russ had to talk about something else. Ammunition! How old it was. The guy says about ten years. Then, get this, he says, And we know it worked, don't we? That was it, pretty much. Then he took off, with his little bag thingy. Poof. Svoboda picked the right one to end with."

"He's done?"

"With the expert testimony. Russ said they have one more witness. Grandpa."

"I thought they'd do that."

"Yeah, right. Are you hungry?"

"No, thanks."

"Now you sound like Mom. It was probably dehydration, there in the market. Can I ask you something? Do you have a boyfriend yet?"

"That's a little off topic, wouldn't you say?"

"I just worry about you sometimes, Laur."

"Why? I date." The word sounded odd to her, comical. She envisioned a date palm, with its sweet brown fruit that rodents loved.

"Is he a musician?"

"No, he works at the theater part-time. Does carpentry and electrical work. He's Ukrainian."

"Cool. Have you told him about any of this?"

"Not yet."

"That's probably smart, though it feels good, at first, to unload on somebody. There's this one guy I told, at the co-op? So now it's going to be with us, like, forever. Plus, he's always bringing it up. How's it goin' now, Lin? I might not even be thinking of it at the time, and this guy goes, So what's happening, any news? And it just wrecks me for about a hundred reasons."

"That might be why I haven't told this person at the theater. The thing is, he reads newspapers to learn English. It's possible he knows about it."

"You like him a lot?" Then, "Your taking the Fifth means, probably, that you do. Well, it's about time."

"The thing is, he has a big family, and they're really tight with one another. They help each other through, oh, nursing programs and school, and send money back to others still in the Ukraine. And they're super-religious. What would *our* family look like to them? His would be horrified, knowing just the basics." Her mouth began shaking.

"I guess I see what you mean. Wait a second. *Svoboda.* Is that a Ukrainian name? If it is, they'd probably be on his side, too, which is even tougher."

"Same region probably." A geographical area she knew little about but imagined to be dense with history, inequities, bloodshed, righteous passion, fanatical beliefs, and some mysterious strength rising from the earth there, itself, maybe, its iron and calcium and phosphorous, who knew what, and also engendering some terrible sensitivity to nuance, shadings. Bogdan had that. It drew her from the start, the way he'd listen to her playing at the theater, his eyes on his work, but his heart, she sensed, in the music. She suspected he'd loved her mainly for that.

Her use of the past tense not lost upon her.

"Lin, I want to believe in Dad."

"Do you really think there's a good chance he's truly innocent?"

"I do." Did she? "Lin, this trial may not prove anything one way or another. The experts tend to just cancel each other out. I mean, look, one says three feet away; another, a few inches to a foot. That's quibbling, don't you think? I mean, when you consider a *struggle* and all that can happen during one."

An image of her father's bloodied shirt came, bringing on a spasm of chills. She turned on her side and shook, under the blankets.

"Can I tell you something, Laur?"

"Sure." She didn't want to hear it.

"I've been experimenting."

"Not drugs?" Laura sensed herself fading despite Lin's alarming words.

"No, God. But the thing is, I'm having trouble concentrating on school stuff."

"Lin."

"I saw this guy doing puppets one day in Ithaca, on the Commons, and he was having a blast with all these little kids around him. It was so cool! He had a little nylon stage he carried in a special pack, and it set up in a minute. Then he got behind it and had these little creatures the kids loved. I watched the show twice, then went to a shop and got some material and made my own puppets. Can I show you? Are you okay enough?"

Laura forced herself to sit up. When she reached for the water glass, her hand and forearm were shaking.

"God, Laur, you're really sick. We'll do it another time."

"No, it's okay. Go get them."

Lin came back into the room carrying a suitcase and a backpack. "I also found out where to buy one of those stages." She set it up, and then Laura was watching an alligator talking to a flamingo.

"Hi! I'm Big Al. I scare people but don't mean to. It's just all these teeth!"

"Hey, Al, my name's Blinky. I like to tuck my head under my feathers and sleep, like this!" Blinky turned her long neck to the side and tucked her beak under a wing. Out came the beak again. "Know what else I can do, Big Al?"

"No, what?"

"Watch." Blinky tucked one leg up and stood straight on the other.

"Wish I could do that! Can you show me how, please, please, please!"

"Well, ah, you see, your legs are a teeny bit short? Don't cry, Al. It's just that we're different. I don't have teeth to snap."

Lin appeared from behind the stage. "It goes on like that, and finally they make up a song about being buddies though they're different. *You tuck, I snap, you fly, I float*—I'm working on the rhymes. What do you think?"

The simplicity of it all, given her sister's weird complexity at times, brought the sting of tears. "It's cute. You did a nice job with the puppets." She took the washcloth from its bowl and covered her brow.

"You think so? Because this is what I want to do now. I have so many ideas for other characters."

"You mean instead of physical therapy?"

"Yeah."

"Lin."

"I never should have told you!"

"Wait a second." She was drifting off again, in the fever haze. "Do it . . . with the therapy."

Laura slept, a prisoner of dream and bits of thought endlessly looping. Somewhere in the labyrinth, she heard Lin's voice again and thought it must be morning. But the bedroom was illuminated with unfamiliar light, its drab white walls transformed into butter yellow. "Have some juice, Laur," her sister was saying. "Then you can rest again."

Laura pushed herself up, movement bringing on the shakes once more. "Your rhymes . . . I could do the music."

"Really?"

Outside, car doors were slamming. Lin went to the window. "They're back. Don't say anything about this, okay? They'll freak." She was quiet a while, looking out the window. "Actually, I'll probably fail at this, too. I shouldn't have wasted all that money. Oh God, why am I so stupid?"

"Lin, you're not."

She began putting away the puppets. "Maybe just going crazy. I've been dreaming about him every night, Laur. Our father. He's just there, and I'm, like, glad to see him. But he's so strange. He just watches me. Staring, like. It's actually awful."

"A dream."

"I know, only it feels so true somehow. Like there's something there that's *true*."

The mental feat of summoning words and the exact right tone that might comfort her sister was too much for Laura now. She understood that this illness was just some bug wreaking havoc on the internal controls; and yet the weakness, the aching helplessness, and above all a growing detachment from her own humbled body told her how it was going to be, one day. Told her how it must have been for her father, though speeded up, that loosening grip on the world.

Lin, you're not going crazy.

She couldn't be sure she'd said the words. Lin was gone, and her dad was there, his broad hand on her forehead, as she swam up through a blur of images. She swallowed the aspirin he'd brought. Then Lin was saying, "Laur? There's a call for you. It's from a Bogdan Urick. Do you want to talk to him? We can help you get downstairs."

She shook her head.

"He sounds so sweet, Laur. Your Ukrainian friend, right? He wants to bring us *soup*."

Again she shook her head. "Tell him not to come."

Sometime later, the chills abated, and Laura lay there, images wheeling. Among them, a bowl of soup with prunes and raisins, and fat doughy clumps floating in a sweet-sour ambrosial broth she could all but taste.

LIN

His halting pace. An aged king ascending his throne in his own good time. When he finally sat facing the gallery, everything about him suggested *bones*. The sallow coloring, the protruding knobs at the hollow cheeks and temples— Though she'd seen him so often in the courtroom since the pre-trial hearing the previous spring, his age still a shock. This man seemed to have no connection whatsoever to the grandfather who'd hunted bear in northern Ontario and who'd swum in icy Lake Michigan each New Year's Day. Nothing, it seemed, connected this person to that long-ago one except, obviously, vengeance.

Svoboda remained seated at the prosecution's table. "Sir, are you related to the deceased?"

In whispery tones Earl Hyland stated, "I am. He is . . . was . . . my son."

"How old was your son at the time of his death?"

"Thirty-two years of age."

"And when did you last see him?"

"Alive . . . or dead?"

"Alive, sir. When did you last see your son alive?"

"I saw him on that morning, the day he died. About nine o'clock he stopped at our house on his way to the office. He had some kielbasa for us."

"Did you enjoy Polish sausage?"

"Oh, sure. Pete knew that."

"What kind of mood was he in?"

"He seemed in a good mood."

Svoboda proceeded calmly, his voice uncharacteristically gentle. "When did you next see your son, sir?"

145

Earl Hyland's mouth twisted downward. "At the camp. I saw his body there on the ground. He was dead."

"Is this the camp where the shooting occurred?"

"Yes, the camp I owned and still do own. He was dead, laying there on the ground."

Lin thought it might stop then, a foolish hope. It went on for several minutes longer. Guns. Earl Hyland's knowledge about them. Pete Hyland's knowledge. The frail man spoke slowly, deliberately, tones nearly without resonance or emotion, yet the context of those words, the silence holding them, made it all eloquent. The tears in her eyes painful, corrosive. She remembered her grandfather's gun cabinet, crafted of golden oak, with a bowed and beveled glass door. The grain of the oak so black, against the gold. In that wood, mountain ranges and riverbeds and flat golden plains. She and Laura had liked to rub their hands up and down the smoothness, which drove their grandmother wild. She'd shoo them away for they were never, ever, to try to open that cabinet even if somehow they managed to find the key. *Those aren't toys, so you girls keep away from there. Go find something else to play with.* And because the guns were not to be touched, nor, eventually, even the cabinet itself, and because they'd never seen their grandfather remove one of the long-barreled guns, they'd learned to ignore the handsome piece of furniture in the parlor, relegate it to the same status as the green-velvet Victorian settee, which they weren't to sit on, either.

"So you trained your son in the use of guns?"

"Yes."

"Was he a safe hunter?"

"He was. I never saw him point a gun at himself or anybody else or hold it wrong."

"Did you train him in gun safety?"

"I did. He always took good care . . ."

The words wisped away. After all the others—scientific, jargon-plagued, formal, gossipy, angry—just those. Lin finally had to let the tears fall onto her fleece jacket.

Russ had no questions for Earl Hyland.

Svoboda stood. "May it please the Court, the State rests."

At the recess Lin crossed the aisle and grasped her grandfather's arm just as he'd gotten himself upright.

"Grampi—Grampi, I'm sorry."

His expression remained frozen in bleakness. When she opened her arms to hug him, he lurched backward and nearly fell. Laura pulled her away.

"God, Lin," Laura said later. "What if the *jurors* had seen!"

"Fuck them. Just fuck the jurors. What do I care if they *saw* or not."

"Lin, you can't just go and do things like that. Not in the courtroom. Please think before you act. Think of Mom and Dad. Think of us!"

"I am thinking of us. I'm thinking of everyone. That's the *problem*."

LAURA

Because her sister was so obviously losing it, Laura needed to do something besides just sitting there all day. The first chance she got, she asked Midge if the names Kinkles and Geffe rang any bells.

He squinted at her, eyebrows, face bunching. "Why?"

"It's something I overheard. People in the grocery store, older people. When they noticed me, they broke off, so I figured it had some bearing." Chilling to realize how easy it is to lie. Words flying into your head and you just saying them.

He rolled a toothpick to the other side of his mouth. "Kinkles. Planes flying in coke and weed from Colombia. Modified Cessnas. Long haulers. Flew under the radar. Made drops at night at his place. He served some time."

"So Kinkles was the guy who'd set it up?"

"Kinkle. One of them. They used his place."

"What about Geffe."

"Geffe? Geffe. D.A. for the county back when Pete Hyland was shot."

"Was he involved?"

"Only as the official who did some investigating."

So on a mild afternoon, the court in recess for the day, she went to the recorder of Deeds office and asked to look up a name in a plat book. Saying the word *Kinkle* sent a small shock wave through the overheated room. All the other women busied themselves with paperwork. The one she'd spoken to went into an adjoining room and returned minutes later with an oversized book she slid across the counter. The dry air in the room fairly crackled.

Half an hour later, Laura had found the gravel road, with its weedy ditches and barb-wire fencing. Bare tree limbs poked upward. No cattle or horses in the rocky pastures, but near a farmhouse shingled with asbestos siding, a pair of draft horses grazing in a small pasture.

Kinkle's.

Beyond the house lay some flat acreage bordered by a meandering tree line. Across the road from the house, a weathered barn served as a garage. A rusting mailbox gave no name, just a route number. Laura parked in a rutted driveway and walked up wooden steps to a side door, which set off a dog's crazed deep barking somewhere within the house. The steps were littered with a tangle of chain, small tools, and plastic pots holding dead petunias. The aluminum storm door was badly dented. A large dog lunged at it from inside, its claws further scraping the Plexiglass. A woman came rushing into the enclosed porch, grabbed the dog's chain collar and hauled him back.

"He's friendly. Just crazy. Get back, you!"

The woman had on jeans and a huge brown sweatshirt. An elastic band held back long hair parted in the center. Cursing, she dragged the dog through the kitchen and shut him in some other room. Barking and whining, he stormed the closed door. "Jake! Shut up!" the woman yelled. "Go lay down!"

"God, I don't know," she said, unlocking the storm door. "He's Jimmy's dog. Wish to hell he'd take him with him, but he just goes and chases deer if you take him out in the woods. And when I chain him, he keeps bustin' the damn chain. So he has to be inside, wreckin' everything. What d'you want? I ain't buyin' nothin'."

It was hard to judge the woman's age. Jeans and sweatshirt, but skin burnt dry by age or tobacco. The hair at the part graying, the rest a faded and limp carrot red. Her small teeth were greenish at the gums and showed serious black pits that had to be painful. "I'm not selling anything," Laura said, feeling bad for the woman who probably hadn't a dime to spare. "Are you Mrs. Kinkle?"

"Who're you?"

My grandparents used to live on this farm. They were from Germany. I just wanted to see the place. The prepared lie. Instead, she said, "My name is Laura Weber."

It took a few seconds for the woman's expression to go from truculent to surprised, even welcoming. "I thought you looked familiar! I saw you on TV! So what d'you want?"

"I was wondering if you could tell me anything about the drug scene around here, twenty or so years ago."

The woman's expression hardened again. "My guy's probably gonna be back in a couple of minutes. I wouldn't be here, if I was you."

"Why not?"

"'Cause people comin' around, askin' questions piss him off."

"I heard you were dealing drugs back then."

"Yeah, right. And we stashed away a million dollars. Don't it look like it?"

The enclosed porch smelled of kerosene fumes. Laura could see an old chrome-edged table in the kitchen, just beyond.

"The thing is, I'd like to know more about that time. It's not for any newspaper or anything. It's for my family. My dad. He's on trial for murder."

"I know that."

"Well, nothing's making much sense. I thought maybe there might be more to it all. More than is coming to the surface, I mean."

The door to the other room banged open and Jake clattered toward Laura.

"Damn it, Jake!" the woman yelled.

The dog, part Rottweiler, danced in front of Laura, growling and whimpering. Slowly she extended her open hand. The dog sniffed, licked, barked, and spun around.

"He likes you. You want 'im? I'll tell Jimmy he just ran away."

"He's a nice dog, but we, oh, have to be in court everyday and—"

"Oh, right. Well, he could stay at your house. You can see what a great dog he is."

"My father, Pete Hyland, was he involved with drugs?"

"Everybody was, back then."

"So that means he was, too?"

"Well, like I said. Everybody who had any bread. Party time!"

"Was there some airstrip here?"

"Oh, wow. Right. Just the field out there. I was, I don't know, seventeen or so, an' just hanging around, but yeah. And my guy served time. I went into deten. We didn't get shit out of it."

"Where did they come from, the drugs? New York?"

"You kidding? South America! No pharmaceuticals, just weed and white stuff. There were these cool small planes? They had these humongous fuel tanks. The whole damn plane was practically nothing but a fuel tank. They'd fly real low, under the radar the whole way. I kid you not. It was neat."

"So you guys sold it?"

"Not us. We just unloaded, and Jimmy, he let them use the field. So they got Jimmy good even though he didn't make hardly nothin' out of it."

"Do you know who did make money from it? And who owned the planes?"

"That I don't know. Like I said, I was just this stoned kid hanging around." She pulled a cigarette from a pack extricated from somewhere beneath the baggy sweatshirt and lit it with a pink lighter.

"Do you know if the D.A. was part of it?"

"The who?" She laughed. "Hey, that was a band back then, remember?"

Laura didn't but saw how the words had stirred happier memories. "D.A. stands for District Attorney."

"Jeez, I don't know. They didn't, like, wear name tags."

"Richard Geffe was his name."

"Don't ring no bells. You need to go, I swear. If Jimmy sees you here and figures I'm talkin' to someone involved in the thing, he's gonna—" She looked out a window toward the woods.

"What?"

"Beat the crap outta me."

"Then I really better go. Listen, if you remember anything— No, never mind. I don't want to get you in trouble. Thanks for your help, Mrs. Kinkle." Laura also didn't want to insult her by offering money. "If you'd like, I could try to find a home for your dog."

"That's okay. I'd probably miss him. Right, Jake? Shit. There he is."

As Laura was backing into the road, a truck, its bed piled high with firewood, was crossing the field and coming toward the house. A black pickup high on its springs. Laura raised dust, speeding away.

LIN

He was the first to be called for the defense, which sent breathy ripples through the courtroom. Russ, seated, asked his questions from the defense table, and her dad responded directly to him, rather than to the jurors. A mistake, Lin thought. Hadn't Russ advised him? His voice, though, *his*. Like some shy high school kid's. Also, subtle echoes of Virginia. The deference and courtesy.

". . . a professor and his wife took me in, after my father's death when I was nineteen and a sophomore at the University of Virginia. My mom had died the year before, and my younger brother was living in Oregon, with relatives. I helped out around the professor's house, doing painting and yard work for them. I also took care of their dog when the professor and his wife traveled."

"I object, your Honor," Svoboda rose to say, "to this taking-care-of-a-dog business as irrelevant."

"You may proceed, Dr. Weber," the judge said.

"Although it might seem I was working for my room and board, I did it because I wanted to. They were good people, and they'd taken me in and treated me like a son, so I did my best to be worthy of their trust and generosity—"

"Your Honor! This is just, 'See what a good guy I am?' "

"You may continue, Dr. Weber."

Svoboda sat down, his slouch registering disdain, even contempt. He'd stopped taking notes and sat well back from his legal pad and pen, arms folded, while her dad told of his wedding to Marcia Lund and then his medical residency at the university hospital in St. Louis, followed by a move to Boston so that he could fulfill his Public Health Service obligation.

153

"At this clinic in Boston, Doctor," Russ said, "what were your duties?"

"My duties consisted of caring for the children of mainly Black and Hispanic women subsisting below the poverty line. I treated everything from the usual childhood illnesses such as ear, eye, and throat infections, to the less usual—problems resulting, for example, from a mother's drug addiction or family abuse. I also developed a nutrition program and pre-natal and post-natal care programs that, by the time we left Boston, were up and running and quite effective."

"Did you, Doctor, see these mothers and children mainly at the clinic?"

"Well, I did something rather unconventional—and probably dangerous, in retrospect. At times, given the specifics of individual cases, I visited them at home."

The gallery seemed to exhale as one.

"Your Honor! I move for a mistrial."

"Denied. But if there is any further sound, *any*, this courtroom will be cleared of all spectators except for one representative of the press."

Russ shook his head the slightest degree and continued. "Can you tell us what were the specifics of some of these homebound cases you visited?"

"Well, in one instance, a mother was afraid of leaving her apartment. Her fear bordered on the pathological but was also grounded in common sense. She lived in a very dangerous neighborhood, drug-infested, crime-ridden. She'd called the clinic and said she hadn't been getting any pre-natal care and wanted to be examined and advised, but was too scared to travel the ten blocks from her apartment. So I went there, with a nurse, and we examined her and gave her vitamins as well as advised her on nutrition. I should add that she had three other children, all in need of care."

"Did you return to care for this woman and her children?"

"Yes, we returned periodically."

"Doctor, did you carry a gun in this dangerous neighborhood?"

"No, I did not."

"Did you home-visit any other patients in that area?"

"Yes. There were a number of children I visited for various reasons. One was—"

"Your Honor, may we approach?"

When the lawyers were through speaking with the judge at the bench and at their places again, the judge said, "Mr. Lowry, please proceed to the defendant's relationship with Mr. Peter Hyland, if you will."

"Your Honor, may I ask one further question relating to my client's work at this period of time?—I assure you its relevancy will be apparent."

"You may—one."

"Thank you. Doctor, there was a particular child who came to your attention—"

"Your Honor! May we approach?"

"Your Honor," Russ said. "I'm trying to establish something about Dr. Weber's character."

"Counsel, approach."

Lin knew what the discussion would be about—the little boy from Boston's inner city who'd been killed by an abusive father and in whose name her dad had started a scholarship fund. Each year, now, a deserving kid from that war zone was able to attend college because of her dad. So far, over twenty had, and most, successfully. Would the jury get to hear of this? She thought not, and was right.

Screw the law. Isn't everything relevant, really? It amazed her that her sister actually had faith in the process.

Then her dad was talking about the move to Tunley and meeting the Hylands. The courtroom was beginning to feel as pressurized as one of those inflated sports arenas. Soon the judge was saying, "At this time we will take a recess of fifteen minutes. Counsel, approach, please."

Jurors filed out. Russ and Svoboda walked up to the judge's high bench, while reporters rushed to their phones and satellite vans. The senior citizens across the aisle exited slowly on stiff legs that made them lurch, some grasping canes, the top halves of their bodies wanting to go forward, the lower part needing to sit back down. Lin turned away when her grandfather passed by slowly, body curving thinly over his cane, his wife alongside him, having to temper her own pace.

Cold air from outside swirled around them. Chatter. Lin looked at her dad, still in the witness chair. Alone. What did he see?

The three of them—silent, waiting, still seated. Lin realized that her mother was holding her hand tightly and with her other, Laura's. An image of a jet about to ditch came to mind. She could see the three of them, heads down, waiting for the slam of ocean.

"I had a law school professor once," the judge began after the recess, "who used to say, 'I love you all as brothers and sisters,' then always added a *but*. So to you, now, I say the same. I love you all as brothers and sisters but during the forthcoming testimony I don't want to hear a peep out of you. No expressions of belief or disbelief, nothing, not a peep. In the event of any sound whatsoever, the sheriff will remove the offending person or persons immediately. And if it happens to any degree that threatens the right of the accused to a fair trial, the sheriff will clear the gallery of everyone save one representative of the press. The Constitution of the United States, the Constitution of the State of Michigan, as well as we ourselves as a society demand a fair and impartial trial. With that understood, let us begin. Mr. Lowry."

Her mother was still clutching Lin's hand as Russ, seated, said, "Dr. Weber, I direct your attention, now, to the date of April 23, 1970. Please tell the ladies and gentlemen of the jury what happened on that date."

Again he looked directly at Russ. "It was my regular afternoon off from the clinic, a Wednesday, but the weather wasn't great. It was cold and drizzly, the kind of day you sometimes get around here in April. Lots of low overcast and some wind, so I wasn't sure that I even wanted to go out to the camp with Pete. He'd set it up for that week and seemed kind of fixated on getting out there. I had an idea what might be going on in his head, and to be honest, I didn't relish the thought of being out there alone with him though, supposedly, another guy was going to come, too. A businessman from Travers City, Charlie Kuchler. He owned some gravel pits. Then I thought, well, if Charlie doesn't show, maybe we could clear the air, Pete and I, talk it over, maybe come to some resolution. I'd been seeing Karen and we were in love. She was miserable, though, because Pete was drinking way too much and had gotten moody. She was even afraid of him, she told me. For one thing, he had all these guns—at least one handgun, two shotguns that I knew of, and a rifle for deer hunting. So there was that. Also, I had no idea what, exactly, Pete knew. I worried that maybe my wife, from whom I was separated, might have talked to him. So maybe, I thought, it might be best to put it all out on the table finally.

"He picked me up in his Jeep—we used to take turns driving out there—and he had the wipers going and the heater on. When we got there, the place looked, well, foreboding. Fog just above the trees. Everything wet. He opened up the cabin and made a fire in the woodstove. I took out the hot dogs and buns we'd bought and started making a little lunch. Charlie wasn't showing, and our small talk was wearing a little thin. You know, how Pete's work was going and how, exactly, do you insure a gravel pit. I felt this great pressure to just clear the air, but Pete, well, Pete seemed out of sorts, moody, a little sullen. So I shut up after a while, thinking it might be the opening he needed. But no. So I asked about his health. I was seeing a lot of bronchitis and other nasty stuff at the clinic. But he said his health was good. So I thought, okay, where to now? By then the fog had lifted a little more and the drizzle had pretty much stopped. He wanted to get out there and do some shooting, so we got our gear and carried everything out to the clearing. The bird-flinging machine, the guns and ammo—we had all kinds of ammo, would pick up whatever was on sale, number four, number eight, whatever. He wanted to try my 16-gauge Winchester because he said he liked the pump action. So I used his 20-gauge side-by-side.

"We shot six or seven rounds of ten birds each, and the guns got too hot, so we left them there on a little table and went back to the cabin. We had a beer each and smoked a few cigarettes. Pete seemed better, and I was relieved though still a little worried. We were still into the small talk. He asked about Boston and if I ever thought of moving back there. He talked about a hunting trip he wanted to go on, up in Saskatchewan. He asked about my divorce, how that was going, and I thought, okay, this is it now. But no. He hopped around to another topic, and I lost courage. In retrospect that was the time for me to speak, not wait for him. It was stupid to let that opportunity go. I don't know why I kept quiet.

"A few minutes later we went out to the clearing again. I shot first this time, then Pete took his turn, and it was my turn again, but this time, instead of loading the machine, he turns to me and says that Marcia had been over to his office. She told him, he said, about Karen and me. Now he wanted to hear it from me, if it was true or not. There were rumors floating around, he said, and he needed to know. He was looking me right in the eye. I knew that I had to tell him. So I did. Karen and I had been seeing one another, I said, but it was more a physical relationship. To this day I regret those words. For one thing, it wasn't the truth. We did love one another. Why I thought saying otherwise would somehow spare him pain, I don't know. It was the exact wrong thing to have done.

"He started pressing me for details, awful questions like how many times and where and when. In my *house*? he said at one point. No, I said. No, Pete. Of course not. Sometimes a motel. Again, the wrong thing to say. Saying *my apartment* might have been better, I don't know. I sensed that I was feeding the flames. But stupidly, I went on, getting into psychological stuff I had no business getting into. I talked about how he'd been away from home so much, on his hunting trips, and the kids just toddlers and needing so much attention. He started getting really angry. So it's my fault, is that it? Is that what the hell you're saying? No, Pete, I said. It just happened. It's no one's fault, really. He got angrier, and then so did I because he wasn't listening to reason at all, just slinging words around like crazy and cursing. It was ugly. But I kept trying to reason with him. She was just lonely, Pete. Lonely, overworked, overwhelmed. That's how it began.

"He screamed at me then. She never told me that! Why didn't she tell me?

"Maybe she tried, I said. God knows, she probably tried but maybe you didn't listen. Or maybe you did but then just went on, business as usual.

"He looked at the guns on the table and then reached up and grabbed the Winchester. It seemed at first he wanted to shoot himself. Then I thought, no, *me*. He wants to kill me. All I knew for sure was that I had to get that gun away from him. I lunged for it, and we struggled a while, and then it went off and he fell backwards."

"Doctor," Russ said, from the table. "Tell us, please, how Pete Hyland was holding that gun."

"By the barrel. He'd grabbed it that way. It was almost like he wanted me to grab the stock."

"Was it your gun?"

"Yes. It was the Winchester 16-gauge he'd been using, so that was the closest one to him."

"Which part of the gun did you grab?"

"I grabbed the stock end."

"How long did you both struggle with the gun?"

"I don't know. Not very long."

"Was he standing, when you two were struggling with the gun?"

"Not at first. He was on the stump. But when we were tugging on the gun, he rose, and when it went off, he fell back."

"What did you do then?"

"I tried to tie off an artery by reaching into his chest, but there was so much blood, I couldn't. He was losing blood fast. I tried to resuscitate but was unsuccessful. So I took the Jeep out to the county road, to a neighbor's about a quarter of a mile away, and he called the rescue people. The Hylands had no phone in their cabin, you see. At first I ran to the cabin only

to find that the keys to the Jeep weren't there. I had to run back
to the clearing and look for them in Pete's pockets. And then
run back to the Jeep and to the neighbor's."

"After going to tell the neighbor, where did you go?"

"Back to the clearing. To Pete. He was dead. There was
no pulse whatsoever. I couldn't believe it had happened in
that way, so fast. It was just unbelievable, and that I, a physician, couldn't do one thing to reverse it. What happened next,
I don't remember in exact sequence. I think I panicked. You
know. Wild heartbeat, shortness of breath, heavy limbs, and
all thought pretty much shutting down except for the horror.
I thought, if you can call it that, *No one will believe me.* I felt
so incredibly alone out there. It was quiet now, so quiet in
those woods. I walked around, maybe hoping to use up some
of that adrenalin. So I shoved my hands in my pocket and
walked around, just moaning. *It was an accident,* I kept saying
to myself. Then something like an idea formed. Maybe I could
say it had been a different kind of accident, and then maybe
people would believe me. So I thought of saying that he'd been
running with the gun and fell. I was afraid, at that point, of so
many things. Above all for Karen, how this would expose her
to so much vicious talk. I was afraid for the children. I was
afraid I'd never be able to practice medicine again. But really,
it was all just a jumble of panicked, wild thoughts, and I was
having bad chest pain, too."

Lin felt the same surge of emotion as she had for her
grandfather. The wreckage there in his voice, his face. Svoboda, though, was sitting with an arm slung around the back
of his spindle chair and one leg outstretched. He hadn't made
a single note during this part of the testimony, had just been
staring at her dad. She imagined the expression: deadly pit
bull. Yet her own heartbeat was easing. The testimony gave
off the shimmer and strangeness of truth, especially the way
the two of them didn't talk about the affair while in the cabin,
and then it all erupted out there, in the clearing. She could
buy that. That happened to people, the smoldering, then words
needing to burst out, finally, no matter the place. It made sense
in another way, too, with its undercurrent of attempted suicide.

What a way to punish someone, to get the final word, and also revenge. Punish them all. *My father.* How he had to have been hurting, to get to that state. And all the while she herself was probably just being a dopey little kid, playing with toys in the sandbox, spilling food all over the place, and asking for Dr. Weber because she wanted someone to play with. The courtroom blurred, then coalesced into splinters of light.

"Doctor," Russ said, still seated. "Later that same year, 1970, did you file a bill of particulars as part of your divorce proceedings in which you denied any extramarital relationship?"

"I did."

"Was that the truth?"

"It was part of the same lie I told the police on April 23rd of that year. I don't know how to explain it any better. At the time of Pete's death in April, I couldn't just go and say to the police that Mrs. Hyland and I were having an affair. No one would have believed me about the shooting, how it really happened. So yes, the affidavit later that year was a lie."

"When you spoke to state police trooper Kahn on April 23rd, 1970, did you lie?"

"Yes."

"Three days after that, on April 26th, when you spoke to Jackson Delrosier, the county investigator, did you lie?"

"Yes, but it was the same lie."

"Nineteen years later, when you and your second wife Karen both talked to the press, answering questions— Do you recall that event, sir?"

"I do, yes."

"When you talked with the press at that time, did you tell the truth about the affair you were having with Mrs. Hyland at the time of Pete Hyland's death?"

"No."

"On each of those occasions, Doctor, why did you not tell the truth?"

"On which— Can you please restate the question?"

"On each of those occasions—the time of the shooting, the time of filing your divorce affidavit, the time of questioning by the state police, and soon after by the county investigator; and then nineteen years later when you and your wife returned to Michigan at the time of the third autopsy of Pete Hyland, and you and your wife spoke with the press, why did you not tell the truth?"

"Because I didn't want Karen to suffer any further pain. I didn't want the children hurt. I didn't think people would believe me about the shooting. How can you tell people you were having a relationship with someone's wife, and then the man is shot after a discussion about his wife, and after a struggle with a gun, and expect them to believe it was an *accident*? Also, I was afraid Karen might feel that she was to blame. So I kept it to myself. I became the lie. That way I could protect everybody."

"So, Doctor, when did you decide to finally tell the truth?"

"Objection!" Svoboda rose to say. "His *version* of the truth. Latest version!"

"Overruled. Answer the question."

"Well, I am on trial for murder, so I had to let it out, finally. I feel awful for my family, but I really had no choice."

"Doctor Weber, are you telling the truth now, as to what happened that day, April 23rd, 1970, at the Lake Marion hunting camp?"

"Yes, I am."

"Did you intentionally, willfully, and with malice and premeditation murder Peter Hyland?"

"No, I did not."

At the recess, seniors got themselves up and began their slow migration to the back doors. Lin overheard one saying, "He's a good actor, isn't he? Boy, this was a good day to come."

She felt her face go hot, but her mother appeared oblivious to the comment. Laura as well. And her dad, waiting for them in the well, looked strangely himself. Neither sagging nor about to break down.

In the restroom adjacent to their room upstairs, Lin doused her face with cold water.

"You okay, Lin?" her sister said.

"I don't know. Maybe. Dad looks better now. I mean than before he testified."

"You think?"

"Sort of relieved."

"Are you?"

"I'm not sure. It does have the weirdness of truth. The way they didn't talk about it at first and then, like, it all comes out while they're shooting— Oh, God."

"What," Laura said.

"I can't believe it." She was whispering.

"*What*, Lin?"

"He's lying again."

"That would be perjury, Lin. He wouldn't, not now!"

"And Svoboda's going to *nail* him." She rubbed her face with both hands.

Laura glanced at the closed door. "How do you know?"

"Those *hearing* protectors! They had blood on them, remember? How could the two of them be talking if he had those things on?"

"Wait a second. Maybe he put those hearing protectors on later, after they argued."

"How could he? He was *shot* right after! Dad said too much! He added all kinds of stuff!"

"Lin. *Lin*. Let's wait for the cross-examination, all right?"

"Did you see Svoboda? He didn't take a single note. He doesn't believe a word of it!"

Laura took a dry paper towel and dabbed at Lin's forehead, her flaring cheeks. "Let's see what Svoboda and Russ do now. Let's not go crazy ahead of time, okay Lin? Please? Calm faces, all right?"

ANTIQUATED HEATING elements along the walls still clicked in frenzy, sending forth dusty heat despite the warm air flowing in through raised storm windows. And Svoboda in a pink dress shirt, Lin saw, his face a matching pink. On the witness stand, her dad sipped from a water glass. He didn't look so good now. Older. Jowly. Hangdog. From a garage somewhere down the street came the *rippp-rippp* of wheel bolts being loosened—or tightened.

The prosecutor hiked up his pants. "Now sir, you testified that it was just before this trial began that you decided to tell this latest story. Is that what you told this jury, sir?"

"*Objection!*"

"Sustained."

"Sir, you . . . did you testify that it was just before the trial began that you decided to change your story?"

"I told the jury, Mr. Svoboda, that it was just before the trial began that I told the truth."

"Well, you should know, sir, that the State of Michigan doesn't accept it as the truth. What you're saying is the truth is just your new version of the truth, is it not?"

"*Objection!*"

"Sustained."

"Did you not tell a different version of the truth before you decided to tell this version just before the trial?"

"I don't understand your question, Mr. Svoboda."

"I am asking if you told another version of the so-called truth before the one you told just before this trial?"

"I have told . . . what I told the jury is that I told a lie before, it was the same lie, a continuation of that lie. And now I have told the truth."

"Sir, did you not tell differing versions, yes or no?"

"It was the same lie."

"Did you not change your story depending on the evidence made known to you, as it developed, and as you knew your current version of the story did not fit it?"

"Objection to the form of the question."

"Overruled. You may answer."

"I'm afraid I don't understand the question, Mr. Svoboda."

Russ must have told him to do that, Lin thought. Balk at Svoboda's ponderous clauses, try to get Svoboda to entangle himself in words that would only serve to confuse the jurors.

"In discovery did you learn that the state had developed evidence of an affair between yourself and Mrs. Hyland prior to Pete Hyland's death?"

"I learned that, yes."

"So is that why you decided to tell the truth about the affair?"

"At the . . . before the trial, I knew I had to tell all of the truth."

"At the press conference you called two years ago, did you lie at that time, saying that Earl Hyland had been spreading vicious rumors about you and your second wife?"

"I don't remember, exactly, what was said then, but yes, I lied about the affair."

"Was that before or after you saw the evidence we had developed concerning your affair with Mrs. Hyland?"

"Before."

"I couldn't hear you, sir. Please repeat your answer."

"*Before.*"

"So you were a liar, boldfaced and calculating, weren't you?"

"Objection!"

"Sustained."

"Not only did you lie outright, but you intentionally impugned a man who'd lost his son, an only child—is that not right?"

"I don't think I impugned."

"You said, and I quote from a transcript of that press conference, 'The man has been spreading lies about us for years.' Are those not your words, sir?"

"Apparently they were."

"So you were, in fact, impugning the man's reputation."

"Objection to the form of the question!"

"Sustained."

"*Were* you in fact impugning the man's reputation?"

"Yes, but I did it to protect my wife and family."

"Did you not also wish to protect yourself?"

"I was thinking primarily of my family."

"So when you received the prosecution's evidence of the blood mist on your boot and the human tissue embedded within the hem of your jeans, did you decide to invent another lie to explain this new evidence?"

The ensuing wrangle took nearly twenty minutes, but eventually Lin heard her dad admitting that, yes, he had seen evidence placing him right alongside Pete Hyland when he was shot, not some hundred yards away.

"So these things were in your mind, were they not?"

"They . . . I don't know."

"It is a statement of the obvious, isn't it?"

"Objection!"

The two legal teams huddled about the bench in a half-circle. One juror went into a coughing fit, and the tipstaff rushed for a cup of water. The pensive juror who liked to look out at the day was doing just that, face to stippled glass awash in gold light. Then lawyers swung around, away from one another, and returned to their tables.

"Did you stage the scene, then, by laying the gun toward the deceased because you hoped to deceive the police?"

"Objection!"

"Overruled. You may answer the question."

"I did not stage the scene."

"Sir, did you perjure yourself on the divorce affidavit's bill of particulars?"

"I lied. I already admitted that."

"You lied with the intention of defrauding the court, did you not?"

"'I don't think so, no."

"You lied to gain advantage in the court, did you not?"

"I lied to protect everybody."

"Were you making allegations under oath, sir, in order to gain something to your advantage, namely your divorce?"

"I lied, yes."

"Did you get your divorce?"

"Yes."

"So you deceived the court with your lies, didn't you?"

"Yes."

"You're pretty good at deceiving people, aren't you?"

'"Objection!"

"Sustained."

"You are, sir, a serial liar, are you not?"

Russ strode to within inches of Svoboda to object, and the gallery went silent.

She thought it would take hours longer to get through it all, excruciating hours—all the words her dad had stated that morning, each sentence turned over and left upended by Svoboda. Days, maybe, before the man would be through with him, shaking him like a rag until the rag became a heap of threads. But strangely, unbelievably, Svoboda was saying, with clear disdain, *No further questions.* Russ echoed the words, though in a far milder tone, and it was over. Lin watched her dad walking back to his place at the defense's table, his face composed.

How could it be over? Nothing about that day? The argument? The blood? The laces? The clay pigeons? Nothing about the weather? The *hearing protectors?*

As spectators stood to leave, Lin sat there, seeing an ear devoid of clotted darkening blood, its whorls pink-rimmed, its cave-like opening to the labyrinth within silvered and waxen but clear of any blood and all sound now, and so the body hearing nothing, no birdsong, no wind, no wailing approach of the EMS rig in the late afternoon of a fine spring day, no fog, no raw mist except for the mist of blood that had already settled and was drawing flies and other insects eager to feed.

LAURA

They were at it again as soon as Laura turned out of the
driveway. Lin going insane, babbling. "All those details . . . he
didn't say any of that last summer. I read the transcript! Just
small talk and pent up feelings . . . why did he have to add so
much? Is he still lying? How can we know for sure, Laur? How
can anyone know? God! What's going on?"

"Maybe the words . . . wanted out."

"What the heck does that mean?"

Laura didn't know for sure. An idiotic thought having to
do with words *wanting* truth. Words *resenting* lies. Nothing,"
she said. "Forget it."

"Actually, I think I know. Each time he says anything, it's
more. But then he goes and blurs it with that stupid cliché, *I
don't know how it happened. It just did.* Laur, what if Dad got
mixed up a little and they really argued in the cabin, which
makes more sense because Pete wouldn't be wearing those
hearing things in the cabin, right? But then, if they have
this fight, they just go out shooting afterward like nothing
happened? Hey, man, let's go and shoot some skeet now.
That's . . . is somebody following us?"

Laura checked her mirror. Distant lights. "No. What did you
want to get at the store, anyway, or did you just want to talk?"

"Mom needs something. Vitamin E, for sure. Actually,
I'd like to get a bottle of John Jameson's, if you really want
to know."

"I don't think you can get that at the health food store."

"The thing is, I'm trying, I really am, but I can't believe
him, Laur. They couldn't have been arguing if our father had
those hearing protectors on."

168

"Svoboda didn't call him on that."

"Which is strange."

"Maybe he just forgot."

"Svoboda? Right. If Dad had just stuck to what he'd said before the trial, it might have worked, Laur. Not talking about it in the cabin, just the small talk, and then being out there and all of a sudden, our father turning on him. That made sense. It would explain those hearing protectors, too. But now—God, he said too much."

Laura thought so, too. Brain, heart—everything—knew this; everything wanted to reject it. And she resented this trip. It was late. Petosky some fifteen miles away. Laura suspected it was just an excuse for Lin to vent. Yet recalling their talk about the puppets when she was sick, their closeness, a blood tie after all, she felt she owed her this, anyway. And besides, holding it all in, too hard, too lonely. "Lin?"

"What?"

No, don't. But words jamming up, in her throat. *If he'd tried to tie off an artery and later shoved his hands in his pockets, wouldn't there have been blood smeared there? Did he wash up at the neighbor's before he went back to the clearing and walked around?* "Let's just go with what Dad said. Wait for the pathologists' reports."

"I'm trying to go with what he says. But it seems there's too many wrong words and not enough right ones. So maybe Mom's too. I hate saying it. The thing is, what do we *do* now? How do we act—I mean, around them. I, for one, am a lousy actor. You know, in my brain I'd like to think it was just embellishment, that business about the weather and about the argument. I'd like to think it happened more or less the way he described before the trial, and then Dad just blew it, later, with the embellishing. But the thing is I can't believe *any* of it now. And what if Dad knows what I'm thinking? Is he going to shoot me, too?"

"Lin! You can't mean that!"

"I don't know what I mean."

"Let's just go back, okay? I don't want to be driving around out here, with all the jerks who hate us. It's late. Let's go back."

"I wanted to get some organic lettuce, too."

"I thought you were done with the food thing."

"Also some grape juice. I'd like to anti-oxidize the hell out of my brain. You can take that literally."

"Then you're going to need a lot more than grape juice."

"Somebody *is* following us."

Laura flicked down the rearview mirror.

"Laur, there's this car right on top of us, practically. Pull over. Maybe they want to pass."

Laura drove partly on the shoulder. That stretch of road had a double yellow line.

"Is it a police car?"

"There'd be a flashing light."

"You think you should just stop and let them by?"

"I'm giving them room. They don't want to, apparently."

Laura locked the car doors but refused to speed up.

"What should we do? This is scary."

"It's just somebody getting their kicks, Lin."

"Let's stop someplace along here. A house or a store, if you see one."

But they were driving through woods, with lanes leading off to cottages somewhere beyond. She had no intention of trying any of those lanes only to find some closed-up cottage.

The vehicle's high beams suddenly swung to the left, and Laura could see a truck coming alongside them. A black truck high on its springs. She was prepared for obscenities but not for the slam that knocked off her car's side mirror.

"He's got a baseball bat or something, Laur!"

A car was approaching in the opposite lane. The pickup dropped behind, tailgating once more.

"Here they come again, Lin. Hang on."

This time the object bashed the side window, right near her face. Glass nicked her cheek and neck, fell into her lap. She sped up. Woods gave way to fields, fenced pastures, and ahead, lights. It looked as if some jetliner had landed there, portholes lighted up.

A dairy barn. She swerved into the barnyard and headed for it, the truck following. A stupid idea. Somehow she'd have to get out of the car and into that barn, and what if no one were there? But the lights gave her hope. She drove up to the barn door and kept hitting the horn. The truck rammed them from behind again and again, but when a man came out of the barn, the truck backed up to the road and tore off. Laura was too shaken to even move. The farmer's face, peering through the car's broken window, terrified her.

He helped them out, finally, and called the state police. They stayed in the barn's milk room for over an hour, waiting, while the dairyman methodically washed his stainless steel milking implements. A piece of rebar, he thought, was what they'd used. He couldn't figure it. Things like that didn't usually happen up there. It was a quiet place. Those boys must have been drinking.

One time years back, he told them, a bunch of them did beat up a colored man. Beat him up bad. Police found the body draped over a guardrail like some burlap bag. Turned out it was somebody from "down below" who'd chanced into a bar. Guys tailed him and his buddy, ran them off the road, and then beat them up. The other one managed to save himself by crawling off and hiding, then getting to a house.

"But that don't usually happen up here."

"No? That's encouraging," Laura said. "I guess we're the exceptions, again."

When the trooper came, Laura gave their names and described what had happened. But she didn't mention Kinkle. After all, it might not have been him, though she was pretty sure it was. And the harassment either a warning or retaliation. Or both. Sickening to think the woman may have been beaten.

The trooper took down Laura's description of the truck and told them to play it safe and not go off on their own anymore, especially at night—given who they were. Also, Laura needed to get her taillights, mirror, and that window fixed. He followed them back to Tunley and waited until they were inside the house. Then he sat out in the patrol car, head bowed over a report. Laura hoped it wouldn't make the local news but supposed it would. Reporters jumping on that kind of story.

"Do you think they were after Dad?" Lin whispered in the kitchen. "Remember that time Dad was a little nervous? Out on the porch? Should we tell them what happened?"

If ever there was a time for self-discipline and silence, or failing that, a few innocuous words, this was it. Instead, appalled at what she was doing, she said, also whispering, "We need to talk about it with them, but not tonight, okay? Let's just calm down a while." Later she'd think those words were like intentionally giving an arsonist a pack of matches.

Their parents were in the living room, their mother on the couch with a book, their dad in the room's only upholstered chair. He put aside his news magazine.

"Were they open?" he asked.

"No," Laura said. "They closed at eight." Another lie to add to the pile.

"Maybe I should make us a fire, or is it too late now?"

"That's okay, Dad, we're pretty beat."

"Well, go get some rest then. Tomorrow's almost here."

It's what he'd always said to them when they were little, Laura remembered. *Hurry up and get to sleep, now, tomorrow's almost here.* His voice rising on the word *sleep* as if it were some sleek train waiting to whisk them off to some great dream.

Lin didn't rise but remained on the couch, sitting next to their mother. Laura was still trembling from what had happened; she thought Lin must be too, maybe even scared to leave.

"You girls look chilled to the bone," he said. "I wish I had made a fire, but it didn't seem that cold. Oh, I wanted to ask—you sleeping okay on that mattress up there, Laura? I was thinking we could try getting you another."

"It's fine, Dad." She was wondering what to say when they saw the damage to her car. "I've been sleeping pretty good."

"Only pretty good?"

"The moon, I think."

"That never bothers me. Lucky, I guess."

Under the flimsy words she could almost hear, *So what do you think about today? Do you feel better about it all now?* She knew what he needed just then—approval, sure evidence of their tenacious faith in him. But she remained silent, and so did Lin. Laura imagined her on some cliff, waiting to dive. Lin raised both hands to her hair and pushed it back into a bunch. *Do it,* Laura thought. *I don't care. Maybe it's time now.* She glanced at her sister, catching her eye, then Lin was saying, "Dad? I have a question."

Karen Weber lifted a page of the book she was pretending to read.

"Just one? That's not bad."

"You said today, in court, that you reached into . . . into the wound and tried to tie off an artery. But there was too much blood and so you couldn't, finally, and so—"

"*Lin,*" their mother said.

"It's all right. Go ahead, honey."

"And so . . . you didn't."

"That's right. I couldn't."

"You said—" she looked away from him, "that you put your hands in your pockets and walked around for a while, or was that after you went to the neighbor's?"

"Maybe I shouldn't have said that because I'm not really sure, but I do know I walked around a while. It must have been after the neighbor's, I half-remember washing up there. Before I went there, though, I was trying to help Pete."

"It's possible you didn't put your hands in your pockets," Lin finally said, "because there wasn't any blood on your jeans."

"You know something? Russ was all over me about that, too. Great minds, I mean you two. I probably did screw up with that detail. Maybe it's how I saw myself walking around out there. How it took root, in a way. Over time, I mean."

It was the kind of thing you might find in a drugstore novel, Laura thought. *He jammed his fists in his pockets and walked around, trying to think . . .* The easy detail, the first thing, maybe, that comes to mind. But his tastes in reading ran more to non-fiction. So maybe that detail had lodged in his mind from teen stories, then just surfaced when he needed *something,* there on the stand.

"Or maybe," Lin said, "you might have put your hands in your pockets earlier, just before you tried to tie off the artery."

"Maybe that's it."

Laura didn't think a physician would do that, wait and ponder. Her dad had said as much.

Her mother stood. "I'm going upstairs."

"We should, too," Laura said. "C'mon, Lin."

"I will in a second."

Laura followed her mother up, the staircase creaking under their weight.

"Mom?" Laura said from the doorway to her parents' bedroom. "Can I come in?"

Her mother sat on one side of the bed, its carved headboard nearly touching the ceiling. A small lamp on the dresser gave a night light's faint glow.

"Lin didn't mean to upset you, Mom. I'm sorry, though."

Her mother lay back and closed her eyes.

She will look like that when she is dying. A thought sinking through her with stony gravity.

"You and your sister had better—" She opened her eyes and massaged under the right one as if the physical act of seeing hurt.

"What, Mom?"

"Just believe him."

"We do."

"Then act like it. I'm tired of all this tension. And you two going off, not wanting to be here, inventing excuses. I'm afraid I know what you're thinking. Just as his brother must be—he won't even come up here. Or even call. After all your dad did for Gordon and my family, too, and no one wanting to come here and maybe be embarrassed. Oh, *they'll* call and offer excuses and pretend to sympathize because your dad did so much for them, setting my one sister's husband up in business—you remember your Uncle Greg—then helping out Marjorie when her husband left her high and dry. Marjorie was eager enough to come out to Hawaii, to recuperate, as she put it, on your dad's money. But where is poor tearful Marjorie now? In a nice condo in San Diego, and oh by the way, your dad helped with the down payment for that, too. So she has her condo, Greg has his dealership, and your Uncle Gordon is a big shot owner of a golf course, courtesy of your dad, but where are all these wonderful people? These so-called relatives. *Busy.* And now you, his *daughters*—"

"Mom, we believe him. We really do."

"Then for heaven's sake show it, Laura. *Say* so—to him. Not just be questioning him. You can see, can't you, what all this is doing to him. Now go. I'm tired."

"We'll do better, Mom. I promise. See you in the morning. I love you." She went to kiss her mother, but her mother turned away.

As she closed the bedroom door, she heard her sister's raised voice, downstairs. "Blood on the hearing protectors, Dad. What does that mean, if you two were discussing or arguing or whatever?" Then her dad's voice, lower so that she could hear only scattered words. . . . *lying . . . evidence . . . state police* . . . Then her sister again, "But that doesn't make sense because they didn't even investigate much back then. So what are you saying?"

Her mother came from her room, arms woven against her thin frame.

"Why didn't you say what you said last summer?" Lin was asking downstairs. "What was all that stuff about rain and fog and hands in pockets? You blew it, you know that? And now nobody knows what the hell happened that day so they're gonna take Svoboda's word for it. Why did you do that? God. I can't believe you got up there and just spun out all that stuff. Why, Dad? How could you do that to yourself? To us? Did you guys argue in the cabin, or what? Because he had those ear protectors on, out there."

"Lin, listen, please. It could be that there was some tampering."

"No. I don't believe that. I think you did. That's what I think. You killed our father. You loved Mom, and you killed him because he was in the way, or the Church was or something, but anyway, you had to do it. That's exactly what I think. And tonight . . . tonight somebody was chasing us with this, I don't know, iron thing, and bashing at Laura's car. Why would they do that? What's going on? Don't touch me, okay? You killed him and then you had Mom and us, a ready-made family. Wasn't that cool. Wasn't that just like—"

Laura heard the slap that stopped the rest of the words. Then her sister was running upstairs, the left side of her face reddening.

"I'm going. I can't stay here. Mom, I'm *sorry*. It's not because of you."

"Lin, you're wrong."

"No, I'm *not*. We've been living with a murderer all these years."

Soon she banged out of her room, backpack over one shoulder. "Don't look at me like that, Laura. You think the same exact thing. Which is why you wanted *me* to ask, didn't you, you coward!" She ran down the stairs and out the front door, leaving it open behind her.

Karen hurried down. Laura grabbed a robe from the bed and followed.

Her dad was standing in front of the ash-strewn fireplace, elbow braced on arm, fingers splayed over one eye, thumb pressed into cheekbone. Karen stood close, rubbing his back.

Laura closed the front door, then went to them. "Mom? Here." She placed the robe over her mother's shoulders. Her own arms were shaky, and her legs. Her dad lowered his hand to help. "You know, all these years I've never once hit you kids. That hurts me worse now than . . . what she said."

"She wants to believe you, Dad."

"Yeah."

"Really. She does."

"What about you?"

"I do." But her eyes slid away from his.

"Come here." He extended his other arm.

"I'm intruding. I should let you—"

"Intruding? We're *family*. That word doesn't apply."

Then she was standing at his other side, his arm around her. *Greg has his dealership . . . your Uncle Gordon, his golf course . . .* Bogdan would understand that. It's what families did. Not set one against another.

"She'll come back," he was saying. "She didn't mean what she said. It's just been too hard on everyone. You see?—this is why I didn't say anything, before."

That night they stayed up late, hoping to hear Lin's car. Sitting before the wood fire her dad had finally made, Laura tried to imagine her sister's entry. She'd be really quiet. But she'd apologize, in her way. And then Laura would too—privately, futilely.

In the kitchen she found the bag of Halloween chocolates they'd bought, in case, but no one had stopped at the house. She took it up to her room and ate them all. Then just before sleep, a thought: her father's pants pocket not bloodied, either. Where the keys to the Jeep supposedly had been.

LIN

To her surprise, it hadn't taken much—merely a photo I.D., proof of age and residency, and a current address on her license, as well as some paperwork. She'd told the gun dealer in Syracuse that her dad used to own one of those and had liked it a lot. The gun dealer, elderly and breathing with a slight whistle in the close confines of his shop, nodded, his eyes distant. On racks along the walls were far more complex shotguns and rifles, expensive guns with stocks in wood to rival that of the finest furniture. Lin thought he was probably glad to see the Winchester go.

She bought some number-four shotgun shells at a sporting goods store and felt definitely strange, carrying the heavy plastic bag back to her car, where the 16-gauge lay in the trunk, swathed in bubble wrap. Just carrying the gun to the car and then going and buying the ammunition left her feeling jangled and uneasy, criminal in fact. She put the plastic bag in the trunk, alongside the gun, then drove slowly out of the mall's parking lot, watching out for cars coming at her, it seemed, from every direction. She supposed it had to do with her naïveté that the sudden presence of a gun in her life—and she its owner—should freak her out to the extent that it obviously was. She was driving like a senior citizen with the shakes. Her father, who had handled guns since he was twelve, at least, had probably felt totally at home around them. What were they but just another kind of sporting equipment, like fishing tackle. You tossed them in your car or truck and took off to wherever. But she didn't even know where to go to test-fire the thing. You couldn't go to a state park, could you? She'd intended to ask the man about that but courage failed her. And too, she'd been scared that it was all too apparent—the old guy would recognize her from some TV news program, put two and two together and just call the cops. She hadn't been able to say anything finally, except *Thanks a lot. See you*, after the man said *You have a good Thanksgiving now.*

At the restaurant on Walton Street in downtown Syracuse, she hung her jacket in the hall near the back door, washed her hands, and entered the steam and chaos of the kitchen. Salad scraps littered the tile floor and one of the stainless steel counters. She took care of those first, knowing how inspectors could materialize anytime, day or night, but usually made an appearance when things were at their worst. Today a Saturday and the place jamming up. Soon she'd prepared twenty-five more salads. One of the owners swung by, found nothing to criticize, and told her to start chopping more veggies for the winter squash soup. "Nuke those, would you? We're down on soups and no time to simmer."

She got to that task, eventually forgetting about that long object in the trunk of her old Mazda.

Nine hours later, in her place at a rooming house near Syracuse University, she turned on the TV her landlady had lent her because, she explained in some leap of logic, she liked young people who weren't afraid of kitchen work. From the eleven o'clock news Lin learned that closing arguments in a local murder trial were set for the following week. The news anchor, an attractive woman with a trendy hairdo, perfect makeup, and understated yet sexy clothing, gave herself a moment to look somber before shaking off the gloom and beginning the next item, something about the reindeer at the Syracuse Zoo being happy in the colder weather. Then she smiled at her co-anchor, and he smiled back at the good time they were having, and this segued into the weather report for the next day.

She lay down on the room's single bed, waiting for the stereo in the next room to start up. Soon the thin wallboard alongside her bed was reverberating, the bones of her chest, too. Which was okay. The music at least decent. "Purple Haze" gave way to something bluesy, and she thought how he was dead, too, Hendrix, stupidly dead, OD'ing in London. Amazing to think:

somebody able to create that kind of music just blowing it all with drugs. But maybe he'd thought that death couldn't finger him, all that sound wrapping him around, all that power drugging the brain with its illusion of immortality.

She imagined her father, a cassette in the tape deck of his Jeep, a young guy, a seller of insurance, Hendrix filling the Jeep as it bumped over gravel roads to the next farm or lakefront cottage. Hendrix wailing *Hey, Joe,* and the lie there, too, in the high of that music.

Well after midnight, she went down to her car and got the gun. Fear made her legs and arms watery. Upstairs again, the door locked, the lights out and the room lit only by the street light, she tried to position the gun so that its muzzle touched her chest while her right hand grasped the trigger. Impossible. Her arm wasn't long enough. No way could you do it holding the gun in the air. Even someone with longer arms. She sat on her bed and held the barrel between her knees. You *could* activate the trigger with a toe—and possibly blow off your head. If you tried for your chest, though, the wound angle would be from low to high, obviously. She remembered the dealer telling her that the magazine could hold five shells and pulling on the pump after firing would lock another in place. Still holding the gun by the barrel, she tried pulling the pump toward the muzzle. It didn't budge. She turned the gun around, drew back the trigger and pulled the rounded wood pump toward herself with her left hand. This time it slid back in a clatter of metal parts impeccably doing their job.

. . . *how was Pete Hyland holding that gun?. . . By the barrel. He'd grabbed it that way.*

A person grabbing from the stock end might cause the barrel to drop lower. If her dad's finger was anywhere near the trigger during the struggle, would Pete's pulling in the opposite direction cause her dad's finger to get caught in the trigger guard, much like a piece of brush, and then accidentally activate the trigger?

Possible. Though unlikely, she finally decided. Why would her father, who'd used guns many times, grab it by the *barrel*? Wouldn't he instinctively grab the stock?

Under normal circumstances, maybe. But if he had wanted to commit suicide and make it look like a murder—no.

But a shell would have to have been locked in place by pulling the pump toward the stock. Had her father, at the barrel end, *pushed* at the pump accidentally—or intentionally—doing that? And then her dad's finger got caught there, firing the gun?

Causing brass pellets to tunnel through tissue and nerves and blood vessels, through the heart, that thickened muscle that had kneaded life into the body every instant, year after year. The heart suddenly halted after some furious spasm. So the instant of death probably not an instant at all but some terrible unraveling that may have seemed endless, as one bodily system after another broke down and life was torn away bit by bit.

She placed the gun on the rug. It was a while before she felt able to get up and take the Winchester back to her car. Outside, she imagined that ten people, at least, saw her, despite the hour. Gun in hand. Unlocking her car and stowing it in the trunk. That's what it must be like to be a criminal. You live in some parallel reality, lugging around the burden of your secrets, like that sailor who'd kept two log books of what was to have been a solo, around-the-world race. Because he'd been having so much trouble with his boat, he decided to stay in the Atlantic, looping around and sending back false reports, false bearings, fictionalizing the entire journey. After his boat was found abandoned and adrift in the mid-Atlantic, people discovered two logs aboard, one falsifying the journey; the other beginning as a truthful account but finally charting the man's descent into a hell of delusion and suicidal intent. So he hadn't been able to do it, hold onto those two versions. Nor, did it seem, could her dad. He said that he became the lie, but from the differing versions he told, it seemed that he was groping his way closer and closer to some truth.

The house quiet finally, she dozed, but soon jerked awake from a vivid dream in which her dad was saying, *You're my girl, aren't you? My big, big, girl!* And she was happy, a kid so happy she couldn't bear to stand still but had to run through the house. *Chase me, Dad! Catch me!*

LAURA

Lin didn't return. Nor was she answering her phone in Ithaca. In court, the defense experts did little to change the numbers on the daily scorecard the local newspaper was keeping. So far the prosecution was "winning" largely because, Laura believed, the defense's experts were either incompetent or lazy. One pathologist got his slides hopelessly mixed up, to Svoboda's derision. Another obviously hadn't taken into consideration the new testimony and was still working on "scenario number one," as Svoboda scornfully put it, the running and falling scenario. After one such ruinous day in court, they were in the kitchen when the old rotary phone attached to the wall there rang.

Her dad rose from the table. A minute later, he replaced the receiver. "That was Russ. Your old babysitter, Janine Nolan, is going to corroborate my story. Pete had indeed wanted to kill me. Get me out there so he could shoot me."

"How . . . could she have known that?" Karen said.

"According to Janine, Pete had told her. She just called Russ from Oklahoma. She's been reading about the trial. Her name's not Nolan now. Something else. I didn't catch it."

"I thought they'd questioned her some time ago."

Laura heard skepticism in her mother's voice, fear.

"I guess," he said, "she didn't tell them everything."

Janine, a young teenager then. Laura had a visceral memory of their red metal wagon bumping over sidewalk cracks, and the jolt as Janine guided it down off a curb. Could hear Lin howling that her butt hurt. Could hear Janine hissing, *You're not supposed to use that word!* And then Janine laughing too, causing Lin to shout, *My butt is hurted!*

A skinny kid. Fine gold hairs dusting tan arms, legs. A woven leather bracelet on one tiny wrist. Ponytail like a thin streak of yellow paint against her T-shirts. Her nose always peeling, the patches pink and sore-looking. And on forehead and cheeks, blue pock marks. *Janine, you got holes in your face. Did you go out in the hail?* Laura hadn't known, then, about chicken pox, but did know about the hail that knocked holes into her grandfather's apples. It had seemed grown-up to ask the question, but when she saw how Janine blinked a couple of times and wouldn't answer, she felt bad. Janine—once such a big part of their lives. Then the strangeness of absence, and the confused lingering sense of loss. *Is Janine in Heaven with God, too?*

That night she tried Lin's number again, but a recording stated that it was no longer in service. She dialed the co-op and someone there told her he'd thought Lin was still in Michigan. She hadn't been in to work—or at school—for several weeks. He had no idea where she might be.

LAURA DIDN'T recognize her, but Janine waved, then Midge had her bag, and she was hugging Laura's mother. Now married to a man named Trost, but still skinny as a teenager. Blond hair in a short punk style. A ring on each finger and thumb. The pock marks still there, half-filled in with makeup. She had on high-heeled boots, tight jeans, and an astrakhan jacket embroidered with vivid designs.

Midge came up alongside Laura as they left the terminal. "Find her something decent to wear tomorrow. And get rid of the rings except for a wedding band, if she's wearing one."

In court the next day, no lengthy buildup, no tedious recitation of credentials. Just a woman taking the stand, stating her name, and beginning her story. She had known both Karen and Pete Hyland as she'd sometimes babysat their children. When she first started babysitting, she'd been fourteen years old. In 1970, she was sixteen.

Except for the hair, Laura thought Janine looked all right in the navy pantsuit Laura's mother had loaned her—Laura's clothes all too large. Janine's hands no longer glittered with metal, and they lay still, one atop the other, as Russ had instructed.

A week or so before the shooting, she had been babysitting the Hyland children. She didn't remember where Mr. and Mrs. Hyland had gone, some formal event, probably, because they'd been dressed up. But Pete Hyland was angry when he got back. Mrs. Hyland hadn't returned with him. It was clear to Janine that he'd been drinking hard stuff. She knew because when her dad drank liquor, he smelled that same exact way, a sharp smell mixed in with breath odor and, sometimes, the minty smell of gum. So she told Mr. Hyland she'd walk home, it was only two blocks, but no, he insisted on driving her. On the way, he yelled about how his wife was making an idiot of him around town, with her paramour. That was his word, *paramour*. At the time, she wasn't exactly sure what it meant but she had an idea. What he was going to do, he said, was take her paramour out to his camp and give him what he deserved. What's that? she asked, and he said, I'm gonna shoot the S.O.B.

The gallery seemed to suck in air as one. Janine brought a tissue to her eyes and lowered her head.

"No further questions, Mrs. Trost," Russ said.

No reporter walked to the back, making floorboards creak. No one coughed or unwrapped candies. No one left the courtroom. In the heavy stillness Laura kept hearing the word *paramour*. Would you use that word when talking to a teenager? Given her father's background in French and that he'd been drinking, supposedly—maybe. Still, the word struck her as off, not true. Straight out of some pulp romance.

Did she come all this way to lie?

Svoboda was in his thunderstorm mode. Collar points flaring, he stood and had a statement marked as an exhibit for the State of Michigan. Then he asked Janine to read it. She did, to herself.

"Mrs. Trost," he said after she'd finished, "when the police came to you for a statement four years ago, you said nothing about this incident. Why not?"

"I don't know. I don't remember exactly what they asked. It was on the phone. I was busy making dinner and was distracted."

"Please read your statement aloud, to the court."

She did, in a subdued voice, telling of the anonymous phone calls to a sixteen-year-old, saying that she shouldn't be babysitting over there because of what was going on. But Mr. Hyland assuring her that any rumors she might be hearing about an affair weren't true.

Again Laura heard the wrong notes glided over yet unmistakably *wrong*. Why would Mr. Hyland talk to her about rumors?—wouldn't it have been more appropriate for Laura's mother to do that? And would people in town really call a young kid to talk about adults having an affair? Wouldn't they call the girl's mother, instead?

The statement went on at length: she'd frequently seen Dr. Weber at the Hyland's. He liked venison, and Mrs. Hyland sometimes made that for him. Often, he came over for lunch when Mr. Hyland was at work and she was over there helping Mrs. Hyland. He liked to eat with the children. Janine never saw any animosity between Mr. Hyland and Dr. Weber.

"All right," Svoboda said. "Would there be animosity in someone's mind if that person says he wants to kill someone else?"

"Yes."

"Why didn't you tell the police four years ago about what Pete Hyland supposedly said to you?"

"There wasn't . . . I didn't ever see animosity between the two of them. That's what the police asked me, if I saw animosity *between* them. I said no."

"You gave them reason to believe there was no affair, that's what you did, is it not?"

"I didn't want to talk to them!"

"Why did you not want to talk to them, Mrs. Trost?"

"Because. Because of what I kept secret for so many years."

"Why did you keep that incident secret, the incident when you were given a ride home by Mr. Hyland?"

"I wanted to help."

"Who did you want to help?"

"The family."

"Did you ever tell Mrs. Hyland about the incident?"

"No."

"Did you ever tell anybody about it?"

"No, not anybody. Until now."

"Did you ever tell the police?"

"Objection! Asked and answered."

"Overruled. You may answer."

"No."

"Did you ever call the attorney general's office and say, Listen I've got something important to tell you?"

"No, I did not."

"Just this past summer we contacted you and you said you did not want to talk to us, is that correct?"

"I didn't want to speak to you."

"Knowing that we wanted to talk with you, you made no effort to contact us, is that correct?"

"Yes."

"But you did make an effort to call Mr. Lowry, is that correct?"

"I called Mr. Lowry after reading about the trial."

"Mrs. Trost, did you ever pay anyone to hide information from a court of law?"

"Objection!"

The sidebar took the rest of the morning. Afterward, Svoboda said that in light of the judge's ruling, he had no further questions. The court recessed for lunch, and Midge got Janine beyond the reporters. Laura asked to go along with them to the airport.

From the backseat of Midge's Buick, Laura said, "Janine, what have you been doing, these past years?"

Janine turned. "Different jobs. Plus I've got four kids."

"Four. Wow."

"Two are from my first marriage."

"Do you work now or are you a stay-at-home mom?"

"Oh, I work. Have to. The thing is, when you've got kids you work harder at home than you do at work. You married?"

"Not yet."

"Better hurry up or it'll be too late for kids. Unless you don't want 'em."

"So what's your job?—outside the home, I mean."

"A day care place. Isn't that a riot? I guess it's in the blood."

"You must like kids."

"Well, they're fun. Sometimes. You guys were, you and Linda. Where is she, anyway? I mean . . . oops, I'm sorry if I—"

"It's okay. She just had to be away for a few days."

Midge sped up. A car tailing him, he said. Probably reporters. The car followed them into the airport parking lot, and two men got out, one with a camcorder. Midge hustled Janine to the security gate. As the female guard looked through Janine's carry-on, Laura said, too low for the reporters to hear, "Janine, really. Why didn't you tell anyone?"

"Because of you guys."

"How would not-telling have helped?"

"And your mom, too. I liked her. I couldn't do that to her. I didn't want her to be the focus of gossip and all."

"You could have said that in court."

"I did, didn't I? I said I wanted to help."

"Was our father, Pete Hyland, really drunk that night?"

"Wrecked."

"Could it have been, you know, the alcohol talking?"

"Maybe, but he sure sounded like he meant it."

"Did he say *paramour*? Or was that your word?"

"It was something like that, I remember."

"Something like it? *What*?"

Security guards were scowling. Laura had to let her go.

Later, her mother asked her to drop off the navy pantsuit at the local Goodwill. She couldn't wear it in court anymore, and in any case didn't want to wear it again. Laura reminded her that if she did donate it to Goodwill, word might get around.

"Then just throw it away."

Laura didn't want to leave it in their garbage and so double-bagged it and took it to the dumpster behind the supermarket. But as soon as she tossed it upward, she felt that somebody was watching. Would go and dig it out and tell the press.

The ways of a guilty conscience.

In his black turtleneck and jeans, Father Harr looked even more like a college kid. There was a book open beside his plate. She apologized for interrupting.

"No, no! Won't you come in and have a cookie? And some tea?" He closed the book. "Thomas Merton. Great writer."

Again she apologized. This time for not having been to Mass in a long while.

"Ah. But here you are now."

A choice of words and tone that seemed right out of old films depicting elderly rectors. Kindly, doddering old men beloved by their parishioners. Faces and hands like candle wax. Bowing, deferential. *Are we all playing roles, then? If so, what was hers—faithful daughter? Nancy Drew?*

He filled a porcelain teacup for her, then got his canister of cookies opened, boyish white fingers struggling with the tight-fitting lid. She felt bad for him, eating alone in the big kitchen with its homey wallpaper and fan-light fixture. The single place setting, the extra pasta in a colander. The bit of lettuce and tomato.

Still, a priest.

"Father, I need to ask your advice. You've probably been following the trial. I don't know, but I'm afraid that I—" Her throat froze around the words.

"If you need to, cry. It's okay. Please."

She fought against the painful swell. "My sister left because she doesn't believe him. I don't know if I can, either. I'm filling up with fear and hatred. The experts are all incompetent or lying, except maybe Svoboda's. They've taken so much of our money, and for what? I hate them. And Russ—he's probably corrupt, too, like the person who was our babysitter. She did that to show off. She doesn't care about our family! She lied, Father. *Paramour*. Where did she get that? From some dumb novel, maybe. Then coming in at the eleventh hour and giving him hope, giving us hope, but doing it for herself. For the thrill, or something. Or maybe Russ paid her. If she really cared about our family, she would have told somebody long ago."

"Um, she was quite young then, wasn't she?" The priest was leaning forward, hands on the table edge. "Young people often don't think. They get frightened and say nothing. And too, your stepfather initially told a far different story."

"Later she wasn't so young. Later she could have said something. How about four years ago, when the investigators were there asking questions. Wouldn't it be natural to just tell everything then?"

"Maybe she was afraid of being prosecuted herself. And way out there in Oklahoma, she might not have known about the hearings and all that preceded the trial."

"Well, but they came looking for information. She must have assumed my dad needed help back then. She's not entirely stupid."

"No, I agree. But is that really at the heart of all your pain?"

"It's only part of it."

"And the other part, or parts?"

"My dad. My parents. I'm losing them. And my sister Lin. We don't even know where she is. And our other sister in Hawaii, at school. Katherine. She never calls us. Mom talks to her, but she doesn't want to talk to my sister or me. We're all just . . . flying apart."

"But you're all still here. Still alive."

"Yes, but nothing's the same!"

"Well, there can be no life without tension and uncertainty. Also change."

"Some families are different. Some families get along, help one another."

"It usually appears that way. Still, how well do you know these other families? Do you know them as well as you know your own?"

"Not really, no."

"That's the thing, isn't it. We tend to think that other people's lives are so terrific. It seems to be part of our hungry human nature to do so." He glanced down at his plate.

She blushed. "And I'm keeping you from your meal."

"Sorry. Bad choice of words. I'm not really all that hungry. I tend not to eat a whole lot."

Lucky you. "The thing is, I'm scared. I mean, the way he's spinning out all these stories."

"But you don't know for sure if he's guilty, at this point. And even if he is, he may be making reparation in ways you can't see."

She held the teacup but didn't lift it. "If he is guilty, are we supposed to just go on *living* with him as if nothing happened? I mean if he's acquitted for some, oh, technical reason, for instance? But that assumes we can *know* for sure!"

"Um, Our Lord would, of course, forgive. Yes?"

Yes, but the vision too awful. A man becoming a father to the children whose father he murdered. Husband to the woman whose husband he had slain.

The *Hamlet* thing.

"Laura, would you like to make a confession?"

No, because then he'd ask her to forgive. "Not right now, Father, but can I ask you something that . . . I don't know if you can answer it."

"I'll try."

"Has he come to you for confession? I mean, here at the rectory?"

She was certain he was going to say yes, but then he rubbed the flaky skin between his eyebrows and met her eyes. "Um, no, he hasn't."

Right. And are you lying too, Father?

A CELLOPHANE-WRAPPED gift basket took up most of the kitchen table. *Lin,* Laura thought. But that was absurd. The postage alone must have cost a small fortune. Then she saw the two greeting cards listing dozens of names. *We on your side, Doctor Weber. We pray for you and your family each day. Charlotte Hoon, staff, and patients.* Laura undid the wrapping and from the artistically arranged pile of tropical fruits, jellies, and candies, she slipped out a box of chocolate-covered macadamia nuts, ate one, then another, and another.

She couldn't get enough. That taste of paradise.

Lost.

LIN

Along a secondary highway leading west from Rochester, ribbons of ground fog hovered over autumnal fields. Pumpkins lay unpicked in one, their leaves curled and gray. In some fields, ivory corn stalks; in others, corn stubble. School buses trundled along, picking up a child or a group of children every so often. Watching them hurry to the buses, she felt a press of emotion that seemed more like some illness finally winning out. The kids so young. Happy to be on the move. Even the most simple arrangement of forms got to her. A half-whiskey barrel on its side, holding what once had been a spill of flowers, before the frosts. The name of a farm obviously the amalgam of a man and a woman's name, *Ken-Mar Farm*. Washing strung on a line leading to a utility pole, numerous pairs of jeans and then a row of T-shirts in different colors. She saw, too, a deer carcass hanging from a crossbeam nailed to tree limbs, rear legs angled at the joint, the stick-like front legs tied together. The head, with its rack of horns, limp to one side. Its belly white. The radio told of another Wall Street scandal. The weather was to be partly sunny that morning, with rain likely that afternoon. She could see it to the northwest, over Ontario, the edge of mauve cloud cover. Interesting, how everything seems to pull you along—the news, the weather, the road—creating the illusion of an infinite line. You don't feel the mesh of time, then. The past is simply a receding shoreline; the future, one in the distance, looming steadily larger until you get there, and then it slides behind and becomes smaller, and there's something else ahead of you and you aim for that.

On and on until all three merge at the instant of death, crashing
together.

Svoboda's *boom*.

THERE WERE the maples, mostly bare limbs now, and the
neat frame houses, their yards raked clear of leaves and once
again a perfect green, and then the courthouse, moated around
by parked cars and news vans. She found a parking space two
blocks away and walked over buckling slabs of sidewalk to its
public entrance.

Conscious of spectators turning toward her, she strode
down the center aisle. In the bench up front, Laura squeezed
her forearm. Her mother smiled the remotest of smiles. Then
Lin was listening to Russ again, the old words. Dirt, grease,
gunk in the barrel. A bore scope not used. Shot cup unpre-
dictability. Pathologists finding carbonaceous deposits—gunpowder residue—along the wound track. The microbiologist
finding carbon deposits. Another pathologist seeing no scalloping, just the presence of embalming fluid along the margins of the wound. All evidence consistent with Ben Weber's
testimony.

Russ's voice calm, perfectly enunciated, neutrally pitched.
But could it convey a passion for honesty, for justice?—this
cool, logical rendering?

No. She understood, then, that she'd needed to hear something more from Russ, at this late hour. Something undeni-
able in the words. But his seemed flimsy, as he rebutted the
defense's arguments point by point, appealing to logic and
common sense. Until an uncharacteristic swerve. "Ladies and
gentlemen, not *one* question asked of Dr. Weber about that day,
not one! A man takes the stand, a man gives up his right to
remain silent, and not one question asked of him about that
day! It actually makes one's stomach turn!"

That much good. Logic trumped for an instant by emotion.

"They have the burden of proof, ladies and gentlemen,
but no questions asked of the defendant. And here's another

matter: where are the boxes of cartridges from that day? Where are the shell casings that were strewn around? Missing. No one knows! So how can we know for sure, ladies and gentlemen, if that more powerful, number-four shot that killed Pete Hyland was the *only* number-four shot used that day? Dr. Weber testified that they often bought shells on sale, kept them all together in a big box, number-four, number-eight. . . ."

It made sense. Gaps in the questioning. Gaps in the evidence. Most of the jurors were sitting well back in their chairs, but two were leaning forward—the man who liked to look out the window, and the elderly woman who used a cane.

". . . distraught, he said, I have to take care of those kids now. . . ."

Alongside her, Laura covertly raised a wad of tissue to her eyes.

And he *had* taken care of them, Lin thought. Had done his best, no complaints there. And here *she* was, a drop-out yet again, with a vacant apartment in Ithaca, a dumpy room in Syracuse, and a gun in the trunk of her car. *What's wrong with this picture is you.* Guilt, anger, everything rotten she'd felt since the beginning of this mess—it all kicked in, and it made no sense to her whatsoever that she'd bought a Winchester 16-gauge. And then in the next minute, it did.

Russ seemed to have reached his conclusion, his voice sinking by degrees at each sentence. "If there are two convincing arguments, ladies and gentlemen, one concluding guilt, another concluding innocence, you are bound to go with the one concluding innocence. . . ."

All but whispering, he might have been the voice of the jurors' collective conscience.

THEY GOT out of their cars and went into the rented house. These comings and goings *en masse*, ponderous in their way, solemn, told her what it must have been like after her father had been killed. The driving to and from the funeral home, people dressed up, not talking much, then to and from the church, the cemetery, the meal put on for family and friends. Ordinary time of comings and goings giving way to the ritual-istic. If her dad was now surprised to find her back, his expres-sion didn't reveal it, distant, even transcendent, as if all worry and anxiety had somehow been burned away.

At the dining room table, Russ said, "It's really the worst moment, for me, in any trial—when I know I won't be able to say another word to the jurors in rebuttal. When I know I've said all I can say and won't be allowed a single word more until after the verdict."

Midge kept steadily working at his chicken and lettuce sandwich. Lin's mother had taken hers apart and was cutting the pieces of chicken into smaller pieces. Laura had one hand on her water glass. Lin was hungry but felt awkward, chewing, trying to swallow. What was Russ doing there, anyway? Didn't he have anything to work on? "Yeah," she said. "That must be really tough."

Her dad raised his head then and seemed to notice her for the first time.

"It is," Russ said. Then, more chewing, more clinking of silverware and cups. Lin excused herself and went up to her former room. It had been cleaned, and the linen changed. She sat in its one chair, near the window.

At the door Laura said, "Are you all right, Lin?"

"Sort of. Actually, that's a lie."

"Can I come in?"

"Sure."

Laura closed the door and sat on the bed. "You're not okay. I can see that."

"Well, I haven't slept for a while."

"Me, neither. The thing is, though, you know how Russ was saying that it's hard not to be able to say anything more, when his part comes to an end? But this might not be the end. That's what appeals are for."

"So if they say he's guilty today, or tomorrow, whenever, we just . . . ignore it."

"I think, Lin, we need to put Mom first. *She* believes him and—"

"How do you know that for sure?"

"The way she stands up for him."

"Do you know what I think? I think *you* think he did it and you're trying to pretend otherwise. You say we have to put Mom first. What about our father? He took care of us, too. He also did one other little thing: gave us birth. His blood is *our* blood."

"You sound like some tribal chieftain or something. Look. Why don't you get some sleep."

"I know who's going to act for him—and who *has* been all along. Svoboda."

"Is that what you came back to see? Clearly, you didn't come back for us, your family."

"I don't have a family anymore."

"Then what are you doing here?"

"I want to talk to him."

"Lin, don't."

SVOBODA'S FIRST few sentences were calm enough, courteous even, as he thanked the jurors for their attention and patience. But then formalities over, he became himself. ". . . We had him every which way from *Sunday* and the guy knew it. So that's when his story changed . . . the evidence showed that he was there, he had to be. So now you need to ask yourself if he told another lie to fit these new facts . . . As for premeditated, it doesn't necessarily mean you think about it for weeks. It means you think about it just as long as it takes you to decide who will live and who will *die*. As for malice, *all* murder is malicious. All murder rises out of ill will, the desire to kill another human being. . . ."

She'd associated *premeditated* with brooding, sleeplessness, weird impulses, urges—until all scruples were finally dissolved in that acid. *Premeditated:* toying with an idea—or an idea toying with you. It's what had been happening to her. But impulses still checked by indecision, doubt, even—strangely—love itself. But here was Svoboda saying that it all could be compressed within an instant, all that anger and doubt and need, into a kind of black hole that, moments later, implodes.

". . . whereas they offer the testimony of the defendant, we offer evidence, physical evidence . . ." Svoboda reviewed it all—downward angle, size of wound hole, absence of tattooing—then castigated the defense pathologists for their many errors. ". . . as long as they get the do re mi. . . ."

". . . Now here is a photograph of Pete Hyland's body. What does this photograph tell us? Look! The shirt is *buttoned*. How do you put your hand in the wound to tie off an artery when the shirt is *still buttoned?* So what is this photograph telling us? It is telling us that the defendant is a *liar.*"

A detail they had missed. Even Russ—maybe. Like her mother, she was visibly shaking.

". . . and *this* photograph—what is this one telling us? Bloodied ear muffs on the hearing protector. Is it in the realm of the likely that Pete Hyland would be wearing a hearing protector while *talking* with another person?" Svoboda went to his table and picked up the hearing protector and shook it. "This, too, tells us that the defendant is lying. Now look at this other photograph. See the area around the ears? It tells us something by what it does *not* show. It does not show *any* blood. Blood everywhere but around the ears. This photograph, too, speaks. It is telling us that Pete Hyland was wearing the hearing protector when he was shot. Like this—"

Russ objecting, Svoboda aimed his pointer at the floor.

"Also, ladies and gentlemen, recall the microscopic dots of blood on the defendant's boots? If the defendant were as close as he testified, he would have been *covered* with blood—shirt, jacket, pants . . ."

Her mother's face seemed carved out of alabaster.

". . . Mr. Lowry asked why the prosecution asked no questions of the defendant. We asked no questions, ladies and gentlemen, because his story stank to high heaven, that's why. And these photographs prove it."

The sky outside looked like some gray churning river, tree limbs caught in it. In the well, Svoboda was flinging his long pointer around, Russ objecting and calling, still, for a mistrial. But Svoboda rampaged on. ". . . how did he kill Pete? What was Pete doing? *Look.* This photograph tells us. See the clay pigeons here on the ground, under the wrist? That's what Pete was doing. Loading the bird-flinging machine. Death was what Weber wanted. He had to make the first shot count. You can't have an accident with two shots, so he . . ."

Outside, cloud cover thinned, allowing a flash of brilliance before knitting together again and shutting it off. Lin was beginning to see how you could do it—go on. You just did. You compose your face. You walk. You say what is expected of you or stay silent. This she did. At the defense table. In the car. At the house. You hold yourself like a sick person going through the motions but, inside, you're somewhere else. It wasn't exactly acting. You just split apart. Twins. But one running silent and deep.

She shoved aside the leftover paella Laura had heated. Its color, its lumpy complexity too evocative of human flesh caught in a screen-like mesh of fabric.

"Would you rather some soup, Lin?" Laura asked.

"I'll get it." Alone in the kitchen, she took a few deep breaths.

"Lin," her dad said behind her. "Thank you. For coming back." He leaned against the counter and watched as she stared at the jumbled contents of a drawer. "Are you okay, honey?"

Fear seemed to be crushing her chest. "Just a little bummed out." *What if he wants to kill me, too? All of us. Then take his own life. Like you read about.* To keep her hands from revealing too much, she clutched the opener and worked at a can of cream of tomato.

"I know what you mean." He tried a smile. "Lin, I need to apologize for hitting you that night. I still hate myself for that."

"It's all right, Dad." She focused on the can, its molded contents.

"Honey, if there's something I can do that'll help, will you please tell me? It hurts me more than I can say to see you so beat up over this."

She found milk in the refrigerator and diluted the condensed soup.

"Honey, give us a hug. If you can." He opened his arms.

She chopped at the thick red substance in the pan and felt nauseous. "I can't, Dad."

"I understand." He picked at his pullover. "You know, we've been through so much these past months. Over the years your mother and I tried to keep you kids safe and happy, and then this—sideswipes us. For other families there are car accidents and diseases. Well, for us, too. But also, this."

Tomatoes supposedly fought cancers. What was the word, *lycopenes?* She really should eat this.

"I told the truth, honey. I—"

The gray pouches under his eyes were iridescent. "There *is* something you can do. Come with me, all right?"

"Where?"

"The camp."

"The *hunting* camp?"

"I'd like you to show me exactly how it happened. Everything."

"I could show you out back here."

"Out there is better. Do this one thing for me, all right?"

"I'll get— But wait a second. Russ wants me here in case something—"

"All right. Out back, then."

From the kitchen doorway Karen said, "I won't allow it, Ben. You girls. I'm ashamed of you."

Laura said, coming up to her, "But Mom, I—"

"I don't want to hear any more from either of you. Linda, just leave. Go back to wherever you were."

"It's all right," Ben said. "I don't mind."

"I do. I'm ashamed of them."

"They have a right to—"

"They do not. They're your daughters."

Lin said, "I'm *father's* daughter. Pete's."

"*Linda.*"

"We *all* deserve the truth, Mom."

"You've heard it."

"Not words! I want to see exactly how it happened."

"Let's go, then."

"*Ben.*"

"It's all right. If it'll help, I'm more than willing."

It wasn't yet dark. Wind thrummed in the bare trees, dry stalks of corn shivering in accompaniment. Leaves caught in weeds at the edge of the field. Karen and Laura stood at screened windows as Lin unwrapped the gun and kicked the bubble wrap to the side.

"Is it loaded?"

"Are you afraid, like on that day?"

"I am, yes."

"Were you afraid for yourself, or for my father?"

"For both of us. Like right now."

"Here. Show me." Using both hands, she extended the gun.

"A Model 12!" He took it. "Where in the world did you get it?"

"Syracuse."

"It's in pretty decent shape. I hope you didn't have to pay a whole lot."

"I don't know. I just paid what he asked—one-fifty."

He pressed the release, opened the magazine, slid it shut. "Well, that's a relief. Okay. Let's do the whole thing from the start. He was getting ready to work the machine for me. Imagine it right over here. It was my turn to shoot, and I was standing to the right of it. Remember I asked him earlier to try *his* gun? You can be me. Take this branch and hold it like you're waiting for a target to come zooming out. *My* gun, the Winchester, is on a table to his left. I'll put it right here, on the ground."

"Dad? I don't remember you saying that before. I mean, you guys switching guns and all."

"You don't, honey? I'm sure I did. Remember how they got the gun marked, in court, *used by Pete Hyland*? But maybe you weren't in court that day."

"Maybe not. So then what happened."

"Well, I'm all set—remember, I'm Pete, so I'll be here, to your left. But instead of him working the machine, he starts talking again. We'd been talking in the cabin, not really arguing but trying to be rational, though I could see your father was losing it. What he said there was that he wasn't going to let your mother divorce him even though she didn't love him anymore. That could change, he said. She might come around again after all this was over."

"What did he mean by 'all this'?"

"Our relationship. He wouldn't look me in the eye, while he was talking. I just let him go on, thinking it might be good for him to blow off steam. I told him I was really sorry, that I hadn't intended for any of it to happen, and that I could understand how he didn't want to lose his wife. Then he warned me to keep away from all of you.

"What crossed my mind first, when he said that, was fear for you girls, I don't know why, a gut reaction, I guess. So I said okay, that's it, then. Fine. Right then I didn't know what I was going to do about it because I really loved your mother and you girls."

"So you lied to him."

"Well, I was trying to calm him down, he was so on edge. Then I suggested we just go back into town. There wasn't any point in being out there, pretending to be good buddies. I was more than a little angry, too. If he really loved you girls all that much, and loved your mother, why all the hunting and fishing trips? And that day, too. Why not stay home, mow the grass, dig a garden, whatever. So I said, Let's go back, Pete. You can spend the rest of the day with your family, then."

"You said that?"

"I did."

"Why didn't you tell all this in court? You said there was this small talk, then you went out shooting, and *then* it came up. And before that you told Russ something about pent-up feelings when you two were there, shooting. And he just turned on you."

"Well, he did."

"But you didn't say anything about the talk in the cabin. You implied that it was just small talk."

"Did I?"

"You did. Each time you tell this story, it comes out different. But anyway, you guys go out shooting after arguing in the cabin? Isn't that kind of strange?"

"Well, it wasn't all-out arguing, remember. It was closer to a discussion sort of thing. And your father wanted to, the day was brightening up, and I thought the worst was over, for the time being. But when we get out there, he starts talking again. He said he was going to get me run out of town. Those were the words he used, as if we were still on the frontier somewhere. That he could get me booted out of town was probably true. He was friends with just about everybody holding any kind of office. So it all starts up again, the talk, as if it were some fire that hadn't been put out all the way."

"So he's really upset."

"Very. In retrospect, I should have just left, at that point. It was idiotic to stay. But you know how, when something starts happening, we don't automatically think it's going to turn out terrible? That was me. I think I said something like, You won't have to do that, Pete. It's over, okay? But apparently he didn't believe me.

"So all right. I'm Pete. You're me. Stand right here, to my right, looking straight ahead."

Lin did.

"Pete is down here, by the flinging machine. The hearing protector is around his neck—"

"You didn't say that before, that he had the hearing protector around his neck. You—"

"I *forgot*, okay? I forgot a lot of stuff, believe me. Things keep coming back at random. Sometimes the details are clear, Lin, and sometimes they're not. Sometimes I think I know, and in the next minute it *slides away*. Anyway, yes, we started arguing again out there, and I think—I *think*—I tried to calm him down again. After all, there we were with guns, so why wouldn't I try to calm him down? But what he must have done, was to jam that hearing protector on, grab the barrel of the gun on the table—which was really my gun, remember?—and I didn't know whether he wanted to commit suicide or shoot me. There was this ungodly cry or yell, and I was so shocked, but still I tried to grab the gun from him.

"Okay. Let's do it. I'm Pete. I'll grab the gun by the barrel. You're me. You're shocked and maybe take a step backward, and there's the gun between us. Like this.

"Pete pulls at it, like this, and you pull in the opposite direction. Pete's still in a kind of crouch, like this, or maybe he's lost his balance a little and is falling backward. And then the gun, it just . . . goes *off*. And Pete's—"

It was as if someone had pushed hard at Ben's chest, knocking him backward. He fell and lay there, still, for too long. Lin threw the shotgun aside and screamed as her mother ran out, then straddled his waist, and with one hand atop the other, struck his chest again and again, fast, then more rapidly. "Call!" she cried between beats. "Number's by the phone . . . *Hurry!*"

LAURA

Lines of time intersecting. It was her father, Pete, lying out there in the grass, and her mother trying to revive him. Their stepdad hadn't done that at all. It was *her*. And so no blood on his clothing. Laura could almost see it. It awaited some final shading in. Her mother had gone out with them. Or had come out there later, telling no one. She must have known or suspected what was going to happen. Maybe she had run up the trail to the clearing and had tried to stop it all. Maybe it was her presence that had been the catalyst. Or maybe *she* had tried to get the gun away and it had fired. *Or she herself* had fired. And so their dad's *I was right up alongside him when he was shot.*

It couldn't have happened that way. She'd been with them—her girls.

Still, Laura couldn't shake the feeling that her mother had been out there. Had somehow seen it all.

And so their dad's confusion and contradictions. That *I didn't know if he wanted to shoot himself or me.* The blur. The smoke bomb detonated by fear and remorse and horror and the need to protect the woman he so loved. And the stories, the *words*, all wrong, and getting their revenge, in time.

After giving directions to the dispatcher, she ran back outside. Her mother was still striking his chest. Lin was kneeling nearby, knuckles in her mouth.

"God, Lin. Why did you—"

Her own superb lie to the self—that *you*.

Lin torched her with a look.

WHILE HE lay in the hospital, the press didn't refer to Karen Weber as a hero. Reporters came and asked what had precipitated the heart attack. Laura found herself in the role of family spokesperson, since neither her mother nor Lin would utter a word to anyone. We don't know, she'd tell them. A history of heart problems. One reporter snuck into the backyard through the cornfield and saw the gun, left where it had fallen, and then that photo appeared in newspapers and even a national magazine.

In the following days she struggled against images: her dad in the hospital, hooked up to machines; the neutral faces of nurses who seemed to be wearing masks, like the jurors. Her mother's gaunt face, shadowed by sleeplessness and who knew what else. Lin's haunted eyes. Her abjectness, now. Laura's own shame took the self-exonerating shape of anger. Whenever Lin spoke, Laura could hardly hear her, the air between them so thickened and distorted by her own anger, black-edged as the wound hole supposedly had been, and her heart fatally damaged. And yet, self-excoriating taunts rising up from some other part of the internal terrain. *You, a* Christian? *Christ-like? Don't make me laugh.* She made coffee and put out three bowls for cereal—hypocrite that she was. Then they would go to the hospital to be with him and pretend they were still a family.

It was during one visit that a thought just came. *Geffe.* Lin had been surfing TV channels, flicking past some courtroom drama, and there it was. *I need to talk to him.*

With it came energy again, and the temptation of hope.

HE LIVED in a large Victorian with a stone tower, Norman in design. Set within the tower, several windows with curved glass. Along the porch on the opposite side hung baskets of ferns. The woman who came to the door was older, with steel-gray hair cut short and stylish. She wore gold hoop earrings, tastefully small, and a tailored wool suit in black and white hound's-tooth. A strong-featured woman—dark eyebrows, eyes, a wide face. Her skin coarse and lined. She held open the outer door, but only slightly.

"I should have called first," Laura said. "My name is Laura Weber. I was hoping to speak with Richard Geffe for just a minute or two."

"I don't know if he's here. I just got back."

"If you wouldn't mind checking to see if he's in, I'd appreciate it."

The woman hesitated as if about to refuse, then let the storm door close but didn't shut the inner door. A chandelier hung in the hall, illuminating the upper portion of dark oak woodwork.

Minutes later, a man walked soundlessly over oriental rugs and opened the storm door for her. Laura stated her name and extended her hand. His was warm and puffy. His face looked bloated as well, the skin stretched and shiny. He wasn't tall, and a gray beard made him appear top heavy. The beard ended in two curls as if in odd compensation for the man's baldness, Laura thought. Or maybe the result of a nervous tic, he unconsciously twisting the ends. Maroon suspenders held up khaki chinos. Under the suspenders, a wrinkled white shirt. His age was hard to determine, given that beard.

Mrs. Geffe reappeared and handed her husband a blue blazer. "Lunch will be soon, Richard."

"Aye, aye, captain!"

The woman didn't smile. Nor did he.

"Come on in," he told Laura, leading the way into what might have been another parlor once but now served as his study. Handsome glass-fronted bookcases lined two walls. A large desk held no papers, but a camelback settee was strewn with hunting magazines. An evergreen scent permeated the air. *Gin.*

He shoved aside the magazines on the settee. "Have a seat."

She took a caned rocker, then was sorry—it was too deep and thrust her back at an uncomfortable angle. "This is fine. Thank you."

The words seemed not to register. He sat on the settee and gazed at her as if daydreaming. "So you're Pete Hyland's daughter?"

"I am." She tried to steady the rocker with her feet.

"Look like him a little."

"I wanted to ask you something about him, if that's okay."

"Can't talk about it much. Orders."

"But the trial . . . it's nearly over."

"In case there's an appeal."

"Oh. Is there anything you *could* tell me about my father, Pete Hyland?"

"People liked him."

"Everyone?"

"Probably everybody, I'd say. It's not cold enough for a fire or else I'd have one. Do, usually, winter days."

"That must be pleasant. The fireplace is beautiful, with that green marble."

"The original mantle, too. The wood for this place came from right around here. Lots'a oaks, back then."

"Is that your daughter, Mr. Geffe?"

On the mantle, a studio portrait of a young woman, sweetly pretty, with a little boy about ten and a younger girl.

"Yup. Way out in Seattle now. Teaches second grade."

"And those are her children, I take it."

"Sure are. Caleb and Angelica. Don't get to see 'em much. His folks live out there so they get to play grandma and grandpa."

"That must be a little hard on you both."

"Oh, we get out there, holidays."

"Mr. Geffe, I realize you can't talk about the case, but I was wondering if there ever was anyone who might have been angry with my father—apart from Dr. Weber, I mean. Somebody who might have had a falling out with him. He was in the insurance business, and sometimes things happen and people aren't compensated. You know—anything like that?"

"I just remembered. I got a clipping of him." He pushed himself up and went to a bookcase.

"Of my father?"

"Yeah, Pete. We were out, the two of us, planting pansies or some damn thing. We both had offices in town, back then. Told my secretary to go and get some flowers for the boxes, you know, in front, and she did. Then she told me that Pete was out there on the sidewalk, planting his own damn flowers. She liked to swear like a trooper. She wasn't about to go and get her nails dirty, she said, in any damn dirt, so I could just plant my own damn flowers, too, if I wanted 'em. Oh, she was full of piss and vinegar, pardon the expression, head a'hair to match, a redhead. So before I know it, I'm out there with this damn teaspoon, trying to plant flowers, and there's Pete, planting something in his box, and this gal from the *Courier* snaps our picture, and then they go and run a story about spring or some damn thing. Here it is. My secretary saved it, liked to tease me."

As he bent close to hand her an open album, he gave off a reek of alcohol, sweat, and something rancid, like olive oil gone bad. She had to turn her head to the side.

"Those were good times, back then. We worked hard but had a lot of laughs, too."

From the doorway, his wife said, "It's time for lunch, Richard."

"Go ahead, if you're hungry."

"No. It's time for *our* lunch. Miss Weber can come back some other day if she wishes."

"I just want to show her this one thing."

The woman waited while Laura, sitting at the edge of the rocker, studied the photo. There was her father, looking like a teenager, shirtsleeves rolled up, hair polished with that day's light. He'd glanced up, smiling, from the oblong flower box. In another photo, the pose identical, flowers identical, was a younger, grinning Richard Geffe, *sans* beard and with hair, sleeves rolled up. *Monkey see, monkey do,* read the caption. The accompanying article was brief, but there wasn't time to scan it, Mrs. Geffe pointedly standing in the doorway. Laura did note the photographer's name.

In the hallway Geffe apologized for not being able to help her out. "I always liked your father. A real good guy. Down to earth. No airs."

"Mr. Geffe, I was wondering, too. Do you know anything about a place called Kinkle's?"

"Richard."

His wife was directly behind him now.

"I'm coming! Hold your damn horses for once!"

WALKING PAST other handsome houses in that neighborhood, she felt certain the woman had been there not to nag about lunch, but to make sure he didn't slip and reveal anything. Geffe's left eyelid had started to twitch. "Nope, sorry. Can't recall that name at all."

Go back to that nursing home.

But when she went there, two days later, she learned that Delrosier had died.

"Really? When did this happen?"

"Yesterday," said the receptionist. Her eyes slid down to her paperwork.

That night, a body-wracking fear. *Kinkle. The black truck. Geffe. Delrosier.* And all of it linking directly to her.

God, let it not be.

CALLING THE newspaper's office and pretending to be a fellow alumna trying to organize a reunion—how easily lies come, when needed!—she learned that Beth Chapman and her husband were living in Boca Raton, Florida. *Would you happen to know the husband's name?* After a while, the obliging woman came back to the phone. She wasn't sure, she apologized. Somebody had told her she thought it was Larry, another had said Jerome Chapman. She supposed you could check out both names in the directory. Or maybe Beth had her own listing.

"Thanks. Thanks so much. I really appreciate it."

"Hope you're able to reach her!"

She drove to a 7-Eleven and found an outdoor phone cubicle that would have to do. It took a while, but she finally got a couple of listings and began calling. After the third call, she reached a woman who said she was Beth Chapman and that, yes, she'd lived and worked in Tunley, Michigan, for many years before retiring.

Laura decided to tell the truth. Lying, at that point, seemed too difficult though it had crossed her mind to say that she was a reporter working on the story.

"Mrs. Chapman? My name is Laura Weber. I'm Pete Hyland's daughter. Do you remember Pete Hyland? You once snapped his photo for the Tunley *Courier*."

After some time, the woman said, "I do remember him, yes."

Laura was relieved to hear her voice and sensed that the woman would talk to her. She sounded like a decent sort. That softness of tone. The hint of reserve.

"Are you aware of the trial going on up here, now? The murder trial having to do with my father's death?"

"I am aware of that, indeed. We still get the paper."

"As Dr. Weber's adopted daughter, I have, I guess you could say, divided loyalties."

"To say the least."

"Right. But I feel that there's so much more to this case than is rising to the surface. Since you took that photo outside his office, I . . . actually, I was wondering if you wrote the article, too."

"I just took the photo. I'm not sure, now, who wrote the story."

She felt at a loss yet didn't want to stop talking with the woman. "Could you tell me anything about that time, Mrs. Chapman? You worked for a small-town newspaper. Maybe you were aware of, oh, something that might have had a bearing on why there wasn't a full investigation back then or, you know, something like that. I had a chance to speak to Jack Delrosier before he died—"

"I'm sorry to hear that he died. He was quite a guy. A wonderful investigator."

"He was? Then why—I mean, he didn't pursue the case and yet all along he thought that my dad, Dr. Weber, did it."

"You're probably too young . . . how old are you?"

"Twenty-five."

"Well, maybe not too young, then, to understand the importance of a pension and health insurance. To older people, having a job with benefits can be a godsend. Jack's wife was chronically ill. She had diabetes with a number of complications. Before becoming county investigator, Jack knocked about some, part-time work as a security guard, that kind of thing. It was tough on them. There was even a fundraiser for Mrs. Delrosier, I recall."

"So when he became county investigator he had benefits?"

"Yes, he did."

"And he didn't want to lose them."

"That's right."

"Because of his wife's illness."

"Mainly because of her, I'd say. It follows that he pretty much had to fall in line."

"Who was his superior?"

The operator came on and said that Laura needed to insert more coins. She did so, afraid that Beth Chapman might have hung up, but no, she was still there.

"The county attorney," she said, "was Jack's boss."

"Geffe? Richard Geffe?"

"Yes."

"And so Mr. Geffe didn't want to pursue the case?" Laura turned to survey the parking lot. A few salt-crusted pickups, a few compacts, but no black vehicle high on its springs. Still, she drew up her parka hood and hunched over the telephone shelf.

"Well, he may have wanted to but didn't. You could put it that way. It's a bit kinder."

"Does it have to do with Kinkle's place?"

"So you know something about that, too."

"Was Geffe involved in drugs?"

"I really shouldn't say."

"That sort of sounds like he was. But why . . . I mean, how would my stepdad have figured in? Had he been into drugs as well?"

"You have to remember that this was in 1970. Still the sixties up there. Some people who owned yachts supposedly did some pretty wild partying out on Lake Michigan."

"Did Geffe?"

"Let's just say that he and his wife were connected socially to those high rollers."

"And my dad, my stepdad, too?"

"Yes, I'm sorry to say. And your mother. A lot of otherwise respectable people were. The times were quite different then. The mores, I guess you could say."

"So my father must have gone, too."

"It was common knowledge, pretty much."

"But Geffe was never charged with anything, was he?"

"No one was except the two pilots bringing in the marijuana and cocaine, the man, James Kinkle, who owned the small farm where the planes landed, and I think a couple of so-called distributors."

"Who investigated it all—not Geffe?"

"The F.B.I."

The more the woman said, the more questions Laura had. Did Geffe help with the investigation? Did he protect his buddies? Was he afraid of what Dr. Weber knew, and so let him off when the shooting happened? Was he afraid even now of what might be said in court? Was *he* ever investigated? And why hadn't she seen anything about it in those back issues of the *Courier*? Had someone squelched the story?

An image of that studio photograph on Geffe's mantle came to mind. "Mrs. Chapman, I have this really awful question to ask. I'm sorry, but I just need to know. Someone in town told me that my stepdad was known to do abortions. Was that going on, too, at the time?—secret abortions? And did he, do you know?"

"He wasn't the only one. There were other doctors involved as well—and nurses. But unfortunately for your stepfather, those parties possibly compromised him. He might not have been in a position to say no. They compromised your father, too, I should add. But Dr. Weber was in the more vulnerable position and I suppose couldn't refuse. If asked."

"You mean, for example, if someone like Richard Geffe asked him to help out his daughter, say?"

"We're speculating here, you realize. But it might not have been Geffe. It could have been any number of others."

"And now the one person who might have done some serious investigating back then is dead."

"Yes. At one time Jack was a very astute man. But powerless by choice, I'm afraid. That's not a very nice thing to say, and I'm sorry, but I think—and again, speculating here—I think someone had him over a barrel. Jack loved his wife. He'd be up at the hospital with her day and night when she went into one of her periodic comas. There would have been no way in the world he could have gotten that kind of treatment, the expensive injections and all without his insurance."

"Everything you're telling me . . . supports the prosecution."

"I shouldn't have said so much. Forgive me. And please remember that it's mostly all speculation."

"Except about the drugs and the abortions and the insurance."

"I don't suppose there's anything I can do for you except to say how sorry I am."

"Do you think Svoboda knows any of this?"

"Quite a lot, I'd say."

"Yet none of it is coming out."

"He may not have much choice, legally. Anything else might be too tricky to prove, in a court of law."

"Mrs. Chapman, if I had said in the beginning that I was a reporter, would you have told me all this?"

"No, of course not."

"How do you know I'm not a reporter?"

"I sensed something in your voice."

"But I could have been lying. I could be lying now."

"Yes, you could."

"So you really can't tell."

"No, not fully. I think a person has to go on faith sometimes."

Her throat closed off sound, and she finally had to just replace the receiver.

In her car she couldn't stop shivering, couldn't move to start the engine. Outside, people hurried into the 7-Eleven, then back out again to idling cars emitting vaporous plumes in the frosty night.

Murder, then? Because of blackmail? And somebody maybe killing Delrosier, not wanting to take a chance, the way he'd been talking?

She finally started the car and managed to drive, though her hands seemed to be bouncing up off the wheel.

But if he's acquitted . . . if he's acquitted . . . Dad . . .

A prayer. And in the rearview mirror, no black truck.

LIN AND LAURA

At the judge's words concerning presumption of innocence, Lin's eyes filled. The knot at the center of her began to ease open. ". . . Being charged with a crime is not evidence of guilt . . . the defendant is innocent until you decide, if you do, that he is guilty. . . ."

What she should have held sacred all along. This was a judge, speaking.

But then the judge was saying, in her school principal's voice, "You may disregard everything the defendant said, or you can accept what you believe to be truthful. You may also take the falsehoods into consideration. There is a saying—*Falsus unum, falsus omnibus.* False in one thing, false in all . . ."

A wild fluttering in her chest, then. She concentrated on holding herself motionless and blocking any more of the treacherous words.

Sometime later—Lin conscious only of some terrible immediacy—the judge wound up her crash course on the law and on the points of this particular case, and the jurors processed out. Russ and his associates approached the bench, as did Svoboda and his team. There they hovered like players around a coach before they, too, all exited, using opposite doors leading from the well. Finally only her dad remained, seated alone at the defense table. He turned to his family and gave his quick wistful smile as they approached, then stood and buttoned his blazer. "I think we can go," he whispered, "but I'm not sure if we should walk past the judge's chambers, or if they want us to go another way."

His face appeared gray, dangerously so. Laura looked around for Midge. The Hylands and their supporters were all

215

still seated, as if not wanting to be tricked into leaving too early. Paramedics stood in back, with a stretcher. Alongside them, the great doors at the public entrance thumped, shutting.

Midge appeared and led them out through the door opposite the one leading to the judge's chambers, while behind them, the Hyland group began making their slow, chatty exodus. Outside, the day still cold, but the frost gone now, leaving lawns wet and glittering. Nylon flags showing turkeys, pumpkins, and pilgrim hats hung from white porches. Stone crocks held bunches of dried flowers and bittersweet berries on their curving vines. On their own front porch and steps, a scattering of brown leaves blown there by the wind. Laura swept the porch, and then it was only eleven o'clock in the morning.

After a few sips of coffee, Karen joined her husband up in their room. In the kitchen Lin offered to start making something for dinner. "It'll pass the time, anyway. I mean, if we cook." She brought several cans from the pantry and set them on the counter.

Laura imagined her parents upstairs, passing the time in their own way, stretched out like figures on a sarcophagus.

"How about meatless chili?" Lin was saying. "On second thought, maybe bean soup would be better. What do you think, Laur?"

The words one thing; the voice another, threatening to dissolve into emotion. What she thought was, she needed to leave the kitchen. Anger was making her shaky, light-headed—anger at herself, mainly, morphing into some large thing, and her sister there, in the path of the storm. Laura turned to go, but Lin was saying, "Look. I'm sorry, okay? I have a feeling you're never going to let it go, but I *am* sorry. *You* were the one who kept, like, egging me on. I had to do something, Laur."

"You knew about his heart and yet— And the reporters having a field day! God, Lin. You never think of consequences."

"I had to know!"

"So do you?"

"It sort of made sense, what Dad said. The way the gun was and everything. But then there's that thing about the blood and the hearing protector. I still can't get around that. I just don't know!" Lin's voice fell to the all-but-inaudible. "I want to believe him, Laur."

"Then go ahead."

"I . . . can't."

Later, Laura would hate herself for her inability to open her arms and comfort Lin as she once had when they were both little—an instinctive generosity of spirit that had, in time, somehow given way to the clotted and cold, the unloving.

"Then you can't." A lash of words wielded with dark pleasure.

Lin pressed fingers against closed eyelids as Laura left the kitchen and went upstairs.

An hour later Lin listened, then replaced the receiver. "That was Russ. A juror broke down. A bad scene, according to him. They're going to have to replace her, so we need to go back to court. He's sending Midge over to pick us up."

Hearing the phone, her father had come downstairs. "He say we all have to be there?"

"Well, you do, he said," Linn answered.

"Stay with your mother, then. Let her nap. I hope the phone didn't wake her."

"I'll go with you," Lin said.

"You don't have to, Lin."

"I know but I want to."

Upstairs, Karen was awake, in the high bed. "What time is it now?" she asked Laura.

"Twenty past two or so," Laura said.

"I thought it might be later."

"Did the phone wake you?"

"I wasn't sleeping."

"Mom, do you want a book or some tea—or, why not both?"

"I thought, they have a verdict already? Then it must be guilty."

Long Day's Journey into Night came to mind, the mother character. Drugged. Haunted. "No, Mom. It just had to do with replacing a juror."

"Since no one came up to get me, I assumed it meant nothing, but then I couldn't sleep. I was always hearing a phone ringing."

"There was just that one call."

"I was half-dreaming, I guess."

"Mom—I'm going to make you a scrambled egg."

"Honey, I'd rather just have a cigarette."

"But you haven't had anything to eat all day."

"Food isn't sitting well."

"Are you nauseous?"

Her mother turned her head toward the room's two windows, with their green shades.

"Mom?"

"Not really, no."

"What does that mean?"

"It means just a little."

"A little."

"It comes and goes. I think it might be a lingering effect of the chemo, that's all."

"Mom, listen. I want you to know that I believe Dad. I know he loves us. I know that he's telling the truth."

Her mother turned back to look at her, then closed her eyes. "I know how you both think."

"Lin believes him. And I, I do, too. He's our dad and always will be no matter what happens today."

She took a cigarette from a pack in the drawer of the night table, lit it, and leaned back against the headboard, smoking. "Your father—Pete—that day when he said he loved me, it broke my heart because I believed him."

"Did you want it not to be true?"

"It might have been better that way. There's too much pain in love. In all emotion. You wonder what's the good of it."

Laura waited but there were no more words. Downstairs, she looked up *custard* in an old cookbook, its pages brown at the margins, and found an entire chapter devoted to the art of making various kinds. It struck her as something akin to knowing how to crochet elaborate borders for bed linens. Heroic, in its own small way. But she applied herself to the task and a while later had the satisfaction of removing from the refrigerator a near-perfect custard in a sauce dish. As she was preparing a tray for her mother, Russ called to say that the juror had been replaced, satisfactorily to all, and the jury was once again sequestered. Laura looked out the kitchen window at the snow, wet and falling straight down against a background of a few remaining gold and green leaves.

What if it goes on for days, like this?

She was in her room, lying down, when the phone again rang downstairs. She ran down to get it. Another juror needed to be replaced. This time her mother wanted to be in court.

Along Main Street people were hurrying toward the courthouse. Inside, media people flowed toward their seats up front. The Hylands were already seated, their supporters entering the benches behind them. Ben took his place at the defense table; Laura, Lin, and Karen sat in their bench up front. As soon as the lawyers had taken their places, the judge called them to a sidebar. Outside, it had stopped snowing. The few remaining leaves glowed.

In the well, Russ was grinning while Svoboda frowned as he left the judge's bench to convey something to the Hylands. Five minutes later, the jury entered and took their places. The judge announced that the jurors had asked for definitions of first-degree murder, third-degree murder, and involuntary manslaughter. After finishing her explanation, the judge stated that a second juror had been replaced, and so deliberations must begin anew, from the beginning.

Laura released her mother's hand and soon they were leaving the courtroom, though not before she overheard a reporter asking two spectators what they were going to do when the trial was over. "Get caught up on my work!" said one woman. "Clean my house!" the other responded. Laura glanced back. The women's smiles said it all—guilty yet pleased.

Then two hours later, another call to the house.

The courtroom's lights, its warmth, a contrast to the deepening cold and November dark outside. The county sheriff seated himself in a chair placed directly behind the defense table. Someone nearby in the gallery was redolent of French fry grease. At the back of the courtroom, paramedics again stood ready, with their stretcher. Gusts of cold air swept through the courtroom whenever the big doors swung open. And then the judge was asking the jurors if they had reached a verdict.

"Yes, your Honor," said the heavy woman who used a cane.

"And this is your verdict?"

"Yes. We find the defendant guilty of first-degree murder."

"And so say you all?"

"Yes," they said in unison.

From the right side of the courtroom came the sound of a fir tree in high wind. Russ requested an individual poll of the jurors, and then each of them, looking directly at the defense table, stated the word firmly, unequivocally. Someone in the gallery uttered the word *Oh!* and then came the single reflexive beat of two palms striking. The sheriff rose to handcuff Ben and lead him out through the exit marked Judge's Chambers. But Russ seemed not to accept any of it. He approached the judge and began speaking to her in private.

Asking for whatever it was he thought might make a difference.

Laura and Lin grasped each other's hand, and Laura, her mother's. Outside somewhere, a bell rang as if tolling a death.

"What do we do now?" their mother asked.

That night the phone's answering machine took message after message—most from journalists and reporters, but also

TV and film producers. Laura later deleted them all, even the one from Bogdan, offering again to come up, and asking her to call him, please. There was some satisfaction in hearing that beep each time. If only reality could be so readily expunged. Something her dad must have thought possible a long time ago, maybe the old chestnut *Love conquers all* goading him on. But probably not. Probably just the moment there, in its fury and immediacy, and he blind to anything else, unable to fathom the depth and breadth of an act that would destroy the same family twice.

She spilled her own hot chocolate down the drain before taking the tray with two mugs into the living room and placing it on the coffee table in front of her mother and Lin, then sitting near them. So far that day she had done all right, she thought, playing the dutiful daughter, the loyal daughter, the loving child she sensed she would never again be.

"Aren't you having any?" her mother asked.

"I finished mine in the kitchen."

Words without substance. Silk from a spider's web, floating away somewhere.

The fire took hold after a while, and it was almost good, sitting there in the quiet—rain, now, outside—no one talking until the sudden pounding on the porch, not at the door, but striking the porch floorboards, and then the windows, shattering one.

Tomatoes. Broken skin, chunks, and juices coursing down windowpanes and sills. Pooling on the dining room floor.

KAREN AND BEN

She folded the geranium pink blazer, white silk blouse, and black slacks she'd worn that day. Tomorrow they'd be thrown out. Then she put on the flannel nightgown Laura had gotten her. At the dressing table, she began removing her makeup.

"Mom? Can I come in a second?"

She went to the bedroom door and opened it.

Laura stood there in pajamas and bathrobe. "Mom, Lin and I have faith that all this'll work out. We just want you to know."

She looked at her daughter but saw the lie instead.

"Do you think," Laura went on, "I mean, would you like if I stayed with you tonight?"

"I'd rather be by myself, honey."

"Are you sure?"

"I'm sure. Thanks."

"Mom, we love you."

Laura extended her arms and Karen did what she knew she must.

"Mom, you're okay, right?"

She nodded.

"The thing is, Dad needs you. So do we."

After Laura went back to her own bedroom, Karen sat in the room's chair and rocked. Their sweaty bodies, she remembered. The inconsolable crying. The kicking. And she just hanging onto them.

She stood after a while and went to Laura's room. Lin was there, asleep in a chair, both her legs tucked up, a blanket over her.

Karen pulled out the dressing table's small bench. "I'll stay a while," she whispered, "until you're able to sleep, too."

Sometime in the night, aching and cold, she got into Laura's bed and lay there, awake, until dawn, then quietly slid off the jouncing mattress and went to her own room.

Still hearing that word even in dream.

Guilty.

HIS OLD buddy the dream was back. He out on the ocean— somewhere off Kona. He'd tried to tell the captain he wasn't there to fish, just wanted to be out on the water, but the guy brushed it off, fixed him a line and said, Go get 'em, Doc! And then some gigantic thing took the bait, it might have been a freighter, the power of it, and the captain strapped him into the chair and told him to go for it, it was a prizewinner, but he didn't want to, tried easing out more and more line, which the thing kept taking. Then he started praying—*praying*—for the damn hook to break, straighten, yank itself out of the bloody mouth, but no, it stayed fixed; and when all the line was out, the captain started the engines and eased the boat toward the thing, and Ben thought that unwise, for obviously it was some damn *whale*, not a marlin at all, and either it would take them down or smash through the boat. *Cut the line. Cut the goddamn line!* But the guy just laughed and kept going. Ben thought of throwing rod and reel overboard, but these, too, had been strapped on. *A dream.* Yet he couldn't break its hold. It wrapped him in sickening despair and didn't spew him out until morning, when, exhausted to the point of panting, he opened his eyes upon his new world.

WORDS

You'd think love a simple thing. To love. Maybe when you're little, it's automatic. But when you're older and something happens and it vanishes, it seems impossible to reclaim. And what is it, anyway? A perception? Something chemical in the brain creating an emotion? Can it ever be recreated? Does one have to work at it?

Faith tested by despair. Love, then, by betrayal?

Peter betrayed Christ three times, yet Christ made him the head of His church.

But I am hardly Him. I cannot see how forgiveness, let alone love, is possible.

Each day I try, though. I visualize you taking Mom's arm, in Tunley, so careful of her. I see you fallen to the ground in the backyard of the Tunley house, the gun there alongside you. I see you up on the witness stand, your face sagging and gray. I see you in the bedroom, in Tunley, when I was so sick that time. Staying there probably all night.

I see all this again and again but feel nothing, literally, as if *nothing* has entered my heart, a chunk of ice, numbing it.

Mom is stirring now, from her nap. She's so disoriented, usually—the dreams must be awful. I always have to tell her my name and where we are—Tom Norwood's, house-sitting. I have to tell her the day of the week and the time, and then we try to get through the remaining hours of the day as best we can.

This is what *your* love, Dad, has—

. . . done. Night again. The afternoon gotten through (no one called, no one visited), our small supper (toast and soup), and so it's evening again, an evening in paradisial Hawaii, flower-scented, the neighborhood dogs quiet for a change, and here I am again, with my anger and my words. In the backyard, palm fronds clattering in trade winds. The fronds all spiky silver daggers. Clouds almost daytime white, in the bleached night sky. You loved these nights, Dad. So did we. The air cooler. The rampant vegetation resting. Somewhere off Leleiwi Point whales and their calves must be migrating south, past the cliffs where the spirits of ancient Hawaiians supposedly linger, watchful and restless as they await their day of return. As our birth father's spirit probably did, in Michigan, for all those years.

I don't believe our father's spirit is at rest yet, though, not while you are still alive.

Did you know that Mom used to let us play with a box of photos that included quite a few of our father? On rainy days when we couldn't go out, we'd tip over the box on the rug and swirl all the old snapshots around. We were always amazed by those of our father. So handsome! So confident-looking! A swimmer. A track star in high school. Blond, like Mom. Tall. Muscular without being gross. But it was scary, too. *This person our father? This . . . stranger?* Mom never talked much about him to us, but we got the idea that she did want us to know a little about him. Be proud of him. There were even some grade report printouts in that box. A lot of A's, Dad, from MSU. In the general calamity when we cleared out Ka Lani, I saved a few of those photos. Here's one of me on the first day of my life. August 12, 1965. In the curve of my father's right arm. Father is slouched in a chair in some room—Mom later told me it was at the hospital in Petosky. I'm your typical newborn—a ruddy prune. Father has this goofy smile as he holds me. The idolized JKF assassinated, American jets napalming North Vietnam, people dying there in merciless numbers, but the solar system whizzing along, and life strewn about this one planet in wild abundance despite our best efforts at destruction. And this stranger, our father, a creator, aligned with life.

What I wonder, sometimes, these long nights, is whether you supplied our father with drugs, our own century's poison. I can ask, right? Even though you'll just lie about it.

Anyway, those photos. How we liked getting them all out of sequence, there on the rug. Making a mess of Time—not realizing that adults do that all the time, and for real.

It's January 22nd and we're being pounded with rain day after day. The house gloomy and damp. Mosquitoes whine outside the screens. Mom just wants to sleep. She took off the diamond you gave her. The big stone kept sliding to the side of her little finger, so thin now, and scraping it raw. I asked if she wanted to keep it in her koa jewelry box. At first she didn't want to remove it. Then, without a word, she slipped it off, so there it is, the only thing in the box. We've had to sell all her other jewelry in order to keep chipping away at the statements Russ keeps sending. God, lawyers are expensive! Where do they get off charging such enormous amounts for an *hour's* work?

But freedom, I guess, doesn't come cheap.

You know, I should be playing my keyboard (the Kawai you gave me, incidentally, has been sold to a dealer in Honolulu), but have no desire for music. Nor does Mom. She doesn't even want the radio on. She did ask what I'm always "working on"—is it something for my students?

I lied (no surprise there) and said it's just a journal. Well, maybe it is. The Journal of Nothing.

But that's not true, either. *Nothing* is made up of many little somethings, isn't it? For example, I'm looking at that beautiful koa box you gave Mom. It was an anniversary gift—remember that time we surprised you in Kona? Actually, Mom orchestrated that surprise, the logistics of getting two daughters living far away on the mainland back to Hawaii in the middle of a school year. I met Lin at Detroit Metro and we flew out together, and then rented a car in Hilo and drove across the island on the moonscape-y Saddle Road. On the way, we picked up Katherine in Kamuela, and then the three of us walked into the open-air lobby of the Mauna Kea Hotel, and there you both were, sitting at this glass-topped case holding shells, drinks in front of you. Warm breezes blowing in. The chirp of birds. You were looking out over the ocean, just beyond the tops of palm trees. It was late afternoon and the ocean shimmered platinum. *Hi, Dad! Hi, Mom!* the three of us said. Tears came to your eyes. *Oh my gosh, I don't believe it!* You stood to hug each of us. *Aren't you girls supposed to be in school or something?*

We laughed. I, for one, absolutely delighted to be so uncharacteristically irresponsible, playing hooky from myriad duties. You standing there, so startled, so happy—Mom, the three of us, so, so happy. I thought I knew, at that moment—could actually *see*—grace. Its bird-of-paradise colors and pulsing energy. Everything else fell away, the little fights Lin and I often got into, my own disappointments (that rejection from Juilliard), even the loss of our birth father and of some other life that might have been. It all dropped from consciousness, where it tended to lurk in the shadows. I hugged you back, not wanting to let go, for I thought I knew what that moment was—a shred, a glimpse, a promise of ultimate, eternal joy.

But—hardly. Rather, something as hollow as those shells in that sealed case.

When you and Mom were sitting there, Dad, looking out over the trees at the ocean, what were you thinking of? The past? The future? The moment? Maybe a terrible mesh of joy and foreboding, past and present, pleasure and unworthiness?

It seems possible that Hell is now, doesn't it.

Thinking this, I can almost pity you.

Is pity the precursor of love?

YOUR BELOVED Katherine has been a real pain lately. Once the sweetest of us three, she's gotten unbelievably selfish, doesn't want to come to Ann Arbor with us, doesn't care, I guess, if she doesn't see you at all in the next who-knows-how-many years. What she wants is to stay at the academy in Kamuela for her senior year, which we obviously can't afford, and Mom doesn't want her out here by herself while she's in Michigan with me. I could go on and on—the phone calls, the tears, the begging, the whining, the accusations—*You don't care how I feel, do you?* And instead of wanting to apply to the U of M, as she's been talking about for years, and majoring in pre-med, it's now Manoa, Manoa, Manoa and marine biology. Well, she's met some guy who obviously helped revise her career plans. No family solidarity for her! When she calls, it's like trying to reason with a five-year-old on the brink of a tantrum. If it's any consolation, she thinks Russ is going to get you off, as she puts it, and you'll be back here soon enough. So she doesn't want to get stuck in Michigan. After every one of Katherine's phone calls, Mom goes into her room and lies down and won't talk for hours.

There's more to it, I suspect, than just the issue of schools. I think she hates me—and Lin, too—because we belong to *that* time. Maybe even Mom, and you, too, Dad. She totally wants to ignore it all, but unfortunately, I'm a reminder, and being in Michigan and visiting you in prison would be a disaster.

Katherine wouldn't even *be here* if it weren't for all of it!

Failure is so easy. And the norm, I'm beginning to see. Anything else, the exception.

And, God, that thought hurts. Worse than my torn fingernails, dried blood there at the quick, which always reminds me of the trial, the Blood Man, and your hands, Dad, darkened and sticky with my father's blood.

Will I mail this? I hope so. I hope I'll find it within me to be that cruel. After all the words you gave us, I feel more than justified in sending you these.

TODAY MOM seemed better, more talkative, wanting to help make dinner, but then I stupidly turned the TV on to the news, and we watched Nelson Mandela being released after his twenty-seven years in a South African prison. I turned it off right after he raised his right fist and smiled in that strong African light. Too late. Mom stood and said she was tired, was going to go lie down—at only six or so in the evening. I couldn't bear to think of her in that room for so many hours, alone, at the mercy of thought. So I talked her into going out on the lanai instead, resting on the chaise. Her little dogs followed and settled themselves one on either side of her, while I got the watering can and orchid food and made up a solution. When we came here in January, I thought she'd be pleased to find so many orchids—cattleyas, dendrobium, a magenta cymbidium, and many phalenopsis in varied shades of pink and magenta. We've had to sell or give away all of Mom's. Now she takes no interest in these. It's as if she doesn't even see them. Maybe doesn't want to. Too much life, beauty, vividness, life flaunting itself. And so, too painful. Like Mandela's power salute.

While out there on the lanai with her, I brought up something that's been on my mind for weeks. The subject of her health. The need for her to see her doctor.

To no avail.

But Mom. You seem so tired all the time, and you're not eating very much at all.

It's not a relapse.

How can you be sure?

I just am.

That's hardly scientific.

I know, but I'm okay.

Just tired?

It's taken a toll.

Would you like me to call Father Bill?

Not really, no. I'm fine.

I can understand her reluctance about Father Bill. Shaky with Parkinson's, his skin with all these gray patches that might be pre-cancerous—enough for him to worry about! He did come to see us once, soon after we moved in here. Well, we hadn't been to Mass in Pahoa, and maybe that worried him. He sat at the edge of the rattan chair in the living room, leaned forward and gave us a little homily about the work of redemption being ongoing. *It didn't just happen way back some two thousand years ago, you know. It happens every day at the Mass. It can happen in our hearts this very moment. But we have to open ourselves to it.*

Words! More words. *How* do you open yourself to it, I wanted to ask. Like opening a window? A door? Where's the handle, the knob?

Anger zooming out toward him—I suppose he could tell, poor man, by that blast of ice cold silence coming from my corner of the room. And Mom didn't seem to have the energy to send forth a few well-meaning words to counterbalance my ugly silence.

Soon he was hurrying through a downpour to his small car. On the kitchen table, a box of groceries from the church pantry—cans of soup, jars of peanut butter and pasta sauce, boxes of pasta, cereal, powdered milk, a few papayas and mangoes.

Now whenever I open one of the cans of soup or jars of pasta sauce, those words come back to me. *The work of redemption . . . ongoing.* Words as infuriating as yours at the trial.

A lie, I want to say to Father Bill. *You are lying.*

The good thing for me is that it does dampen appetite.

Still, it moved me a little to think of him in the pantry at the church hall, selecting cans of soup with his trembly hands, packing the box high, then hefting it up and carrying it to his car.

Coming with groceries and a few solemn, if meaningless, words.

TOM NORWOOD is a professor at UH-Hilo, Dad. I don't think you know him, you and Mom having traveled in different circles. He has a nice little house, everything cared for and kept up. It's a small yard, with some ficus and a banana tree on one side; plumeria, of course, and on the other side, a cropped banyan kept bonsai-trimmed, its wide trunk a gray cave of merging stalactites and stalagmites. There's a big clamshell set on ochre gravel and filled with water for birds. At the bottom of the yard, a clump of poinsettias, with their blood-red petals. I don't have to tell you what I think, each time I catch myself looking at them.

But for Tom and his wife Evelyn, they're just flowers, no doubt. Pretty, against the low stone wall. I imagine the two of them walking around this place, their first night back, seeing it all with new eyes, embracing it all with renewed gratitude, maybe even wonder. Their little tropical sanctum. Their *home.*

I WAS making Mom a plumeria lei this afternoon—remember how she used to pick up blossoms around the church in Pahoa?—after years in the Islands, still amazed by those sweet-smelling blossoms, like some tourist. I thought it might cheer her a little and so tried to get her to help string the flowers, but she wasn't interested. Anyway, the phone rang. Russ, I thought. I *hate* when he calls because it's always some legal gobbledegook to show how hard he's been working to earn his thousands. But it wasn't Russ. It was dear Katherine again, this time with another request. She wants to go on a class trip to Honolulu. She hadn't signed up for it last fall, but now somebody had a change of plans and could she please buy his flight ticket and hotel voucher? *I really wanted to go, Laura, but was afraid to ask you and Mom. I knew you'd flip out. But now it's like it was meant to be. And I won't even have to pay the full cost. The guy is willing to take a whole lot less.*

I flat-out said no. Which started the tears flowing again. *You're so mean, Laura. I can't believe how mean you are. Dad would want me to be happy.*

Dad spoiled us. The spoiling time is over. Where are we going to get this two hundred dollars? We need every damn penny for flight tickets back and for living expenses until I can start earning something again.

I hate you.

So there it was. A bit of truth, anyway.

I don't care.

But that was a lie. That cold chunk at the center of me apparently isn't frozen quite through yet, given the pain and alarm at those words.

Katherine, please listen. We've sold everything, remember? The furniture, the rugs, Dad's car, Mom's car, the dishes, pots, pans, and silverware. All their stuff—except for Dad's medical books and that painting Mom loves.

Well, maybe Mom could sell that.

Do you really want Mom to give up her last painting? Her favorite one, so you can go on a stupid class trip for a couple of days?

Yes, it's exactly what sweet Kate wants. She's trying to sway me by saying it's her last year here, so she has to go.

Which contradicts the whole thing about Manoa and marine biology, etc.

Mom wanted to know who called, and I stupidly told her.

How much does she need?

A lot. Two hundred. Plus some extra.

Couldn't we take that out of our travel fund?

I said she should come here instead and just do some surfing. We could take Tom's car and go out to Isaac Hale. Bring a picnic lunch.

But it must mean so much to her, given all this.

Then Mom started crying, the tears filling up the reservoir and spilling over and she hardly aware of them.

There's that one watercolor yet, Laura. In my room.

Mom. You want to sell that so she can just go to Honolulu for a couple of days?

Mom nodded.

Katherine's response? *If Mom wants to do it, you have to let her, Laura. You're not her jailor. Maybe she doesn't really like that painting all that much anyway. Maybe it's no big deal.*

And now I feel almost murderous and am wondering if it's anything like what you felt, Dad. Just rage and helplessness. I *can't* keep Mom buoyed up, apparently. I *can't* fix Katherine's heart, her brain. I *can't* keep us together, body and spirit, keep us a real *family*, Dad. And I can't fix my own heart and brain, either.

And the painting? What happened with the painting? I'll tell you. I put it in Tom's car, drove into Hilo's old section, and sold it to this cool-dude California transplant who's a total shit. Haggled with him. He wanted to steal it, of course. *Oh, I don't know. Her stuff isn't bringing those prices these days. Maybe a couple of years ago, when the market for this sort of thing was a little firmer.*

Bullshit, I said. Yes, I did. Me, Laura, now the vulgarian. But it was bullshit. That painting, as you must remember, is gorgeous, a clarity and purity to break the heart. If you have to put a price on it, it has to be way up there in the high hundreds at least. No. Thousands. And that is what I told the guy.

What did we get? I'll bet you're dying to know.

Three hundred and fifty.

Mom's response? *Well, that's enough then, isn't it?*

Here's the thing that kills me. Another thing. What if you're really innocent and all this we're going through now is baseless? Like some natural disaster that just happens. And what if I send you these words and you're innocent, and these knife-y words just stick in *your* heart and kill you and the sin is on me forever and forever? And then *I* am the murderer.

Oooh. Irony of ironies.

So when I can't sleep, guess what I think about? The trial, Dad. All your words. Sometimes I entertain the notion that you truly forgot what in fact happened and just slung words around because you were deathly scared. And they turned out to be the wrong words. Simple as that.

The truth is always simple, that one investigator said. It's lies that are complex.

I keep asking myself why we lie. Simple self-preservation? Or the image we have of ourselves in our heads?—that we are good, decent, worthy?

Is that how you see yourself, Dad, still? Did you lie because of Mom? Because you loved her—and us—too much?
Or not enough.

THIS EVENING Mrs. Hoon came to give Mom a bath, shampoo, and trim because Mom won't go to a salon. It's obvious why. She's afraid she'll run into some of her old friends. Mom doesn't want me to help her bathe or fix her hair, either. Why?—I'm not sure. Maybe she needs a break from me. Maybe she's afraid I'll nag her (some more) about her declining weight, her need to see a doctor. Maybe she's just ashamed to let me see her naked, as if it'll reveal too much. Or else, she simply likes having Mrs. Hoon here. She's so cheerful, that high, exuberant giggle of hers! And she always saves up stories about her grandkids for Mom.

Also it's a relief for me, too, when she's here. I can take Sophie and Max for their walk without worrying that Mom might do something drastic with a razor blade she found hidden away. This is definitely a worry. I keep anything potentially dangerous hidden, cleansers, razor blades, etc. But there's the knife drawer, and I can't exactly hide all those, so I'm here, or Mrs. Hoon is, and that's pretty much it for our social life.

Actually, yesterday Mom had a phone call from Adele Simekin, Dr. Simekin's wife. I was glad to hear her voice and handed the phone to Mom with hope, then listened from the kitchen. Here's how it went:

Mom: *Oh, better, thanks . . . it'll take time, I realize, yes.*

Followed by quite a lengthy silence. I imagined Adele filling Mom in on why she hadn't called sooner. Getting her two boys packed up for school, maybe. House renovations, maybe. Traveling. Busy, busy, busy.

Then Mom again, finally: *That would be nice, sure, whenever. We're just . . . here. Call anytime.*

When we had the estate sale out at Ka Lani, and some of Mom's friends stopped by, I made a point of telling them where we'd be staying until Katherine was finished with her junior year. It hurt. But I did it. So far, Adele has been the only one to call.

Afterward, I asked Mom if she'd like to invite someone over here. I could make a little lunch, and they could visit.

A spark of hope, imagining it—Mom and a friend on the lanai, with the orchids and her two dogs.

I don't think so, honey. I'm an embarrassment to people.

Mom, that's not true.

It is. Besides, it'd take too much out of me.

Maybe that part is true. The effort to hold up. Put some kind of good face on it all.

Just as you had to, Dad.

Have to.

M<small>RS</small>. H<small>OON</small> always brings us something when she comes. Yesterday it was a bag of perfect mangoes. She just leaves things on the counter, never makes a big production of it. Six papaya. A pineapple. A tinfoil pie plate of almond cookies or the oatmeal raisin bars she likes to make. Often a container of soup so delicately spiced and fragrant I totally despair over my own meager culinary ability. Yesterday, Mom said she wished we had something to give her.

But Mom, she enjoys coming to see you.

Still, it would be nice if we could reciprocate somehow.

It gave me an idea—giving piano lessons to one of Mrs. Hoon's grandchildren, if anyone's interested. Then Mom told me she has ten.

Ten! They wouldn't all want lessons, would they?

They may.

Let me think about it a bit. That seems like a lot of little kids to teach.

Mom gave me a disappointed look, so I'm going to take the plunge and ask Mrs. Hoon about it. The idea scares and exhilarates me. *Can* I even teach anymore? Summon up the energy, the enthusiasm? It needs to come from the heart, after all. But exhilaration, too, because teaching somebody

might help bring *me* back from whatever brink I've been tee-
tering on.

So I told Mom I'd talk to Mrs. Hoon about it. Mom seemed
a *little* happy despite her retreat, as usual, after her brief foray
into the outer world. It's as if there was so much before, so
many words, so much thought and emotion, that she can only
tolerate a few now, and we'd just used those up. But I got up
the courage to put in one of Tom's tapes. *Les Sylphides.*

Chopin's music. I'd all but forgotten how it cuts straight
to the heart.

Tonight I'm actually weepy, writing this.

And now I want to be playing again. Really playing. *Being*
in that other dimension of consciousness, the one that—

Okay, *pace,* Father Bill—Maybe redeems all this.

Iᴛ's Hᴏʟʏ Week already, early this year. The moon full, the
tides high. The ocean sways heavily, under its silver coating.
I'm thinking of Jesus, in His last week on earth. Knowing his
betrayer. Knowing his terrible death, just there, a few hours
away. And he goes into his beloved Gethsemene to pray that
the cup be taken from him. In his human form, he despaired.
Then accepted the despair.

God, let me, too.

Mom has no desire to attend Holy Week services, so I offered
to read a few passages from Genesis, remembering how passages from that book are read at the Easter vigil. That amazing
story. Darkness parting and a strand of light appearing, then
another, and another, and the strands twirling and braiding
themselves into stars, moons, planets, earth, fire, water, and
out of each thing arising a host of other things, a plethora, a
cosmos. Called into being.

Called into being.

And for a reason. A purpose.

Which I'm not at all sure about, now.

After reading, I thought of hiding some small chocolate eggs
for Mom to find. It might be fun for her—and Katherine, too—

to look for them among the orchid pots on Sunday morning. Also, I'm going to make a white cake with shredded coconut and jelly beans on top.

Maybe the opening of the heart is in simple *doing*.

Just . . . break through the tyranny of *thought*.

But really—can it be that simple?

Eastre, I recall reading, was a goddess, and there was a vernal festival in her honor, celebrating rebirth. The craving for which must be embedded within our souls. Our DNA, maybe. Begin again. Begin anew.

The work of redemption is ongoing.

You wanted to begin anew, didn't you, Dad, after the shooting. Yet you brought us here, where people don't celebrate the globe of light rising as if by magic from the sea each day, but rather its magisterial sinking back into it.

A thought bringing with it an image of my father that day, that fine April day. Recognizing his betrayer, his death right there—*you*—as the late afternoon sun hovered just above the spring-new woods.

TODAY MOM complained of a sore throat. It's unusual for her to complain, so it must really hurt. I nagged her again about going to see Dr. Giardi.

I'd rather not, honey.

How about if I give him a call tomorrow. Maybe you can talk to him on the phone.

Mom said nothing. That's her way, ignore me. Sort of like a teenager but without the sullenness.

So I'm going to call him, Dad. Try to get him to come over here. She's lost another two pounds. I've been making custards and puddings and milkshakes and still she's losing weight. Sometimes I get the scary thought that she's trying to starve herself to death. *I'm not hungry . . . drank all my water . . . I know, but water's not enough, Mom! . . . Maybe later I'll have some soup . . .* That's how it goes with us, but when you call, on your day, guess what? We lie to you. We say everything's all right, things are okay. And I bet you still lie to us, don't you, with your *hanging in there* stuff.

Sometimes I think Mom has been cursed, literally by some *kahuna* practicing dark magic. People who believe they've been cursed go into decline. It's all in the power of suggestion, apparently. Or maybe Mom has cursed herself.

God, these are weird thoughts. What I really think is that the cancer is back. And she doesn't care. Maybe *wants* it back.

Mom was sitting on the rattan couch today, an old quilting magazine on her lap but her eyes spacey. I wondered if she was thinking about it all again—dumb thought. She's probably *always* thinking about it. So maybe talking a little about it might help.

Mom? When you were married to our father, did he love you a lot?

These words startled Mom, and I immediately regretted them. She reminded me of a bird realizing it's flown into somebody's house and doesn't know how to get out.

But then she nodded.

And you, him?

Again she nodded.

It felt true! Mom talking, in her way. Maybe truth could lead to more truth.

And you two were happy.

We were. At one time.

Do you think, Mom, that . . . he might have killed himself that day?

I wanted to think that.

But couldn't?

No.

Why not?

Because it happened as your dad said.

Mom? Can I ask you something else. It's about Dad. What was he like when you two first met?

Happy. Cheerful.

Always?
Always.
We must have liked that, Lin and I.
You adored him.
Adored?
You couldn't wait to go to the clinic and see him.
Did he give out those little prizes or stickers?
His nurse did, yes, but more than that, he just really liked kids.
But he had none of his own.
No.
Did he fall in love with you first, or you with him?
I think . . . he fell in love with you.
Me! What do you mean, Mom?
I mean, with you and Lin both.
But why us? He must have seen lots of little kids at the clinic.
Maybe it was everything combined. I mean you, too, Mom.
Maybe.
Did our father love us?
Of course.
Not as much, though?
Not in the same way. You were his little girls and he loved you,
but he had his work, too.
But so did Dad.
Your Dad was needier because . . .
Because why, Mom?
Because he didn't have two little girls like you. Both blond, but
one so serious and the other so silly. You were like sun and moon,
both beautiful each in your own way. Really, I shouldn't have kept
going there with you.
Why did you?
At first, I thought it wouldn't matter. I trusted his profession-
alism. I trusted my own good judgment. I had no sense of the depth
of his need.

Mom pressed an index finger to each eye, then drew the
throw over her shoulders.

I felt bad for bringing her down, further down, so I looked
through Tom's video collection and found a couple of old *Monty*

Python's Flying Circus tapes—even though it's Good Friday. I've read somewhere that laughter is supposed to help one heal. We watched a few zany sketches, and Mom smiled a little at John Cleese doing his Funny Walk through London. I did, too, then immediately slipped back into the torture chamber of thought. That *I think he fell in love with you . . . you and Lin both.*

It hurts. It really hurts to think of this *adoration* of you when we were little kids. Imagine: you're a man whose wife is drifting away somehow, and even your little kids, too. How would you feel? What gnawing misery? Your wife might be able to hide it, somewhat. But little kids? They can be hideously cruel, in their innocence. *Daddy, Daddy, look what Ben gave us today!*

Tonight my thoughts scatter back to the personal when I try to meditate on His agony and death. That He died for us. To save us. *Redeem us.*

The thing is, if you're redeemed once—by such a horrendous death—why the need to keep *on* being redeemed?

The work of redemption is ongoing.

Meaning, never quite finished?

Because we are so hopelessly—or all but—imperfect?

One good thing, however, did happen today. It was when I got Mom tucked in bed. I brought her a cup of beef and barley soup and she actually sipped some, then lay back. *Don't give up, Mom,* I told her. *Please don't give up.* I kissed her on the brow as she always did with us, after our prayers.

I want to tell you that I felt something for Mom tonight. Something so powerful it can only be love. Here is what I am going to do. I am going to get Mom well, and I am going to find out the truth.

And here is what I fear, Dad. That I am betraying you by my lack of faith in you—and am betraying Mom because she loves you. And before all this, we betrayed our father, Lin and I, with our *adoration* of you.

HOLY SATURDAY. The air sulphurous. An acrid stench that burns the back of the throat and the membranes of the nose.

Mom has been coughing terribly. The goddess Pele rampaging again, and Kilauea rumbling. Seismologists are predicting a major eruption. We don't know if Hilo is threatened, but if the flow does come this way, there aren't any barriers to stop it. Where will I take Mom? Panic is zooming around my chest. A shelter somewhere? Katherine is supposed to be here tonight. She'd be better off staying up in Kamuela.

I diverted myself from doomsday scenarios by frosting the white cake I made from scratch, as Mom always did for us at Easter when we were little. Then I sprinkled on shredded coconut and on top of that arranged pink, green, orange, red, and lavender jelly beans. The black ones I threw away.

Mrs. Hoon called, apologizing for the lateness. Two of her grandchildren are excited about the piano lessons. *One is sixteen—Emilia—the other, nine, Christine. Real good kids.*

Oh, I'm sure they are.

You'll see! But will it bother your mother?

I don't think so.

Well, if it does, you tell me, yeah? Now what about music? Where can I get them something to learn on?

When we'd sorted out which music store to try and what to look for, I gently replaced the receiver but worried whether I should have told Mrs. Hoon about Dr. Giardi coming on Monday.

Katherine. I dreaded her coming. Hated to think of having to look her in the eye—my thoughts so poisonous about her dumb trip. I still see that watercolor on the guy's counter. But—Katherine's being here seemed good, in fact, for Mom. They talked a lot about school, Katherine recounting exams and projects and a funny assembly where the teachers dressed up as football players. I let them have the lanai to themselves for a while, then as Mom napped, I tried to talk with Katherine about the painting and my anger and Michigan.

Katherine, the thing is, that painting is so gorgeous but beyond that, it's what it signified. It was Mom's last beautiful thing, apart from her diamond, and it kind of stood in for everything else. You know?

*Are we still on that, Laur? Mom's not upset at all about selling
it. I even asked her and she said no. You're making such a big deal
over it, jeez.*

*She's . . . being kind, Katherine. She doesn't want you feeling
bad.*

No, she wasn't just being kind. She meant it.

*Okay. All right. She meant it. The thing I really want to talk to
you about is her health.*

She seems pretty much the same, just thinner.

*And really tired, despite the good show she put on for you today.
She doesn't want to see Dr. Giardi, but he's coming tomorrow—I've
asked him to. In Michigan, though, she might be more amenable to
some doctor who doesn't know her story. I really think you should
come with us, Kath. Do your senior year in Ann Arbor, we'll see how
the appeal goes, and we can all visit Dad regularly—*

Laur, I talked to Mom. She understands. It's all right with her.

That you stay here?

Yeah.

*But we don't have the money, Katherine. Unless you want Mom
to sell her diamond, too.*

*C'mon Laur, give me a break, okay? I worked it out and told
Mom. I've been taking all these AP courses so I can graduate early if
I want, and there's a scholarship at Manoa I can apply for, too.*

Is that what you and Mom were talking about?

*Uh-huh. She wants me to live my life. That's exactly what she
said. I told her—*

After a while I stopped listening. Katherine was just being
a kid infatuated with herself.

Soon after we returned from taking Katherine to the airport, you called.

Mom lay on the chaise out on the lanai, listening to you
telling her . . . what? The weather in Michigan (snowy, sunny,
slushy, rainy?). The Easter Vigil service (was there one?). Did
you receive Holy Communion again?"

I heard her telling you about the egg hunt and the cake.
When it was my turn, I said things are going just great here.
Such a lie. I have to say that I'm ashamed of myself. I guess I

do want to talk to you about Mom, tell you the truth, ask your advice as I always did in the past. Another part of me, though, just can't shake it. The need to claw you with these words.

Your voice—so unchanged. Soft. Upbeat. *How're you doing out there, honey? You know that Island saying, Lucky you live Hawaii? Here, there's lots of snow. Some of us had a snowball fight out in the exercise yard. Well, that's Michigan for you, right? I can't wait to see you guys, though. Oh, by the way, Russ tells me he's making some progress. Things are beginning to seem promising. I'll explain in a letter. But it's looking pretty good.*

I did tell you about Kilauea. I didn't know what else to say.

Well, Katherine's aloft, heading northwestward to Honolulu now. I envy her. So much so it causes a tightening in the chest, a burn under the eyelids. She seems so free of it all, Dad. She really believes you were framed and that Russ will get you off sooner or later. She doesn't care about the trial, has never asked to see a transcript of it. For her, our life has been only temporarily altered.

She and her classmates boarded the plane wearing shorts, T-shirts, and flip-flops. It struck me as a pure act of faith and caused me to remember that inter-island jet that ripped open, in flight, and that passenger who got sucked out of the cabin thousands of feet over the Pacific. So I've said a prayer for her. She's such an innocent.

But still, I'm disappointed in her. She's too old now for *innocence*. At some point in one's life it becomes vapidity, doesn't it? Or is the word *vacuity*.

Yet her faith in you, if that's what one can call it, seems amazing.

Blind faith.

Or maybe it's just your garden-variety selfishness.

ON EASTER Sunday, the rain-wet, clipped dome of Tom's banyan tree looked like a fireworks display, one of those umbrellas of arcing light. Doves sipped from the big clamshell birdbaths. Off and on during the day I found myself thinking of Bogdan and his family—the young man who phoned me in Tunley, remember?—when I was so sick with the flu or whatever? I was thinking of them going to Mass as a family, the paschal candle burning there, to one side of an altar all but hidden by Easter lilies. The trumpet blooms waxy white and scenting the entire church with an ethereal fragrance. I could see them having their midday dinner of Easter ham and cinnamon coffee cake and sweet and sour noodle soup and various sweet delicacies, the tablecloth white as those church lilies, and displayed upon it a basket of gorgeously painted Easter eggs, their designs bringing this time in alignment with that ancient one; and even before, stretching back in time to that moment when some upright being crouched, for the first time, before a small egg and watched life appear.

Bogdan sitting there, at the table, surrounded by sisters all either nurses or studying to be nurses—while he, nightly, slowly reads his thick English engineering books. At one end of the table, his mother. At the other, his father. Both formally dressed. His mother's silver hair wound high on her head and pinned there. Color in her cheeks from the cooking, the steam in the kitchen. His father quietly amazed by the life, so much life, he has somehow engendered, *Thanks be to God!*

A family. *Albeit* my own idealized version of one, maybe. And one I will probably never be able to share—because of you.

Mom said we probably should have gone to church today; so after making her some tea and whole wheat toast, I took the Bible from Tom's shelf and read that passage from Luke in which Mary of Magdala and the two other women take spices to the tomb of Joseph of Arimathea, where the crucified body of Jesus had been placed, but find the stone rolled back and the tomb empty except for two men in brilliant garments. "Why do you search for the Living One among the dead?" one asks the women. "He is not here; he has been raised up." The figures tell the women to recall His words while he was still in

Galilee, how he would be raised up on the third day. The terrified women bow, then hurry back and tell the apostles about this marvel. The apostles think the women are talking nonsense because, after all, they're just women. Peter runs to the tomb and finds nothing but the linen Jesus had been wrapped in.

Mom said, *The Jewish officials no doubt believed it had all been staged.*

I didn't want to get into that conversation so opened the Bible again, remembering that John had a slightly different version of the events of that mysterious morning. Finding the passage, I read how Mary Magdalene, seeing the empty tomb, stood there weeping even though she was witnessing something extraordinary—two figures, angels!—in dazzling robes. Still, she weeps. Why? they ask her. She tells them because someone has taken away "the Lord" and she doesn't know where. Then something makes her turn around. Another figure. This time, it seems, a man, a gardener. He asks her why she's weeping and what is it she is looking for. She tells him that if he's the one who has taken the body away, please tell her where. The man then shocks her by saying, "Mary!" She responds with the Hebrew word, *"Rabbouni!"* Teacher. She mustn't touch him nor try to cling to him, he warns. He has "not yet ascended to the Father." But she is to go and tell his "brothers" what she has seen and heard.

There, I thought as I closed the Bible. A few words for Easter Sunday. Now what?

Mom said, quietly, *You know, I used to believe. I mean, in all that.*

It's okay, Mom.

No. It's not.

This evening Bogdan called. Hearing his voice, I couldn't speak at first. Surprise, but also a rush of anguish, maybe, that I'd been holding back for so long. Also, I'd expected the call to be from Lin, or Katherine, and so was wholly disoriented. But I had been thinking so much about him, and his family, all day, all that thought must have somehow transmitted itself.

Laura, I call to wish you and your family a blessed Easter.

How did you . . . find this number?
I talk to your sister. Well, I must tell you, she calls me.
Lin called you?
Yes. She calls to tell me how you are and what you are doing for your mother and your sister. It is most good, I think.
It's just . . . necessary.
My heart had much . . . worry. Now I hear your voice, and is better.

I found myself afraid to talk to him, afraid to encourage him in any bettering of his heart. I did not tell him about Mom. I did not tell him that Dad was hopeful that some legal strategy could be put together that would place us all, eventually, in a courtroom again and in the newspapers and on TV. I did not tell him anything about my heart and its angry lurches. I simply listened to his voice, took it in as one might that of a child's voice, all sweetness and simplicity.

TODAY, EASTER Monday, Dr. Giardi told me he wants Mom to go to the hospital for tests. I explained that Mom has no health insurance so we'll have to borrow the money, though we do have some for an initial payment.

Words bringing the sting of stupid tears. Giardi, a prim *narrow* man. This is how I always see him, but really, he's only thin and tallish—you must remember—and *always* neatly put together—white shirt, not aloha wear—bow tie and tan slacks. Elegant small moustache. Elegant haircut. Elegant leather sandals and dark socks. Dr. Giardi looked at his beautiful olive-toned fingers a second and said, *Don't worry about it for now. We'll work something out.*

His dark eyes flitted toward mine, then quickly away.

Charity. More charity. And it was all I could do not to start bawling.

The thing is, you're going to have to convince her to go, I told him.

We'd been out on the lanai, near whispering. Dr. Giardi went back in to talk to Mom. I stayed out there, weighted with dread. *It must be something really bad.* Then I remembered that in a few minutes one of Mrs. Hoon's grandchildren was coming for her first lesson. I went in and dusted the keyboard, then washed and dried my face. Dr. Giardi emerged from Mom's room and I walked out to his car with him.

Laura, it's up to you to convince her. I didn't have much luck, but you may. I have to tell you, I think it's crucial.

Can you tell me anything specific?

He shook his head, just a bit. *Not yet.*

A lie. Clearly, a lie. Like Svoboda, he knows plenty.

SOON AFTER Dr. Giardi's car left the driveway, Mrs. Hoon's appeared, and I had to pretend interest, even enthusiasm. Her eldest granddaughter, Emilia, is a sophomore in high school and wants to be an elementary schoolteacher, and of course she reminds me of Bogdan's sisters—their sweet quiet strength. She has patience, even serenity. Today whenever she made a mistake, and she made a lot, she merely rolled her top lip under, but her body didn't tense, her eyes didn't cloud. The mistakes didn't shame her in the least; she simply leaned forward and tried again. Out of sheer determination, maybe. Or else some inherent belief that if she persists, it'll all turn out well.

In other words, faith.

I should be taking lessons from *her.* And she's so very pretty, too, in her quietness. The heavy black hair, the long limbs. Her simple trusting nature. I could go on and on in praise of this child. The truth is, I wish she were my own.

And, oh, I'm beginning to understand how a child can exert a magnetic force. How it must have been with us and you, Dad. How painful the need and how it underscores *absence.*

WELL, KALAPANA—and not Hilo—is right in the path of the lava flow. Some people there want to move the little church. Others are saying that Pele will spare it. Meanwhile, the flow of a'a lava proceeds down toward the village at a slow but inexorable speed. It's a huge berm of that clinkery stuff, glowing red and smoking. Hundreds of feet wide and tens of feet high. As it advances, lantana trees and o'hia burst into flame from the terrible heat, then are inundated. The same with houses. The tall elephant grass burns and then is crushed by the great black wall. The sound effects are equally awful, a grinding, crackling sizzle as the mass of a'a crunches down through jungle growth like some massive living thing from a sci-fi movie.

Actually, a vision of hell if ever there was one.

Mom and I watched this awful news, we couldn't help ourselves. Kamainas in leis stood before the wooden church in the village, gesturing. Beyond them, the ocean was in its sapphire mode, waiting to receive the fire. The black sand beach and its coco palms will be no more. Up on Kilauea, people have been throwing sacrifices into the caldron, bottles of gin, plumeria and anthurium, even live chickens.

This last hurts the heart more—my heart, anyway—than the probable loss of the beach in Kalapana, the small wooden structure that is the church.

Mom, let's turn this off for now, okay?

She nodded.

What day is it? she wanted to know.

It's Monday, Mom.

Monday? I thought Saturday.

No, just Monday.

What did we do today?

Today? I pretended to think though I knew very well.

Oh, I remember. I gave a lesson to Emilia, Mrs. Hoon's granddaughter. And Dr. Giardi came. He said that he'd like to get you in for some tests. Remember, Mom? And I said we'd discuss it and get back to him tomorrow morning.

Overload, and Mom sinking under it. I went to her and raised her legs onto the couch. I covered her clean frailty with the Hawaiian quilt Mrs. Hoon has made for her. The Tree of

Life pattern. Yellow and orange squares and triangles on a field of white.

Mom? Why not close your eyes and nap for a while.

Honey, it wasn't his fault.

I believe that, Mom.

It's not a question of belief. It's fact.

Yes, I know. But then I said, *What . . . fact, Mom?* When she didn't say anything further, I asked—the thought just coming suddenly—*Were you there, Mom? Did you see what happened?*

I was with you children that day. I was home.

Right. How could you have seen anything, then.

I wonder if there are competing visions—or versions—in Mom's head.

I sometimes imagine the truth locked away within you, Dad. It's there, but you refuse to retrieve it. Maybe won't even acknowledge that it's there. And when you die, it'll be buried with you. And your body will decompose, as our father's did, but no one will autopsy yours to search it out. And then it, too, will be gone. And no one will ever know—for certain.

Mom, I said when her eyes refused to close. *We should do something. What about quilting? Or—painting. Maybe you and I could take, I don't know, a course or something.*

Laura, I don't want to have any tests done. Promise me you won't take me there for tests.

But why not? Maybe there's something they can help with. Please, don't worry about money. We'll just borrow if we need to.

I don't want Dr. Giardi's charity. I would like, though, to try painting. I've never painted in my life.

Well, me neither. Except when I was little. You probably did, too, then. We could try. It'll be fun. But Mom, a test at the hospital—

No. Promise me.

Why is she being like this?

Aɴʏ ᴘᴀɪɴᴛɪɴɢ course would probably be too expensive for both of us. But maybe I could pick up a few brushes and paints

on sale. It's a thought, as they say. Feels good—for a change—
like a stone you pick up and decide to keep.

Tonight, when I went in to check on Mom, she was sleeping
nicely, one arm crooked loosely over the blanket and sheet, the
other tucked under, her still-beautiful face turned toward the
light from the hall. Parents looking in on a sleeping child must
feel something similar to what I did, tonight. Awe at the degree
of restfulness a body can achieve, all that bound it during the
day unloosened. And all trace of storms, the day's shifting
weather, erased.

Mom, I love you. I want you to be well. Please let me help you.

A SMALL box from Lin arrived today: the St. John's wort
capsules. Why *St. John's?* Did the saint find it in the wilder-
ness? Or, give to this particular species its healing properties?
A *wort* is simply some plant that's used in compounds.

I suppose it couldn't hurt her . . . and may even help.

But I have little faith in it. Either for myself or for Mom.
And I suppose what is needed, with such folk remedies, is the
element of *belief.*

I'M THINKING, again, about the time you first told me about
the shooting. We were at the tide pools—remember those
swimming-pool-sized tide pools? In the near distance, great
waves exploded against the broken-off shelf of lava. I'm not
sure why I brought up the subject of my birth father that afternoon. It might have been simply because I had your full attention, and feeling grown up, wanted some topic of conversation.
Whatever the case, you didn't seem put off at all. It was more
like you actually welcomed the chance to talk about it.

In the sun, the ocean thumping away, I was comforted
by your words. My father had fallen and the gun went off.
Nothing but grass, trees, sunlight, and a man who had been
my father.

You and I sat on our mats, one of the placid tide pools shimmering before us. And I loved you.

April 2. Mom and I are painting. I found some materials in a consignment shop catering mainly to kids. In a bin of art supplies, a set of watercolor paints, brushes, and a block of Aquarelle Arches paper. Somebody obviously had big-time ideas, buying French paper, 100-percent cotton, cold-pressed, which must mean something. Or else, and this a sad thought, some artist might have died, and a family member had just dumped all the supplies. The clerk thought nothing of the two-dollar price for the lot.

Mom and I like to watch color seep into the paper, spreading in mysterious and sometimes beautiful ways. We're concentrating on skies now. I took a book out of the library that tells how to let the paper work for you. You're supposed to go with things a little, surrender a measure of control. After skies we plan to attempt some waves. On our palates are blues of various sorts that we mix ourselves. I notice how we're avoiding the reds.

But anyway, skies, waves, and then—who knows?—maybe trees, houses, gardens with poinsettia and anthurium.

Mom said today, *You know, I've always wanted to do this.*

Me, too. And now here we are.

But such a long way around, getting here.

I know, but we're here, and that's something, anyway, right?

She touched the tip of her brush to a wet section of paper and created a circular shape that at once began extending itself, blue tendrils reaching out into whiteness.

Do you think I'll ever be able to paint a flower?

What she had inadvertently made was lovely, even beautiful. I'm still astonished. *You're doing it right now, Mom. Look.*

We both did, for a long while, and I felt all but overcome by hope and love.

Mom, I've been thinking about the hospital—

Laura, no.

Just for a day or so?
Laura, I'm fine. I'm getting better.
Dr. Giardi called today and—
If he calls again, tell him I'm better.
Maybe we can discuss it again later.
I don't want to discuss it anymore.
Then Mom went back to dabbing bits of blue on white and watching them grow.

THE BLACK wall of smoking, grinding a'a advances ever closer to Kalapana. In an act of despair, or hope, villagers have gotten their small church up on blocks and are moving it a safe distance away. People have been scooping up containers of black sand and digging up hibiscus shrubs and ti plants, the power of these plants no match for Pele's rage. And people have been carting out their belongings and shuttering their small houses. It tears at the heart, the reverence paid to these humble places. Like beloved animals that must be left behind, to the flames.

APRIL 3. This morning Mom asked if we were going to paint. Actually asked. So I set everything out—the block of paper, our few brushes and tubes of colors, our palette, our thin boards for holding the paper, our water glasses and napkins—and Mom immediately began creating her flowers. Touching the damp paper here and there, she'd pause to watch the process working on its own, before dabbing on another bit of color. Then she took the tube of red, as yet unopened by us. This she opened and squeezed a drop into a well on the palette, then added some water. We watched it pool. She stirred it with her brush.

My pulse quickened.

She applied a dot of red onto the white. The tendrils fanned out. She placed another dot of red on the paper. It grew.

What are you trying to make, there?

I thought . . . an anthurium.

How about if we try rolling the brush somehow?

Mom rolled her brush against the paper, downward then inward. She did the same on the other side, only in the opposite direction and created the shape of a heart.

There, Mom! I think you have it.

After a while she picked up a different brush, touched it to some green and made a surprisingly swift downward stroke. A stem. A simple, straight, definitive stem. Delicate yet razor-sharp.

It was my fault.

What do you mean, Mom?

He did it for me.

Are you saying, do you mean to say, Dad shot our father?

Whatever happened, he did it for me.

But Mom, you didn't do it, so you can't really say it was your fault.

But it was.

You're blaming yourself but you shouldn't.

No. I should.

I took the paper and slid it out of sight, then taped a new piece of paper to her board. But Mom was through painting for today—and speaking.

Hᴏsᴘɪᴛᴀʟ.

I don't know the date. The verdict—cancer of both lungs. Possibly elsewhere.

There was so much blood. Her little dogs in a panic. I had to keep lifting them off her bed while Mrs. Hoon and I waited for the ambulance. Even then, Mom kept saying *No, no.*

I can hardly write these words, my hand is still shaking so bad. I have just agreed to a feeding tube. She's very malnourished, they told me. For now, though, an IV.

Dad talked to her though she's in a coma.

A *coma!* What have I done, not getting her here sooner.

He didn't yell at me. Just wanted to talk to her.

But Dad, she's—
Just put the phone to her ear. Do it, honey. Please just do it.
I thought, no. Don't. Why should I?
But then I did—for Mom. I leaned against the raised side of her bed and held the phone to her ear, the receiver's lower end angled down toward her mouth. After a while, I took the phone. The connection had been broken. There was just that airy sound of empty space.
I hate you, Dad, I said into it.

A VIGIL again, as in Petosky, when you had your heart attack during the trial. I don't know if I did the right thing, saying they could feed her. As the eldest, I had to make this decision, but I don't know. And why Giardi didn't consult with you, I also don't know. Maybe convicted murderers have no rights in this regard. Mom seems netted by these tubes. Should I have just let her die more quickly—and then live with *that* decision? Should I have denied the feeding tube?
Deny my mother *food*?
Lin thinks I should have. She says that Mom would have wanted that even though she didn't explicitly say so in her living will. She, Lin, is going to try to get here.
What do you mean, try?
Well, you know, the flight. I'll have to borrow some money.
Look. I'll call the airline and book your flight. I have enough in my account. It was for our trip back, but now—
Are you sure she's—
*Lin—*I stopped myself. This wasn't the time. *I'll get your flight and call you right back. Stay by the phone.*

KATHERINE, AT least, thinks I did the right thing. She's here in Mom's room, sitting by the window and working on a laptop. Mom is getting morphine, but that's hardly a radical measure. And Dr. Giardi insists that it's necessary for her comfort. There's no question of any surgery, he told me, not only because of Mom's living will, but because of the extent to which both lungs have been affected.

She's dying.

Mrs. Hoon has the dogs and is watering Tom's orchids now, as once she watered Mom's. Mrs. Hoon our earth mother. Just there. Always there. Mrs. Hoon, you are wonderful, but why, why, couldn't we have taken Mom to the hospital sooner? At least to a doctor. Read the signs sooner? The question haunts me: If we had gotten her to the hospital sooner, could they have helped? Maybe the doctors in Honolulu?

How is it we can fail one another like this? And now I have to call people. Mom's mother and father, those traitors. Her sister and brother. Must I call anyone, though?

It's the decent thing. Maybe even the moral thing.

So what.

The trial and all it held seems very far away now. Is this how it was for you, Dad, after the shooting? Time taking you away from the epicenter?

Sometimes Katherine goes down to the cafeteria to work on her laptop. When she comes back, she seems rested, detached from this reality. Maybe it's some kind of denial. What do I know? Or maybe—and this is an evil thought—she senses freedom not far off.

When it's my turn to leave for a while, I usually just wander the corridors and observe, from a distance, other people's lives. Then I come back to the room again, and here it is waiting for me—my own.

At least Mom seems at peace now. I look at her and hope that her dreams are kind. I put lotion on her hands and her face. I fluff her hair a little, against the pillow.

I keep looking for Lin.

At the appointed time, I call you, Dad , and put the phone to Mom's ear and remember, suddenly, the hearing protector on father's head that day, so distant now, and see you leaning toward him, just as Svoboda said you did, leaning toward him and firing the shotgun.

It has become the predominant vision. Simplicity winning out.

Father Bill came this morning and gave Mom the Sacrament of the Sick. With his shaky right hand, he anointed her face and hands with holy oil and said several prayers. Readying her for the journey.

Why can't I get over the notion that she has willed herself sick?

But maybe she hasn't. Maybe the two things aren't related at all—her illness and what happened so long ago. Maybe it's just my own pathetic need to connect the dots.

Today a nurse asked how I'm doing. In her tone, something more, or deeper, than mere professional interest. My body registered her sincerity, the concern, and all but buckled. *Fine,* I was barely able to say. *Doing okay.* Then I holed up in a bathroom and cried. I suppose they're trained to observe the family, be watchful for danger signs. When I finally returned to the room, the nurse was still there. A beautiful girl of mixed race.

Anything you need, you let us know, yeah?

Okay. But I didn't know what to ask for. Nothing seemed relevant.

A minute later Lin walked through the door just as the nurse was leaving. Lin opened her arms, and I mine and we hung onto one another for a long while. Her hair smelled of jet fumes and stale aircraft cabin air. I thought of her having come so far—a continent, an ocean.

Katherine here?

Downstairs, in the cafeteria.

How's Mom?

The same, more or less.

But Mom's eyes were open and she was looking at us. *Girls,* she said. *Be nice to one another. You're sisters, remember?*

We stared at her. Mom surfacing from her coma but where was she? In what decade? I've heard people say there can be a kind of recovery shortly after Last Rites—brief, usually, but a few minutes of lucidity, anyway, and repose. Still, it gave me hope, a pang of it.

Mom, we are being nice to one another. I'm so glad Lin came to see us. She's going to stay here with us until you get better.

Honey, I need to tell you both something. Your dad is innocent. He killed no one. It was me. I did it. Your dad loves you so much. Never forget that. Love him back. Promise me.

I was stunned into silence, but Lin said, *We promise, Mom. We won't forget how much he loves us. We love him, too.*

Then Mom began fading again. Her eyelids fluttered shut. One hand went up to the oxygen tube, then fell back.

We kept hanging onto one another as if afraid that if we let go, rancor, distrust, hatred, those demons, would slide in between us. But finally, Lin loosened her hold, then went over to Mom's side and stooped a bit, maybe not wanting to tower over the bed.

God, Lin, I loved you for that.

Mom? It's Lin. I'm here. I've come to see you, Mom.

Mom's eyelids didn't even flicker.

Still, I was afraid of what Lin might do next, how she might dramatize it all, but surprisingly, she just stood, stepped back, and turned to me.

I saw anguish there, in her face. A great stunned grief. Her eyes dark with it, her skin nearly bloodless.

Lin, come sit down.

What an idiot I've been. At least you got to be with her, Laur. You and Katherine.

Here. Sit down. I'll go find you some juice or something.

But I didn't want to leave her there, alone, and so called for the nurse and asked her to bring Lin something. The young nurse seemed happy to have been asked, and again I felt that stab of something so powerful it fairly takes the breath.

It has to be love, or something close. Some current leaping from one to another. Maybe it's this we're alive for. This and nothing else.

When Lin had some of the juice, I ventured a few words. *Lin, we're all here now, and Mom is still alive. And she knows. She knows we're here. So it's not too late.*

Lin held the plastic cup with both hands and kept looking down. After a while I knew she was crying. I slid my chair closer to hers, and we just sat like that until Katherine came in, with her laptop.

I wanted to heave the thing out the window.

Then Lin whispered, *Laur? He's here. In the lounge. He flew out with me.*

I looked at her. *Who did? Not Dad?*

No. God. Your guy. What a nice person. You never told me.

I wiped my face and walked out of Mom's room. He was in a small lounge off the corridor, outside the ICU unit, just sitting there, hands clasped between his knees, while a patient who'd pulled in his IV stand with its two plastic bags of fluid and its bag of collected urine watched a baseball game. I took a few steps into the lounge, and Bogdan looked up, then stood.

Forgive me. My heart, Laura. I have to come.

What's the matter with your heart?

It worries. It unsettles itself. I should be here before only—I don't know why. It was not so good of me. Not good.

He seemed pale. So pale and fair. Almost a vision. Some icon lacking only the thickly-painted gilt halo.

Your sister, she tells me to. My sisters tell me. My mother.

Your mother?

Yes. They all tell me. They give me for the flight. I bring something for you.

From his carry-on, he brought forth a small pastry box.

She makes this for you. She says, Eat. You will feel better. She wants everyone to eat, our mother. We are all too skinny and she worries.

Too skinny. Well, that's not me.

A cake, flattened on one side, its icing melted somewhat. There would be nutmeats inside, raisins, citron.

Thank you.

I had to sit down. Then he did, alongside me.

I am here now. I will do whatever you wish. Whatever you say. Only do not say to go away, please. That, I cannot do.

His hand as trembly as Father Bill's as he took mine.

Bogdan, I wish you to stay.

And it was true. And I wanting also the delicate sweetness of that cake, the sweetness evocative of some ancient land that has endured much.

LATER BOGDAN went to the house to look after Sophie and Max. Lin and I were alone in the lounge when she said, *What did Mom mean, Laura, that she did it? Do you think that's true? How could it be? She was with us that day, wasn't she? Or did she take off for a while and leave us with a babysitter. With Janine. And maybe Janine was covering for her, then, in court, with her story. Oh God. How can it be so complicated? Would Mom lie now?*

I told Lin what I thought. That in her mind Mom took responsibility for it all. Whatever happened that day, she was the cause, if not in a court of law.

I wish I could believe it had been an accident, Laur. Sometimes I'm sort of able to, then it's gone and all the other stuff rushes back in.

I know.

The thing too large for our puny words.

WE WERE astounded, later this afternoon, to see Mrs. Hoon come into the room with a Hawaiian man none of us recognized.

How were you able to get in? I asked.

She smiled, though sadly. *They all know Mr. Kamanoulu.*

Mr. Kamanoulu did not resemble a priest, Hawaiian or otherwise. He looked, well, child-like, even mildly retarded. An egg-shaped head, bald; light blue eyes—*blue?* I wondered— an egg-like upper body and spindly legs in tan shorts. Flowered shirt and flip-flops. His head, arms, and legs looked like polished if rippled teak. Walking, for him seemed more like tipping gently from side to side. But he offered each of us a beatific smile. Mrs. Hoon led Mr. Kamanoulu to the side of Mom's bed. He didn't look down at her, but upward, blue eyes raised to the ceiling, and he extended his right arm upward, too, and began chanting something beautiful that began, *e ki'i, eki'i, o Makalapua* . . .

I tried to hold onto each word, but they merged and flowed by. Words rinsing me in warmth. Mr. Kamanoulu intoned a final phrase and then remained standing in the same pose. It seemed he might be receiving some reply only he could hear. After a while, he gazed down upon Mom and lowered his right arm, then reached forward and placed it on her forehead. Her eyes did not open. The monitors showed no change as Mr. Kamanoulu chanted, *E Kane mehani, ke Akua noho I ka Lani* . . .

I recognized only the last few syllables, *ka Lani,* heaven, or heavenly, as in the name for our old plantation house. Mr. Kamanoulu drew a long breath, leaned close to Mom's head and exhaled. Then he straightened, turned away from the bed, and gave us all the same full smile as he had earlier. In the next minute, he was tilting from side to side as he made his exit.

I followed. *Mr. Kamanoulu! What were those prayers?*

He turned back, smiled again, but then turned away and kept going down the hall toward the elevator, his flip-flops snapping against his bare feet. The Asian nurse appeared and took my arm. *He was saying these words just now,* I told her. *Do you know what they mean?*

It has to do with forgiveness. He was praying to the god Kane, begging him to forgive your mother's sins.

Then he breathed on her, on her face.

Oh yeah. He does that sometimes. It's, I don't know— They have power, these healers. All very scientific!

She meant kindness, I sensed. Not disparagement.

Gratitude, then. Its easing.

LATE TONIGHT, in the lounge, Lin said, *I got this really weird letter a week or so ago, Laur. It sort of scared me. I forgot to mention it when you called about Mom.*

What did it say?

Just one word, Geffe. It was sent weeks ago, addressed to just my name and the college. Postmarked Tunley.

It just said Geffe? Nothing else?

No, nothing. In pencil, printed on a sheet of paper from one of those supermarket tablets. The envelope was, like, just an envelope. My name and the address were printed, too. There was no zip code or anything. Somehow this person must have found out that I go to school there. Why would someone write to me? And does he or she think this Geffe person maybe did it? Didn't you once mention a name like that?

I think I know who sent it. A woman there, out in the country. I went out and talked to her. I was going to ask that she contact me, but then thought better of it because of her husband. He was the one, by the way, who smashed my car that night. I'm pretty sure.

Why would she write to me, Laur?

Maybe she didn't know how to reach me, after we left. She must have seen your name and the name of your college, in an article. I don't know. When I went to her place, she didn't say much except that there was a lot of cocaine and marijuana around at the time, and parties. Everybody was into it, pretty much, anybody with money. But as for names, she said she was too young back then to know names.

Or stoned.

Probably. When I asked who was making money on it, she said she didn't know. She and her boyfriend were just unloading these small planes that would come in, and then distributing the stuff to various places—or people, I guess.

So this Geffe guy might have been the one making the money?

Maybe. But then again, maybe not.

What does he have to do with Dad?

Geffe was the county's district attorney back then.

Oh. Then . . . then what if he was the one who shot our father? You know, like he was out there that day, and father might have threatened him with telling about the cocaine or something, and he just shot him, and then Dad covered for him, and then he didn't investigate. And that's why Dad's story has been swerving all over the place. Because it was a lie to begin with. And—

That sort of ran through my head, too, for a while. But now I don't think so.

Why not?

I'm not sure. I went to see him, too. And there's even more to the story.

What are you two talking about? Katherine asked from the doorway.

She was standing just inside the lounge, the laptop clutched like a purse at her side.

I had to make a quick decision. Lie, or tell the truth. The hell with it, I thought. Wasn't it time we stopped lying to protect one another? Besides, she might have been standing there for a while.

Lin got an anonymous letter that had only one word written in it. It's the name of a man who was the county's district attorney twenty-some years ago.

Then I told them what I'd learned about the parties, Jack Delrosier, and the rumors of abortions performed by Dad and maybe other doctors as well. *People might have covered up for Dad because they owed him. And because they didn't want him retaliating with anything that he knew. It would have been a big scandal. On the other hand, it could be that they covered up for him because he was a doctor and they liked him as a person.*

But Laur, Katherine said, *what if Geffe was the one who did it, and that's what the person who sent the letter wants to tell us?*

I relayed my impressions of Geffe. Someone drowning in booze. Someone not all that bright. Not all that strong-willed. I couldn't see him shooting anyone in cold blood. Also, I just couldn't conceive of a district attorney committing murder. Drugs, maybe. The abortion *quid pro quo,* maybe. But not murder.

Still, a possibility.

But no, Svoboda would have been all over him long before now.

Katherine was saying, *But there might be a reason for the drinking, now, and that just might be why. Because he did it.*

I finally said, *Katherine, you're old enough. You make up your own mind, okay?*

So you think Dad did do it.

I'm not saying that.

Yes, you are. And you do think that! So do you, Lin, don't you?

I dreaded what might come. The wild words. The who-knew-what. But she said, *I'm here for Mom, now, Katherine. For us. Not to go over all that.*

But you brought it up. You got a letter, you said.

Anonymous letters tend not to mean that much. It could have been just some prank.

Good for you, I thought. Oh, good for you.

Katherine's eyes were filling. *I hate this!* she said in her petulant-child tone. I went to her and drew her into the room, and then Katherine and I were sitting alongside one another on the couch and Lin nearby on a chair. I had my arm around her, and Lin, reaching over, did too. Messages came and went on the PA. People passed by the open door. Nurses. Orderlies. Visitors. After a while we went back into Mom's room, filing in damp-faced and exhausted.

It was only late afternoon though it felt much later. Out the window, a view of Hilo Bay. Sitting there I had visions of how it might yet be: Mom recovered, and if not at Ka Lani, then a similar house we'd find. And you, Dad, freed after an appeal and practicing medicine again and healing little kids once more, here in Hilo. Katherine—Katherine at the University of Hawaii and going out on the ocean to study its invisible currents and mysterious life. Lin here, too, doing physical therapy in Hilo. And I—well, the strangeness of this Bogdan thing in the middle of all the rest.

Mom DID come out of another coma only to give us false hope again. She squeezed my hand with her bony one and didn't want to let go. Her wasted arm was bruised purple from the intravenous tube I wanted to yank out for the pain it might be causing. The skin of her face so sallow and waxen it was like looking at some plastic model of a face. Sometimes her left hand would drift there and pull the oxygen tube prongs from her nose. Then a nurse tied her arm to the bed's railing, which disturbed all of us. The bed's sides now had foam padding, for Mom had started to go into convulsions.

Russ called to tell us he'd been unable to get Dad out on temporary parole.

The Asian nurse continued to be kind as we took turns staying with Mom. We napped, off and on, and the heaviness I'd become mutated into lightness where nothing mattered but Mom, and that we were here, the three of us, for her.

She died quietly. It was my turn to be with her when I saw the numbers on the blood pressure monitor start to fall. A buzzer went off, and a nurse rushed in. She took a look at the numbers, then switched off the buzzer. *Get your sisters.*

Then we stood as close to Mom as we could, each of us grasping Mom's right hand while the numbers continued sinking, and the green designs on the heart monitor widened, unraveling.

Mom! I wanted to say. Come back. We'll go to Michigan and see Dad. But she was going in another direction, clearly. So I said what I thought she needed to hear. *Mom, it's okay. Just go. We're here, Linda, Katherine, and I. We're here, Mom, together. We'll take care of one another and Dad, too. You can go.*

I had hold of Lin and hung on, fixing her against me, willing both my sisters not to break down as the numbers, in the single digits now, floated earthward.

Afterward, Katherine and Lin cried. Someone closed the door so we could wail as much as we needed to. But I didn't. I was somewhere beyond tears. A place where death was all but visible. The mystery of nothingness right there, manifest.

Mrs. Hoon drove us back to Tom Norwood's house. As we opened the door, Mom's little dogs raced to us, looking for her. And there was Bogdan, with the table set.

Epilogue

Laura parked her car in the lot adjoining the prison and stepped out into whipping blasts of wind. To the west, storm clouds piling up. Would he hear any of it? Probably not. The image of a concrete vault, the kind that holds caskets, came to mind. She shook it off and walked, in the gritty wind, toward the entrance. Inside, she went through security, along with several women in capris and tank tops in jewel colors, beads in their hair, and large gold hoops in their ears. Laura had on white slacks and a long-sleeved shirt. Dowdy by comparison, yet the observation carried no emotional weight, no self-censure. It was nearly pure observation except that she felt sad for these women—all that effort, the doomed attempt.

The women seemed edgy, their antipathy palpable as they shoved over, with hauteur, their purses and hoop ear rings to a prison official. Then it was Laura's turn to surrender her purse, which contained a packet of words she intended to leave with a prison official on her way out. Soon they were passing through a security arch beyond which a female official swept them with an electronic wand. In a waiting room of plastic chairs, the women in capris loudly, profanely, voiced their complaints. An odor of heated flesh, perfume, cigarette smoke, and anger pervaded the room. Other women entered, some with children, the little girls in fancy dresses, a few boys with gel-spiked hair. Finally they were all allowed to walk single-file down a gray hallway with steel doors on either side, to a large open room where seated men waited behind a length of Plexiglass divided into narrow cubicles.

He was in the fourth on the right. Laura slid out the orange molded chair and sat. His eyes went watery, reddening, and

265

she looked, instead, at one side of his face. Swollen. Flushed.
A piece of bloody tissue stuck to the jaw.

He raised a telephone-like receiver to his ear. She picked
up the one on her side. "Laura, did she say anything? At
the end?"

"She wasn't conscious much of the time."

He looked down for a moment. "Nothing, then?"

Lies of omission. Would she ever see this man again? She
thought not. They were no longer a family. Why go on pretending? But then the image of her mother in that hospital bed.
Her love for this man. And the promise Laura had made. *We'll
take care of one another and Dad, too.*

"She loved you."

"She said that? To you girls?"

"Not exactly, but we all knew. She wanted us to believe in
you. And she told us to—" Laura couldn't finish.

"To what, honey?"

"Well, when Lin arrived at the hospital, Mom surfaced for
a while. She told us that you're innocent and that you love us
very much."

Bracing his arm, he lowered his head against fingers and
thumb and sat that way for some time. Laura finally spoke
again. "Mom also said that she did it. Is that *true*?"

"She told you that?"

"Yes, but we weren't sure about her mental state. She was
getting a lot of medication at that point. Also, just a minute
or so earlier she talked to us as if we still were little kids. So
I don't know. But she did say that you didn't kill anyone. She
did, she said. 'It was me,' she said. 'I was the one who did
it.' And earlier, while we were still at Tom's house, we were
painting one day and she said it was all her fault."

"Oh, God." The grimace wrenched his face to one side.
You—I hope you told her that wasn't true. Did you? Not let
her go on thinking that at the end?"

"I did, the time we were painting, but in the hospital she
asked us to promise something and so we did, and then she
just faded again."

"What did she want you to promise?"

Laura took a long breath. "To love you."

He closed his eyes. "I don't see how you can keep that promise. I won't hold you to it."

"Katherine, well, Katherine has never doubted you."

"But you have."

"Yes."

"You've a right to. I wrecked everything. Took everything away when I'd wanted to give you everything. Love. Happiness. A wonderful home. A terrific life. You name it, it would be yours. And now you've lost your mother, too."

He shook his head and leaned back in his chair. "Honey, your mother did nothing wrong. Never think that she did. *Never.* It was me. Totally and completely." He dropped the receiver and pushed at his face with both hands, then started punching himself, dislodging the bit of tissue. A guard came over and told him to stop. When he didn't, the guard looked in the direction of two other guards, and they soon had him out of the chair and moving toward a steel door. His shoulders were hunched up on either side of his neck. His head was down.

The woman alongside Laura, one of the group who'd had to surrender her ear rings, turned her head slightly. "Fuckers," she whispered, then turned back to her man.

Outside, a midday twilight. The sky to the west a blue-gray wall. Laura took the on-ramp for I-94 East and soon had to turn the wipers to their highest speed, and even then they were nearly powerless against smoky rain coating the windshield like ice. Soon hail was bouncing off the hood of her car, whitening highway and fields. Lightning poured into the earth. Nearing an overpass, she braked and pulled over. Lowered her head to hands still clenching the wheel. In the passenger seat, her purse, with its words.

H<small>E KEPT</small> slugging himself—arms, face, stomach, but his body numb to physical pain. The brain, though, radiating hurt.

As on that day. *That day.* The quiet, except for the crazed flies.
Pete there, a dead man. Utterly, utterly silenced. Stilled. And
he willing it *not* to be, just as moments before he'd willed the
exact opposite. *Die, you bastard. You don't love her. You don't love
them. I do!* Because Pete wouldn't give them up, because of his
vindictiveness, his glee, his *relishing* his *right,* his sanctimonious
Catholicism, because . . . because . . . of everything, the day,
the spring, its softness, its faint colors, the sweet air, the new
growth underfoot, the warm wind, *the warmth after that fucking
long winter up there,* because of that one moment, an opening,
a way in, a *yes* to his *no,* because Pete was so blind to what
was, now, what everything had become, because of his smug-
ness, his turning his back and just carrying on, in that day,
lord of the manor, because of the way the sun made his hair
even lighter, white-gold, a wealth, a goddamn *wealth,* and he
reveling in it, and so the trigger squeezing back and back, for
it had seemed right, had seemed justified, had seemed the only
thing to do, in that wide, warm day, the only damn thing.

The light in his cell flickered several times, then went out.
Inmates on the cell block screamed and made haunted-house
sounds. He pressed against sudden pain seizing his chest,
filling it from clavicle to bowels. The nitro was near at hand
on a shelf, the stainless steel shelf just inches away, above the
sink. If he stood, despite the jackknifing pain, he need only
take one step and extend his arm, his hand. He could will this,
had done so before. A few seconds, yet, before the shut down.
Do it for them.

A generator somewhere kicked in, and dull yellow light
came on.

Do it . . . for . . . But saw in it the lie. How it wouldn't be
for them. Not now. Not after it all. He had time, though. Time
to tear off the cot's blanket. Lie down and curl himself around
the pain. A nap, it would look like, a face-to-the-wall nap. Had
time to remember that time in Kona, at the hotel, the girls sur-
prising them—*fifty is five perfect tens.* The light that day. Out
over the water, the palms, the terrace. Silver haze. As on one

of those clear, still, Canadian-cold days in Michigan, the snow fairly alive with light and the blue air, too.

He felt more than heard himself crying out. The sound distant because he was walking and had been for a while, walking away from the carapace of him lying there twisted, under the twisted blanket, and the girls were with him, three little girls, and she, too, and the light in their hair was something you never forget.

SALT SPRAY floated in the air like sheer curtains. Massive waves cast up glittering fountains after each great thud. Below the cliff, chunks of black stone appeared to tumble down to the seething ocean.

"Katherine," Laura said, "it may not work, here. In this wind."

"I know. I'm going to take them out there." She pointed to a pinnacle of basalt about thirty feet beyond the foaming surf. Leading to it, a natural bridge of the volcanic stone, narrow, slightly arched.

"Are you kidding?" Lin said.

"Fishermen do it all the time. Watch."

Laura and Lin stood at the cliff edge while Katherine climbed down through the broken rocks, then negotiated the bridge like a tightrope walker, a koa wood box in each hand. When she reached the pinnacle, black and silver against blue of ocean, she turned to face them. A glassy wave tipped over into an avalanche of white water, then burst against the rocks before falling back and becoming part of another giant sliding in. Katherine watched it forming, then dropped the box in her right hand into its swell—their mother's ashes and their stepfather's. Then she tossed the other box in—the bit of Michigan earth from the gravesite of their father. The swell spilled over into white turbulence. Katherine balanced her way back, wet hair blown by the wind, legs and arms and face gleaming. Laura extended her hand and pulled her up, then the three of them stood in salt spray, the cliff shaking underneath them.

A wild, churning solitude, Laura thought. The ashes would be pulverized, or might hang in the air with sea spray, then fall to the cliff rock, or might sway in that violent cradle until they became the sea itself. "It seems kind of purgatorial," she said. "This place."

"Well, it is a sacred place," Katherine said. Her rapt face told them she believed this. The sisters stood on either side of her then, their arms linked behind her, as waves broke and a small fishing boat passed, just beyond the pinnacle. Laura looked down at the wet lava cliff, pocked and fissured but glistening. She thought of how much they had been through, those past months. All the words. All that emotional back-and-forth.

"Laur," Lin said. "Say something."

After a moment, Laura understood. But what words could possibly be adequate?

"Lord," she finally said, "forgive us all."

Her sisters turned to her and when she said nothing further, both said *Amen*. A stillness entered her. She moved back from the cliff edge and sat on ironwood pine needles and looked out over the ocean, at the frieze of cloud on the horizon, now pink. Lin and Katherine followed and sat alongside her.

Lin said, "I just remembered how Dad would never let us stray off paths whenever we were at any place like this. He was always afraid we'd fall into some hidden lava tube and break our necks. He'd be like, *Girls! Girls! Don't run!* Or else, *Time to leave now!* after about, like, five minutes."

"He hated it when I started surfing, too," Katherine said. "And then I gashed my leg at Kapoho. Remember? He went, like, crazy." She rubbed the meandering scar, white against golden tan on her right leg.

"But still he let you do it," Lin said.

It's what a family does, Laura realized. Recounts its stories. The surviving. She reached for Lin's hand and then Katherine's. It was good, their hands in hers. The ocean's heartbeat. The jingle of water on stone. The salt mist that one might, in some fanciful thought, take as guardian spirits. Around them, now, the scent of moist volcanic soil. Sharper, more strident than that of wet soil on the mainland. It seemed that the earth here still remembered its fiery genesis in the caldron of the earth and lay dreaming of that time, the brilliant fluidity and terrible heat before its devolution into black rock, stilled, frozen, and then its humbling breakage into grains between which hair-like roots moved, finding their way in darkness, lapping moisture and minerals, and these becoming the unknowable world of this now.

Thoughts evoking memory. She reading her Earth Science textbook when she was eleven or twelve and deducing a frightening conclusion.

Dad, is it really true that these islands are sliding toward the northwest and are going to sink back into the Earth's core one day?

Let me see that book.

Then, *Okay. It says here the plates are moving, and so, yeah, the islands are on one of the plates, and we're on one of the islands. But, hey, the whole process is gonna take millions of years. That's a long, long time from now, honey bun. No need to worry. And in the meantime— Look!* Motioning toward a window at Ka Lani, the green splendor beyond the screen. *We have . . .*

His voice tightening around the words, unable to give them breath for a moment.

. . . all this.

He'd kissed the top of her head and left her to her homework, but she'd sat there unmoving a while, like now; shaken, like now, by a mystery so enormous and complex it seemed altogether beyond comprehension.

And now, too, in wave-seethe and gush, his words again—

. . . all this.

Going, once more, straight to the heart.

ACKNOWLEDGEMENTS

I'm most grateful to Judith and Martin Shepard of The Permanent Press for their encouragement over the years, their astute editorial comments, and for their decades-long commitment to literary fiction.

My thanks, as well, to Robert G. Donald, a dealer in vintage firearms, who took the time to instruct me in the workings of a Winchester 16-gauge shotgun. Any inaccuracies in its depiction in this novel are entirely the fault of the author, who had never before handled a real gun of any kind.

To Joslyn Pine, my gratitude for her keen eye and copy-editing skill. Likewise, thanks to Susan Ahlquist for her meticulous typesetting.

And finally, to my husband and first reader, Jerry, an award for patience and endurance as well as my deepest gratitude. Over the years he has read through several drafts of this work and has offered valuable insights and always helpful criticism. His sustaining presence in our family's life as well as in this writer's life has been a gift beyond measure.